PRAISE FOR STINA LINDENBLATT

This One Moment

"A thrill ride that kept me on the edge of my seat, *This One Moment* is hot, intense, and filled with emotion—contemporary romance at its finest. Nolan stole my heart from page one, and Hailey was a heroine with whom I could truly identify. I was in reader heaven!"—*New York Times* bestselling author Rachel Harris

"A well-written story that kept me entertained from start to finish."—*Harlequin Junkie*

"I loved this book; this is romance at its best, this is that perfect ending we all read romance for, this is an absolutely beautifully told love story."—*Guilty Pleasures Book Reviews*

"Very satisfying . . . Stina Lindenblatt is a new author to me and a very good one I may add. . . . I will sure keep an eye on her in the future. She is really worth it!"—*Collector of Book Boyfriends & Girlfriends*

"The story is amazing and the suspense is thrilling."—*Just One More Chapter*

"Filled with emotion, intensity, a lot of sexual tension and the perfect amount of heat."—*About That Story*

My Song for You

"Romantic angst powers this fast-paced novel, and readers will return to the series to learn more about the enigmatic side characters whose own stories are waiting to be told."
—*Publishers Weekly*

"The author has an amazing and deep connection with her characters.... I loved every single page."—*Extreme Damage Blog*

"From the first to the last page—greatness unfolded."—*Ellie Is Uhm . . . A Bookworm*

"Filled with romance, misunderstandings, lies and a whole lot of heat . . . [*My Song for You*] has everything to satisfy the romance itch in all of us."—*Twin Spin*

"Six stars—Stina Lindenblatt has a skill to write heroes with some depth like few can."—*Collectors of Book Boyfriends & Girlfriends*

"Oooh, a secret baby story with a twist . . . and I liked that twist. I also really liked that this was somewhat of a friends-to-lovers story. . . A really good, entertaining read and I enjoyed it a lot. I'd definitely recommend it."—*Smitten with Reading*

I Need You Tonight

"Ms. Lindenblatt has penned another remarkable read for this series. . . . Full of exquisite heat and passion, and the ending brought happy tears to my eyes. . . . I would highly recommend *I Need You Tonight*."—*Book Magic*

"*I Need You Tonight* is one of those books that you go into thinking one thing and end up getting your mind blown because you were not expecting the emotion that this made you feel. Honestly, this had to have been the best book of the series because of that."—*Life of a Crazy Mom*

"[Stina Lindenblatt's] writing shows superb talent and care for both the storyline and her characters. This is not a book you want to pass the chance at reading."—*Ellie Is Uhm . . . A Bookworm*

"There are so many, many things that I loved about this story. . . . I hadn't realized I'd been missing and I was craving the Pushing Limits boys until this one came along. And it came with a bang!"—*Collectors of Book Boyfriends & Girlfriends*

ALSO BY STINA LINDENBLATT

Contemporary Romances

Pushing Limits Series

My Song For You

I Need You Tonight

Carson Brothers Series

One More Chance

One More Secret

One More Betrayal

Lost in You Series

Tell Me When

Let Me Know

Romantic Comedy Novels

By The Bay Series

Decidedly Off Limits

Decidedly with Baby

Decidedly with Love

Decidedly with Mistletoe

Decidedly by Chance

Decidedly with Luck

Decidedly with Wishes

Visit stinalindenblattauthor.com for more books

THIS ONE MOMENT

STINA LINDENBLATT

To Ralph,
Thank you for all your love and support.
And thank you for all you do for our family. xox

THIS ONE MOMENT

1

NOLAN

The arena locker room crackled with unspent energy. I grabbed my guitar and strummed a few random chords, experimenting more than anything.

But it wasn't enough.

I'd been edgy for the past hour. Normally it wasn't like this before our band, Pushing Limits, took the stage. Usually I could clear my head of everything that didn't belong there before the show began. Then all that mattered was the music and the fans.

I closed my eyes and pretended the stale air didn't smell like hockey players fresh off the ice after an intensive workout. Instead, the room reminded me of sugar cookies. A room from my distant past.

The random chords transformed into the melody I'd been playing around with for the last two days, after I'd managed to sneak off somewhere quiet.

"Dude, that's really good." Mason drummed along, tapping the beat on his knees.

I stopped playing and cracked open my eyelids, the moment over.

The tattooed drummer draped his arms around the shoulders of the two groupies cuddled up to him. "Hey, why'd you stop?"

"He's right," Jared said, eyes gleaming like those of a pirate who'd just discovered buried treasure. "You've been holding back on me."

I returned the guitar to its case and propped it next to me on the wooden bench running along the wall. "Sorry, that's all I've got so far." Which was a huge amount compared to what I'd written over the past few months. Touring wasn't exactly productive for songwriting.

My phone buzzed in my rear jeans pocket. I removed it and checked who'd texted me. Brandon, my best friend from back home.

> Brandon: Call me! It's important.

I ignored the text and shoved the phone back into my pocket. I'd deal with it later, after the show.

Resting my head against the cold concrete wall, I closed my eyes again. Exhaustion sat on the bench beside me, ready to crash the party as the five of us prepared to go onstage. And it wasn't just hanging around me. I'd seen it on the guys' faces for the past few weeks. The next stop on this touring train? An extra-long break with a side order of sleep.

Giggles broke out across from me. I peered through half-closed eyes at Mason and his friends. The blond groupie sitting next to him pushed herself off the stained orange couch and walked over to me, her gaze ripping the plain black T-shirt and jeans off my body.

Not that I was much better.

Her tight Pushing Limits T-shirt, which she'd cut into a tank top, revealed cleavage a guy could easily get lost in. I wouldn't be surprised if Mason had already tried.

"Hi, Tyler. I'm Rachel." She sat next to me and rested her

hand on my stomach, just above the waistband of my jeans. My muscles instinctively tightened for a second, then relaxed.

I cocked my head to the side and gave her the lazy grin Mas had dubbed my panty-dropping smile. Hey, whatever worked. "Hi, Rachel. Ready for the show?"

"I'd say," she practically purred. "You're my favorite singer. And guitarist."

I leaned in and murmured against her ear, "Well, thank you."

She sucked in a sharp breath, her fingers curling into my stomach muscles, taut from years of pushing myself to the limit when I worked out. "Wow, you're fit. And hard." The last word came out as a seductive exhale.

Chuckling, I stood. Unlike Mason, I never fucked just before a show. The moment I hit the stage, I was raw energy. Fucking before that would only dull the edge.

I glanced around the room. Mason was busy with the brunette now on his lap. Jared and Aaron were talking to a roadie, Jared flipping a guitar pick between his fingers and across the back of his hand, like he always did just before a show. Kirk was chatting with another groupie who had sweet-talked her way backstage. All the guys were preoccupied, none paying attention to me.

"Maybe I'll see you after the show," I told the blonde. I grabbed my black sports bag from the floor next to my feet and walked to the far end of the bench. Fortunately, she didn't follow me. She returned to the couch, smiling to herself.

I unzipped the bag and removed the laminated photo. The picture was slightly battered between the two plastic sheets, the result of me not having had the foresight to laminate it sooner. Along with my acoustic guitar, which I used for a few songs during the show, I always brought Hailey's picture with me onstage.

A lifeline.

The one nobody knew about.

In it, we were sitting on my bed, both of us seventeen years old. Hailey was holding my guitar on her lap, trying to play it. I was straddling her from behind, repositioning her fingers on the D chord for the tenth time. Hailey was laughing because no matter what she did, the chord always fell flat. That's when my mom had snuck into my room and snapped the photo.

It was the only one I had of Hailey. It was one of the few possessions I'd taken when I escaped my hometown six years ago. Hailey's picture was the only thing that had kept me going all these years.

The dressing room door opened and a roadie entered. He scanned the occupants until his gaze narrowed in on me. "Mr. Remar wants to talk to you."

"Now's not a good time," I told him, slipping the photo into my back jeans pocket.

He shrugged, not having a response, because ultimately it didn't matter if this was a good time or not. If the president of the record label wanted to talk to me, I'd better move my ass and be there five minutes ago. Both the roadie and I knew that.

The guys all made a move for the door. The roadie put his hand up like he was directing traffic. "He only wants to speak with Tyler," he said, referring to me.

I shook my head. "If it has to do with the band, then he needs to talk to all of us."

"You already planning your solo album?" Mason said, laughing.

Jared raised an eyebrow, either echoing Mason's question or silently asking me what this was about. Hell if I knew. Yes, I was the lead singer for Pushing Limits, but the band belonged to both Jared and me. Not only had we created the band five years ago, we'd cowritten half the songs on our debut album. The rest I'd written on my own.

The roadie's sigh was the long impatient sound of someone

with a million things to do in the next five minutes. He didn't care either way what we did. He was only the messenger. He'd let Remar chew us out for ignoring the request if that was what we chose to do.

"Can you bring my guitar if I'm not back in time?" I asked Jared, the member of the band least likely to forget my request.

He nodded. Then one corner of his mouth quirked up. "Good luck."

"God, I hope I don't need it."

He patted me sympathetically on the back as I walked out of the room, but he didn't look too disappointed to be missing out on the fun with Remar.

I followed the roadie down the hallway, past the back of the stage. From the sound of it, fans were piling into the arena, screaming and chanting the name of our band as well as the headlining band, Crazy Piper. This was the heart of the building, the love of music pulsating throughout.

Backstage was a rush of people, still preparing for the show. Two bulked-up guys kept a stern eye on things, ever ready for fans trying to sneak backstage. One security guard nodded at me as I walked past, which was more interaction than I was getting from the roadie. He was too busy yapping on his phone about his love life, or lack of, to remember I was with him.

We rode the elevator to the second floor and walked down a surprisingly empty hallway. His cowboy boots clacked against the tile, the sound echoing against the dull brown walls. In contrast to the noisy energy in the dressing room and the arena, here the energy was nonexistent. Sucked away. Forgotten.

If it hadn't been for the roadie talking animatedly on the phone about some lusty brunette he had the hots for, it would've felt like I was being escorted down death row. But while I might've felt like sleeping for all eternity, I suspected that wasn't the reason for my impromptu visit with Remar.

The roadie stopped at a plain black door. The phone in my

back pocket buzzed again. I managed to ignore the temptation to check it.

Before I could ask the roadie if this was where I was supposed to meet Remar, he knocked on the door. There was a muffled reply, and the roadie opened the door. He waved me in, then left me to face the three men in the room alone.

Ronald Remar was seated at the opposite end of the long conference table. Two suits, whom I vaguely recognized from our first meeting, flanked him. The tall skinny man had on wire-rimmed glasses, while the dumpy guy looked like he'd been dragged back from his Mexican vacation, where he had taken great pride in getting a bad sunburn. His short white hair was clipped close to his skull and matched Remar's hair perfectly.

The president of the record label waved for me to move closer but made no indication I should sit.

"You wanted to talk to me?" I didn't know why, but I had a feeling I wouldn't like what he had to tell me. Especially since my bandmates had been excluded from this little get-together.

"That's right, Mr. Kincaid," Remar said, choosing to use my real name instead of my stage moniker. To the rest of the world, including my bandmates, I was Tyler Erickson.

"The label has decided, based on the tour's success and the success of your last two singles, to move up the release date of your next album," Remar explained. "We want to strike while the band is still hot."

I frowned. "How much earlier are we talking about?"

He leaned forward in his chair, elbows on the table, hands interlocked. His silver Rolex gleamed in the overhead light. "We've booked the studio for December twenty-seventh." In four weeks. Three months ahead of schedule. "We've been extremely lucky to land Daniel Maynard, thanks to his recent divorce." A satisfied smile slithered onto Remar's face, as if he personally was responsible for the demise of the producer's marriage. Although I wouldn't have been surprised if he had been. Rumor had it Remar was on wife number five. Presumably he knew a trick or two about wrecking marriages, especially his own. "You do know who Daniel Maynard is, right?"

Just the greatest producer in the United States when it came to rock music. He had produced the albums of some of my favorite bands, and they'd all gone straight to the top of the charts, every fucking time.

I nodded. "I do."

"Good. Then you understand how important this opportunity is for the band. And how important it is that you're ready to record the album come December twenty-seventh. We've managed to book him for a week. Then he won't be available until the following October. Is it correct to assume you'll be ready?" His tone indicated the question was rhetorical. We would be ready or else our contract would be canceled. That was why the two suits were here: to remind me that if the album wasn't ready when the label expected it to be ready, we could say goodbye to the record deal.

"Don't worry. We'll be ready."

"Perfect. Make sure that you are."

I waited for him to say something more, maybe give me a reason why he wanted to talk to only me instead of the entire band. But after a few seconds it became clear I'd been dismissed.

Relieved to escape the chilly regard of everyone in the room and get ready to do what I lived for, I headed for the door.

"And before I forget," Remar said in the tone of someone who was incapable of forgetting, "there's a reporter here from *Rock News*. I granted her a brief interview with you and the band for after your show. Please don't disappoint her."

"No, sir." I hoped she didn't mind interviewing five guys coming down from an adrenaline high. Five guys who tended to forget their filters while coming down from the high, Mason being the worst of us.

And since when did Remar book our interviews? Our publicist was responsible for that, the same way she was responsible for making sure the world knew me only as Tyler Erickson. Although that wasn't an especially tough a job, even with social media. *Thank you, Mom, for being so gung-ho to home-school me.*

Pushing the thought of Remar from my head, because there was no point in trying to figure out anything to do with the man, I left the room. I respected his decisions. So far they hadn't been wrong. But next time I saw him, I'd make sure he understood I wasn't the boss of the band. It was a democracy. The band and the music weren't just mine. They belonged to each of us, each adding his own vision to the mix.

No sooner had I shut the door behind me than my phone played a classical tune. *What the hell?* I pulled it from my pocket, mentally kicking myself for letting Aaron borrow the phone. Only he would have reprogrammed it to play classical music.

I checked the screen. Brandon. Again. He knew I had a show tonight, so for him to be this desperate to talk to me meant that whatever he had to tell me was damn important.

"What's up?" I asked, half wondering if it would've been better to ignore the call the way I had ignored his texts.

"Shit, Nolan. I've been trying to get hold of you."

"Yeah, got that. Sorry. Had to meet the president of the label for a little chat." I pressed the elevator down button. "What's such a big deal it couldn't keep?"

"It's Hailey."

My heart slammed against my rib cage at the urgent sound of his voice. What about Hailey?

"She's in a coma."

2

NOLAN

Six Years Ago

When it came to the law of best friends, the unwritten rule stated that if you fell in love with her, you should never *ever* tell her the truth. To do so would only fuck things up. If you violated that rule and she didn't feel the same way, you would've lost the one person who meant the world to you. And if she did feel the same way and things didn't work out in the end, where would that leave you?

Royally screwed, that's where.

I flopped down next to Hailey on her parents' couch and pretended her scent didn't affect me. *Good luck with that.* I didn't know where it came from—maybe her shampoo, or maybe the spray stuff girls loved dousing on their bodies. All I knew was it reminded me of my mom's sugar cookies. And I loved Mom's sugar cookies.

"How was soccer practice?" I asked, attempting to distract her from what had happened today. The TV was on, but it was obvious Hailey wasn't seeing anything on the screen. Not unless she'd suddenly developed an interest in spiders after years of freaking out whenever she saw one.

My best friend, the girl I'd secretly been in love with for the past two years, shrugged. "It was okay, I guess." The rough sound of her voice made my heart sink. Hailey lived for soccer practices and games—the same way I lived to play music.

"I talked to my boss and managed to switch the Saturday schedule around, so that I can come watch you play."

That got a small smile out of her. To get him to say yes, I'd had to agree to take the closing shift at the music store every Friday night for the next month. And there might have been something about teaching his fourteen-year-old niece to play the guitar.

"Do you want to see a movie tonight?" I knew Hailey was free. Kayla, her other best friend, had a date. Tonight Hailey was all mine.

She shrugged again. I took that as a yes.

"Wanna see *Firewall*?" The new gangster movie sounded good but wasn't her thing.

She gave me the look, the one that said I knew exactly what her opinion of the movie would be.

"Tell you what," I said. "Winner picks the movie. Deal?"

One corner of her lips curled up. It wasn't the beautiful smile that always warmed my heart, but it would do. It meant my plan was working. I was about to distract her big-time. "Deal."

I jumped up from the couch and pulled her to her feet, her soft hand in my callused one. I clicked the TV off and followed her downstairs to the game room. The foosball table, which her parents had owned for like a hundred years (because they didn't believe in video games), sat in the middle of the hardwood floor, waiting for her to whip my ass. Even off the field, Hailey was a soccer superstar.

"You can pick the color," she said.

I snorted. As if the color of my team would make a difference. "Blue."

I sent my goalie a mental message that I would melt him in the fire pit in Hailey's backyard if I lost. I didn't want to see the movie I knew Hailey would pick. I was okay with chick flicks if they meant I'd get laid, but with Hailey, there would be no getting laid, no matter how much I might've wanted it.

Smiling, Hailey got into position. Confidence clung to her like the red-hot bikini she loved to wear. Realizing I would lose if I didn't get my head back in the game, I focused on the plastic players on the foosball table.

"You want to go first?" Hailey asked.

I gestured at her. "Ladies first."

"Okay. Three . . . two . . . one." She pushed the small ball through the hole in the side of the table, aiming toward her row of players.

I twisted the handle, forcing my stiff-bodied players to kick the ball.

But Hailey was faster. She got one of her players into position, and it nailed the ball with its feet. The ball rushed past my players faster than I could move one to block the kick.

Hailey gained possession of the ball, and with the sharp clank of plastic hitting plastic, the ball flew toward my goal. I attempted to prevent her from scoring, but instead clipped the ball and scored on myself.

I hung my head in utter shame while Hailey laughed the warm, sweet sound that always made everything all right—even when the stakes were this high.

I retrieved the ball from the return hole at my end of the table and poked it through the game-play hole. For a few glorious moments I had ownership of it, until Hailey stole the ball away. Her players expertly maneuvered it back to my goal.

This time I didn't score on myself. I didn't have to. Hailey hammered the ball past my goalie.

And for the first time since I'd come over to see how she was doing, Hailey grinned.

Which made losing to her worth it.

3

NOLAN

Present

"**W**hat do you mean?" I barely got the words out, ice pushing through my body with each beat of my heart. Brandon couldn't have been any clearer when he said Hailey was in a coma, but it didn't stop me from hoping I'd misheard him.

"I don't know all the details, other than she was attacked and it was bad."

"What do you mean, attacked?" *Somebody put their hands on my girl?*

"That's all I know. Right now her parents aren't saying much, not even to Kayla. I only know 'cause Kayla called me." Hailey's parents would've called me if I had kept in contact after I escaped Northbridge. But I hadn't kept in contact with anyone other than Brandon.

Not even with Hailey.

I dragged my fingers through my hair, pushing the messy strands out of my eyes. If I thought the energy in the hallway had been sucked dry before, that was nothing compared to now. Even the overhead lighting failed to buzz with life. "Is she going to…?" I couldn't finish the sentence because I wasn't sure if I really wanted to know the answer. Especially not when I still had to perform tonight. "I'll be there as soon as I can get away after the show." The elevator door pinged open, and I stepped inside the empty space.

"Are you sure you want to do that?" His tone was gentle yet heavy with doubt. He knew how much I'd rather avoid returning home. Too many memories existed there—and there was a lot more I couldn't remember.

The police had tried to find out what happened the night my old man went apeshit, but I couldn't remember. They called it dissociative amnesia. A fancy term for "too scared shitless to want to remember" was my guess.

"I have to, for Hailey." Even if she'd hate me for stepping back into her life after I'd turned my back on her for so long.

I stalked out of the elevator, rejoining the world of the living. A burly man yelled last-minute instructions down the hallway to a roadie rushing in the opposite direction.

"I'll call you once I know what time my flight's landing." I ended the call as a boisterous noise headed toward me. A new found, if not temporary, energy rolled off my bandmates.

"Yo, man," Mason boomed, much like his beloved drums when he pounded on them. "Show time."

Which meant I couldn't book my flight home until after we were finished with the show, and once the interview with the reporter was over. *Shit.*

"So what did the old man want to see you about?" Mason asked.

"I'll tell you later." I wasn't ready to be the bearer of fucked-up news just yet. The least I could do, before I told them the truth, was let them think they were getting a long break, like we'd originally planned.

Jared handed me my guitar. With him, like with the rest of

the band, fatigue peeked out from behind the glow of pre-performance excitement, ready to crush us if we let it. Thank God tonight was the last show of the grueling touring schedule, which had lasted over a year. At the rate we'd been going, I didn't think we could've lasted much longer before one of us collapsed from the strain of it all.

The roadies at the bottom of the metal stairs leading to the stage handed Jared and Kirk their instruments. I exchanged my guitar, which they would hold on to until I needed it, for my microphone.

In anticipation of our arrival, the arena lights darkened. I could almost taste the audience's restlessness for the show to begin. A loud murmur of voices filled the air, inching me toward the zone I needed to be in for the performance to be a success. I hoped to hell I could flip over to autopilot and pull this shit off. I could do this set in my sleep. It was hard to shove from my damn head the image of Hailey lying broken and unconscious. But I had to do it for the band. They didn't need me to screw up our last show.

We needed to go out with a bang.

The announcer introduced the band, and the audience cheered, filling the arena with their growing excitement. As Mason stepped onto the stage, I turned off my cell phone and shoved it back in my pocket.

Kirk and Aaron were the next ones out, and both were met with the same level of enthusiasm that greeted Mason. Jared turned back to me and we fist-bumped.

"Let's go fuck this place." I grinned at him, the storm of emotions twisting inside me, giving me a stomachache.

Jared's grin met my fake one. "Here's to fucking the place." He turned around and walked out to thunderous applause.

I took a deep breath, pressed my hand for a brief moment against the pocket with Hailey's picture, and eased the air out of my lungs as the band started to play. *Okay, Nolan. You can do this.*

I strutted onstage, the heat of the stage lights trying to warm my cold insides as I sang the opening lyrics to our debut song. The fans went wild. Especially the girls. Arms stretched toward me, the girls screamed and sang along with the upbeat melody and words. It was a song about chasing after a passion and making it yours. It was a song about success and what it took to get there. It was a song everyone could relate to, which was why it had done well on the charts.

I worked the stage, moving my body in time to the music, smiling at the girls. Making love to each one with my eyes. That only made them scream louder.

The song ended. "Hello, L.A. Are you ready to party?" I yelled into the microphone, then held it out for the audience to answer. The concert was sold out, and even though not everyone was here yet since we were just the opening act, the arena was already three-quarters full.

Answering my question, the place went wild with cheers, whistles, and hoots. "I can't hear you," I said, laughing. I cupped my hand against my ear, and I swear the answering noise could've cracked the roof.

Mason took this as the cue for the next song and seamlessly segued into the new beat on his drums. Another round of cheers charged the air as people recognized the song, and I continued feeding off the energy bouncing around the arena.

I strutted across the stage, song after song. The passion around me—from the band, the roadies behind the show, the fans—consumed me, helped me stay in the moment, helped me push aside the world outside the arena walls.

And then came the opening strains of the song I'd been dreading. Hailey's song. I'd written it for her before I left North-bridge, not that she knew my love for her had inspired the lyrics. "This One Moment" was our biggest hit. Everyone expected us to play it. It was the ballad that had critics comparing us to the bands I respected and admired.

The stage lights dimmed. A spotlight poured down on me, but it wasn't enough to push away the darkness growing inside me. I placed the mic in the stand and poured every emotion inside me into the song, as I did every time I sang it. The pain in my words was clear from the emotion in my voice. Girls mouthed the words, as if they too could relate to them. I closed my eyes, blocking out their faces. Only one face filled my thoughts every time I sang the lyrics.

And she was now in a coma.

That thought just about brought me to my knees. But somehow I kept myself together as I finished the song—the final one of the set, thank God.

The last notes of the music rang out over the audience, and the crowd burst into the loudest cheering of the night. I'd be surprised if the applause for Crazy Piper could top this.

We waved our appreciation to the audience and left the stage so the crew could set up for the main act. As I climbed down the last step, the roadie handed me my guitar, already in its case.

I high-fived my bandmates, our usual post-performance tradition. "Don't go too far," I told them. "Remar told me some reporter from *Rock News* wants to interview us."

The guys groaned. Post-concert interviews were the worst. Everyone wanted to get out of there and relax, not answer a bunch of ridiculous questions.

"Can't Mason at least shower first?" Kirk said, smirking at the drummer. "He reeks like something from my old hockey bag."

Mason leaned closer to the dark-haired bassist and lifted his arm so his armpit was near Kirk's face. "And I bet it's turning you on something fierce."

Kirk shoved him. "Save it for the women, asshole."

"No clue," I said, answering Kirk's question and ignoring their antics, even though normally I would've joined in. "Gotta do something first. Catch up with you in a few." I started to make a beeline for a side corridor, where I wouldn't be overheard, to book my plane ticket.

I didn't get that far.

A girl stepped away from the wall she'd been leaning against near the stage. She wasn't the usual variety of female who hung around concerts, hoping to see her much-beloved stars and possibly get lucky. Her straight blond hair hung to her shoulders and she had nice tits, but nothing compared to most of Mason's girls. Even her outfit was different from what most girls who hung around backstage wore. She had on jeans and a thin cardigan, and looked like she'd be more comfortable in a library than at a rock concert. Only the media badge hanging around her neck betrayed her reason for being here.

Shit.

She held out her hand to me. "Hi. I'm Jodi Merrill with *Rock News.*"

I shook her hand, though I'm sure she regretted that considering I'd just played a forty-minute set under hot stage lights and I was positive I'd sweated at least two gallons of fluid. But if my sweaty hand disgusted her, she didn't show it. "Tyler Erickson."

She also shook hands with each of the guys, not once flinching at how sweaty they were, and indicated for us to follow her, away from the backstage craziness.

Pretending to listen to her glowing review of the concert, I fought back the need to remove Hailey's picture from my pocket and examine it. It wasn't as if that would save the girl I loved. All it would accomplish was to let everyone know she existed.

A few minutes later we were sitting in a room with nothing more than a table and several plastic chairs. Nothing like where

Remar had been waiting for me. But as sparse as the room was, life and energy weren't taking a vacation. They were all around me, doing their best to soothe my agitation at being here instead of being on the phone with the airline.

Jodi placed her iPhone in front of her on the table. "Is it okay if I record the interview?"

"Sure, go ahead," I said. Not that it ever made a difference. Even when they recorded the interviews, reporters still kept quoting us out of context.

My knee began bouncing, counting away the seconds the interview was delaying my escape.

"First off, thank you for agreeing to let me interview you guys."

I almost snorted at that. The way I saw it, we hadn't been given a choice.

The interview proceeded as they normally do. Jodi first asked us about our musical influences. Next came the questions about our pasts, which I faked as usual.

"Have you always lived in L.A.?" She looked at each one of us, but paused on me for what felt like the longest.

"Yes." I practically held my breath at where this could possibly be going, but she apparently took what I said at face value. Jared, Kirk, and Mason replied the same.

"I'm from small-town Illinois," Aaron said. "But I moved to L.A. when I didn't get into Juilliard."

"Do you ever regret that you didn't make it in?" she asked him.

"Hell, no. Originally I wanted to compose movie music, but rocking the stage night after night is way more fun."

"And more likely to get him laid," I said with a chuckle.

The rest of the guys laughed. My knee bounced faster. *C'mon, end the interview.* I kept silently repeating the words to myself, hoping to send her a subliminal message.

Jodi rolled her eyes. "So, what was the spark about each of you that made you want to put together the band?"

"Jared and I had known each other for a few months," I said, trying not to groan out loud at my failed attempts at subliminal messages, "after the girls we were seeing at the time decided we should meet. We were both musicians playing the L.A. scene, but neither of us was in a regular band. We were just jamming around with other musicians. I'd been writing my own songs for years, but I'd never played them for anyone." *Other than for Hailey.* "It was only with Jared's encouragement that I finally played them for him."

"I knew Tyler was a great singer and not a bad guitar player," Jared explained, "but I had no idea about the depths of his talent. Not until I heard his songs. That's when I knew he shouldn't be wasting his time playing with cover bands. So I told him as much."

I burst out laughing. "Actually, what he really said was that we had a chance to make it big if I'd stop screwing around with covers. But I realized he was right. I already knew we worked well together onstage, and once we started collaborating on songs, we knew we had what it took to get where we wanted to be. But we needed a bassist and drummer. We'd seen Kirk and Mason playing around the circuit with numerous other bands. None of the bands seemed right for them. I knew Kirk was a business major, and figured he'd bring more to the table than just his musical talent."

Kirk snorted. "Face it. You only asked me 'cause you guys needed a manager."

I grinned at him. "Damn straight." I looked back at Jodi. "It was the best decision Jared and I made. Without Kirk, we would be just another band trying to be heard in the crowded L.A. music scene. He got us seen." Mason slapped his buddy on the back.

"Aaron joined us after he approached us one night at a gig,"

I went on, "and told us we needed him. We were skeptical at first when we heard he was a classically trained pianist, but we gave him a chance to audition and he proved himself right."

Aaron chuckled. "I'm always right. Eventually you guys will realize that." He high-fived Kirk, his biggest supporter in the band.

The interview continued with some thought-provoking questions about our lyrics and ambitions for future projects.

"Right now we're just focused on writing songs for our next album. Beyond that . . . well, who knows," I said, biting back the urge to check the time. I could practically hear the seconds ticking. And as each second passed, my restlessness climbed a hundredfold. If this interview didn't end soon, I'd have to feign a sudden illness.

"More and more singers have dabbled in Broadway and Hollywood. Have you considered becoming an actor, Tyler?"

Considered? I am one, every freakin' day. I shook my head. "It's all about the music for me."

"What about the rest of you?"

They just shrugged. I doubt it was something that had entered any of their minds.

Then came the questions I always dreaded: the girlfriend ones.

"Of the five of you, only Tyler has a girlfriend. Tell me, Tyler, what's it like to be dating Alyssa Graham?"

"We're just friends."

In Hollywood and the music industry that was the code for "Yes, we're fucking each other's brains out, but we don't want anyone to know about it." But in our case, it wasn't even true. We actually were just friends, or more like acquaintances. But the paparazzi loved her, and before I knew it, I'd been romantically linked with her. I quickly learned that explaining myself was pointless. People wanted to believe whatever suited them, and Jodi was no exception.

She nodded in a way meant to signal she understood what I was saying, but the gleam in her eyes told the opposite. She was as much in love with the fictitious romance between Alyssa and me as everyone else was. It didn't help that Alyssa was doing nothing to dispute the erroneous belief.

Jodi asked the guys several questions about girls in general and about what they looked for in a possible mate.

"I don't know," Mason said. "I like being a free agent."

Unable to hold back any longer, I removed my phone from my back pocket and checked the time while the guys laughed at Mason's answer.

Would this interview ever end?

4

NOLAN

My question was answered several minutes later when Jodi thanked us and we were free to go.

"I'll catch up with you later," I told the guys. Once they were out of hearing range, I called the airline and booked the next available flight home.

All I had time for was a quick wash in the men's bathroom before I had to leave for the airport. Fortunately, I had a spare T-shirt and antiperspirant in my bag, which I picked up on my way to the bathroom, so the person who sat next to me on the plane wouldn't be suffering too much.

As I walked to the back entrance, my gym bag slung over my shoulder, I sent Brandon a text, letting him know when my flight to Northbridge would land. I was booked on the 11:55 flight, with a connection in Atlanta, but wouldn't arrive until 10:30 tomorrow morning. But at least I could head straight to the hospital. By then it'd be visiting hours.

Now that Crazy Piper was performing onstage, their music vibrating through the walls and the floor, the area was empty of both crew and VIP fans who were allowed backstage. No one cared that I was leaving. My part of the evening was over.

A security guard at the end of the hallway walked toward me. He nodded at me, an acknowledgment to have a good evening. I nodded back.

As my cab sped toward the airport, Brandon responded to my text.

> Brandon: See you tomorrow. Will pick you up
> at airport.

> Me: Any news about Hailey?

> Brandon: Sorry. Nothing.

Jared sent me a text as the cab approached the airport, asking me where I'd bailed to. I ignored it. I didn't feel like lying, but I also didn't want to tell him the truth.

Before climbing out of the cab, I pulled on my sunglasses and my nondescript baseball cap, paid the driver, and high-tailed it to check-in.

As much as I hated it, I was forced to check my guitar. I would've left it with Jared, along with my other gear, but figured I could at least work on some songs while I was away. With the record label's deadline looming over me, I couldn't treat this trip like a vacation. Every minute I wasn't with Hailey would require me to work my ass off, creating new songs.

I hurried to my gate, stopping on the way to grab a soda—something with caffeine. I did my best to avoid checking out the tabloids while in line to pay, but the headline "Baby in Tyler Erickson and Alyssa Graham's Future?" was enough for me to grab an issue and pay for it along with the drink.

On the tabloid's cover, the magazine had drawn a circle around Alyssa's stomach and scrawled the words "Baby Bump Alert!" If she was pregnant, and it was hard to tell from the photo if she was or not, I could guarantee the baby wasn't mine.

Not only had we never fucked each other, I always used condoms.

At the gate, I avoided the waiting area, preferring to stay away from the crowd. I stood near the window and stared at the night sky. My mind raced back to the last time I'd been in my hometown. Hailey had driven me to the airport and told me to call her as soon as I got to L.A. I never did. And I never responded to the numerous texts she sent me over the next four months. I couldn't, as much as it killed me. I was no longer the guy she had known since third grade. Besides, Hailey knew I was alive. She had ambushed Brandon, demanding to know what was going on—the same question he frequently asked me but which I'd never been able to answer.

The flight boarded a few minutes later. I waited until my section was called to commence boarding, then approached the line. If anyone recognized me, they kept it to themselves, and the woman checking boarding passes looked like she was probably the furthest thing from being a fan of the band.

I followed the other passengers onto the plane and located my seat near the back, next to the window. I was barely settled when a woman in her late fifties pulled her suitcase to my row and inspected the overhead compartment. Her gaze jerked to her luggage, then back to the compartment. Releasing a long, hard sigh, she bent down and picked up the bag.

"Do you need help with that?" I asked.

"Yes, please." She smiled, and my heart pinched at how much her smile reminded me of my mom, as did her floral perfume.

As if the trip wouldn't be painful enough.

I helped her with the luggage, then sat down again and leafed through the tabloid until I found the article I'd been searching for. Inwardly I groaned. If I didn't know better, I'd be convinced from reading this that Alyssa and I were very much in love. And yes, the photo of her kissing me, which wasn't what it looked like, didn't help my case either.

"You know none of that is true, right?" The woman, who had sat next to me while I was reading, tipped her head toward the tabloid in my hand. "It's all fiction. Every word of it," she tutted, making me feel ashamed for reading it even though I knew nothing in the magazine was true. "I can't believe people waste their money on that garbage. If they didn't do that, the magazines wouldn't have the need to print hurtful articles and pictures."

"You're right. They wouldn't." I expected her to continue her anti-tabloid rant, maybe indicate that she recognized me as the guy in the magazine. But she didn't. She yawned and closed her eyes. Within minutes, as we pulled away from the gate, her breathing became slow and even.

Exhaustion pulled up a chair, the adrenaline rush from over two hours ago beginning to fade. I shoved the tabloid into the seat pocket in front of me and removed the picture of Hailey from the front pocket in my notebook, the place where I normally kept it. I stroked my finger across her high cheekbone. But the laminated photo was a poor substitute for the flesh-and-blood girl. All the girls I had been with in the past few years had been a poor substitute for the real Hailey. And none of them had cared. They'd only been interested in Tyler Erickson, rising rock star.

That was fine by me. I didn't have the time or interest in something more substantial than that. My career came first.

I opened my notebook. The least I could do while traveling home was work on lyrics for a new song. God knows I hadn't written much while we were on the road. It wasn't practical. You would've thought that with mile after mile of endless highways on the tour, we would've had plenty of time to write. But inspiration for new songs had been sadly lacking.

And it had been that way even before the tour.

BOTH FLIGHTS WERE UNEVENTFUL, BUT BY THE TIME WE LANDED in Northbridge, Minnesota, I was ready to sleep for a hundred-plus years. It showed in the crappy lyrics I'd managed to scrawl in my notebook. No chart topper there.

I grabbed my sports bag and the woman's suitcase from the overhead compartment, and waited for the passengers in front of me to disembark. As far as I was concerned, they couldn't move fast enough.

As I waited, I turned on my phone to check if Brandon had called. He hadn't, but Jared had. As much as I wanted to avoid this, I couldn't delay it much longer. Even Jared had his limits as to how much of my bullshit he would take.

"Hey, you called," I said after he answered the phone.

"Where the hell are you?" he replied, sounding like his annoying morning-person self, even though he would've returned to our apartment well after midnight. "You never came home last night."

I smirked. "Sorry, Mom. Didn't realize I needed to check in with you."

"Ha ha. Was Mason right? Did you go off with that reporter?"

The line of people in front of me began moving. I followed, eager to get to the baggage claim before they started unloading the luggage. "Why would Mason think that?" I said, stalling.

"Because you held back when the rest of us left. What was he supposed to believe?"

"She wasn't my type." I didn't have a type, other than the woman with long brown hair who was in a coma.

I entered the building and followed the stream of passengers headed for the baggage claim area.

"US flight 745 to New York City is now getting ready to

board," a female voice announced on the PA system. "Please have your boarding passes and photo ID ready."

"Why the hell are you at the airport?" Jared asked.

Shit. "Family emergency." Not that I had family here or anywhere. Both of my parents had been only children.

"Sorry to hear that. When are you coming back?"

I cringed. "I don't know."

"Well, as long as you're back in time for us to start working on new material. But that shouldn't be a problem. It's not like you're planning to be gone for two months, right?"

Double shit. "We don't have two months." My words were cautious, a rabbit waiting for a rattler to strike. "Remar told me the label managed to hire Daniel Maynard to produce our album." I didn't need to tell Jared who Maynard was. Jared's biggest dream was to one day work with the producer. "We're due in the studio December twenty-seventh."

"Fuck. And when were you planning on telling me this?"

Ignoring the escalator and the passengers herding onto it, I trotted down the stairs. "You make it sound like I was keeping it a secret. I just found out last night, before the concert. I'd planned to tell you sooner but didn't have a chance. Look, as soon as I know when I can come home, I'll let you know. And in the meantime, I'll work on some songs here. There's this wonderful invention called Skype. If worse comes to worst, we can use that." It wasn't ideal, but it was the best solution I could come up with until I knew more about Hailey's condition.

Jared muttered, "We're screwed." For now I had to agree with him, but wisely kept that to myself. "So why did Remar want to talk to you and not the rest of the band?"

"Hell if I know. I also have no idea why he arranged the interview instead of Jennifer doing it. I would've thought PR work was beneath him."

"Good point."

"But next time he pulls that stunt, I'll remind him we're a

group, not a solo act." The last thing I wanted was unfounded resentment among the guys. We were friends. I wanted it to stay that way.

I told Jared I'd talk to him soon, and ended the call.

I tracked down the flight's assigned baggage carousel. Brandon had beaten me to it and was waiting for me, a weak smile on his face. I gave him a one-armed hug.

"Sorry, dude. No news yet," he said, already knowing what my first question would be.

"How could this have happened?"

"I don't know. The police interviewed me this morning. They're trying to figure out why she was in Westgate. That's all I know."

"Westgate? Why the hell would she be there?" The only people who hung out in that part of town were drug dealers and prostitutes. The last I'd heard, Hailey was neither of those.

"Hell if I know. It's not like Hailey keeps me updated on her life. I haven't talked to her much in the past six years. Not after she figured out I was keeping things about you from her." He shot me a look to remind me how much he'd hated lying to her.

I ignored it and grabbed my guitar off the conveyor belt. Now I was almost complete. As complete as I would ever be.

"Was she . . . ?" I swallowed hard, unable to say the next part but needing to know all the same.

Brandon shook his head. "According to my mom, there were no signs of sexual assault or rape."

I let out a long breath, and for the first time since Brandon had told me the news about Hailey, a small amount of tension unknotted from my muscles.

We didn't say much else as Brandon drove me to the hospital, mostly because I was exhausted from the combination of touring, last night's show, and then traveling hard since I boarded the plane in L.A. Not once had I slept during the two flights, my mind constantly on Hailey.

"Just so you know," Brandon said, "you can only stay at my place for three days."

I lifted an eyebrow. "What, I'm cramping your style?"

He snorted. "Hardly. It's my roommate." *Ah, the roommate from Nerdsville.* "He's a real stickler for rules, and my apartment will only let us have guests for up to three days. If he wasn't coming back on Wednesday, it wouldn't be an issue. They'd never know."

"That's okay. I'll find somewhere else to stay."

"You still have . . ." His words fizzled at my glare.

"I'm not staying there, so don't even suggest it."

"You haven't even tried to sell it."

I shrugged. End of discussion.

Brandon pulled into the hospital parking lot thirty minutes later and took me to the ER, where his mom worked as a nurse. Hailey was in neurology, but he figured my best shot at seeing her would be through his mom. He didn't know if Hailey's parents were at the hospital to grant me permission to see her, and we didn't want to bug them if they weren't. I loved her parents and they had always treated me like a son, but I didn't know what they thought about me after my father had exchanged his engineering career for the title of mass murderer. Maybe they wondered if I would turn out like him.

Fuck knows I'd frequently wondered that myself.

With my hat and sunglasses on, I sat on a plastic chair away from the crowd. No one paid attention to me, not even to glance in my direction. Everybody there was caught up in the frustration of having to wait so long—caught up in their own private hell.

After I talked to Brandon's mom for a few minutes, she sent me upstairs to neurology.

Pushing on the door to Hailey's room, I removed my hat and sunglasses. A colorful display of flowers, taking up every available surface, greeted me, along with the nose-twitching combination of disinfectant and roses. The people who sent them couldn't have known Hailey very well. The Hailey I remembered thought roses were a cliché.

Hailey's mom glanced up from the seat next to the bed. Her eyes were red from either crying or lack of sleep, or maybe both.

"I'm so glad you came, Nolan." She stood and threw her arms around me in the way I always remembered her doing, and a pain I hadn't experienced in six years sliced through me. It had been a long time since someone had hugged me this way, this sincerely. Girls were always trying to hug me once they recognized me. But that was because of who I was. Hailey's mom didn't care about any of that. "How did you know?" she asked, pulling away.

"Brandon called me last night. I came as soon as I could get a flight here."

I looked down at the girl I loved, and my heart almost cracked in two. Whoever had attacked her had done a number on her, but behind the bruised, puffy face and the thin oxygen tube attached under her nose, she was the same beautiful girl I remembered. The same beautiful girl I had known, deep down, I would return to when the time was right. Once my life was less complicated with the band and touring. Once I no longer feared reliving the memories from the night I'd lost my family.

Her long brown hair was still shiny and inviting. I itched to stroke my fingers through it to see if it was as silky as it had been six years ago. I longed to lean close to her and see if she still smelled like my favorite sugar cookies, sweet with a hint of vanilla.

"What do you want to make?" she had asked me just before our last Christmas together. We'd been standing hip to hip in her parents' kitchen, poring over a recipe book while she took a break from her studies. "Gingersnaps or chocolate chip cookies?"

"If we make star-shaped sugar cookies," I said, fighting the craving to kiss her, to let her know how I felt about her, "then we can decorate them."

She giggled. "You mean then you can eat all the frosting."

I'd smirked. "That too." Hailey had known me too well.

"What happened?" I asked her mom now. "Do the cops have any leads?"

With her gaze on Hailey, Mrs. Wilkins shook her head. "The last we heard from her was when she was at your house. My husband had asked her to go there and locate some information off a legal document he said you needed." I knew about that. My lawyer had contacted him because I was considering finally selling the place. "She found it, told him what he needed to know, and then was headed out to meet up with someone before going to work. She never showed up at the sports center for her shift." She wrapped her arms around herself. "They found her and her abandoned car in Westgate."

"Who was she supposed to meet?"

"She never said, and Jim didn't think to ask." She gave me a small smile. "It's good to see you back. Are you going to be here for long?"

Apparently Hailey had never told her mom that after I'd left the college town, I ignored Hailey's attempts to communicate with me. She'd never told her mom how I had treated her like she'd never existed, like she'd never consumed my waking thoughts all this time.

I continued watching Hailey's slow, rhythmic breathing. She looked peaceful. A princess sleeping until true love's kiss woke her up, like in Hailey's favorite fairy tale. I wished it had been as simple as that.

"I'm not sure yet." I wasn't sure if Mrs. Wilkins was asking how long I'd be staying here in the hospital or in Northbridge, and I couldn't be bothered to ask which one she meant.

I finally looked back up at her. Her eyelids were drifting

shut, and I was surprised she was still standing. "Have you gone home at all since she was admitted?"

She shook her head and glanced at her daughter.

"You should go home and get some rest. I'll stay with her until you get back." What I really wanted was to be alone with Hailey so I could apologize for all my screw-ups. But I'd only do that while she was in a coma and wouldn't remember everything I told her once she woke up. At least I didn't think she'd remember.

Her mom smiled at me, the effort weak at best. "Thanks for coming, Nolan. It will mean everything to her."

I didn't believe that, but I nodded anyway.

Once I was finally alone with Hailey, I leaned down and brushed my lips against hers, doing the one thing I'd fantasized about for as long as I could remember.

As expected, Hailey's eyelids didn't flutter open like in the fairy tale.

I took the seat her mom had vacated and wrapped my fingers around the hand free of the IV, then brushed a stray strand of hair off Hailey's face.

"Hey, Forget-Me-Not," I said, using the nickname I'd given her when we were kids and she had been obsessed with the tiny blue flower. "I've missed you." I gently stroked my thumb against the back of her hand. "I'm so sorry I blocked you out of my life. Just know that I didn't want to, but I couldn't survive here anymore and . . . and I knew you deserved better than me." I glanced back at the flowers. Funeral flowers. "I couldn't take the pressure of trying to remember that night . . . nor did I want to remember it."

All I could hope for was that my return to Northbridge wouldn't drag me back into the nightmare.

That my return wouldn't trigger the memory of the night my mother and sister died.

5

HAILEY

I was dreaming.

That was the only way I could explain it. I could hear Nolan's voice in my head even though it couldn't be him. The guy who'd been my best friend, who'd always known how to make me laugh, and whom I'd been falling for, had moved away six years ago and had never spoken to me again.

No, this guy's voice definitely did *not* belong to Nolan.

I wished I could even pretend it had been a long time since I'd seen him, since I'd heard him, and that was why my memory wasn't so clear. But that would be a lie. Ever since his band started getting radio time, I'd paid attention to everything that was Nolan. Except now he was Tyler Erickson.

A guy I didn't recognize, but a guy I missed all the same.

I strained to hear what the voice was saying. The words were garbled, like whoever was talking to me was on the other side of a sheet of glass separating us.

How long he'd been talking to me was a mystery. I kept drifting in and out of awareness. But each time I drifted back, the voice was clearer, as were the words, to the point where I was positive it was Nolan.

Then the beautiful, breathtaking melody of an acoustic guitar filled every part of me with longing. It was one of my favorite songs. Always had been since the first time Nolan sang it to me. Back then, I had imagined that he'd written "This One Moment" about me, about us. That the love I heard in the lyrics and in his voice had been directed at me.

Three weeks later he'd disappeared from my life and I realized I'd been wrong. The song wasn't about anyone in particular. He hadn't been in love with me.

The voice, the one filling my dreams, started singing again, and the emotions I always felt when I heard the song became a jumbled mess.

I wanted the song to stop.

I didn't want the song to stop.

The corners of my lips curved up in a slight smile. Warm callused fingers gently brushed the back of my hand.

"Hailey? Hey, babe, are you gonna open your beautiful eyes for me?" Nolan's deep voice sank into my body, hugging my bones tight, and the full-bodied richness melted me to the core.

I wanted to do as he asked. Even if he was just a dream, I wanted to open my eyes and see him. Really see him.

With all the strength I could muster in my achy body, which felt like someone had mistaken me for a soccer ball and kept kicking it against the wall, I cracked open my eyelids.

A bright light pounded on my brain and my head screamed in pain. I let my eyelids drift shut.

The fingers stroking my hand moved to my face, and a thumb brushed against my cheek. "Hey, Forget-Me-Not. Am I gonna have to kiss you like the prince kissed Sleeping Beauty?"

Yes, please.

Apparently I hadn't just answered that in my mind like I'd thought I had. A warm breath kissed my mouth first, before a pair of real lips, as soft as I'd imagined they would be, briefly touched mine.

Then all too quickly they pulled away, leaving behind the crisp lingering scent that reminded me of lemons and sunshine. Nolan's scent.

I turned my head, taking care not to move it too fast and cause the pain to worsen. I opened my eyes again, the movement slow. This time the light wasn't as bright as before. It took a moment or two for the world to come into focus. The IV attached to the back of my hand. The rough sheets, thin, almost weightless, not at all like my comfy bedding at home. The bland white walls with the two nondescript beige doors. The only real color in the room came from the explosion of flowers on the nightstand and the windowsill.

Behind me, I heard a regular beeping noise from the heart rate monitor. I hadn't noticed the sound until now, so I had no idea if it had kept the same steady beat when those warm lips touched mine. God, I hoped the damn thing hadn't sped up. Shoot me now if it had.

Once my eyes adjusted to the room and the light without another flash of pain stabbing my head, I turned toward Nolan. He hadn't changed much since he'd left Northbridge. He still looked very much like the guy I had grown up with. The guy who had practiced dribbling the soccer ball with me hours after everyone else had gone home. The guy who hadn't laughed at how much I sucked when he tried to teach me to play the guitar. And the guy I had fantasized kissing, night after night. His light brown hair was shaggier than back then, which only made him sexier. His normally smooth face was rough with a day or two of growth, which also made him sexier. And I knew without removing his shirt that his body was as lean and muscular as before.

Seeing him in front of me hurt almost as much the dull throb in my head. I hadn't realized how much I missed him until now. The glossy-picture version, the music-video version, the TV-interview version were all weak facsimiles of the real deal.

"Hey, pretty girl. Fancy meeting you here." The sexy, mischievous smile I clearly remembered from six years ago slipped onto his face. And this time the heart rate monitor did betray the upkick of my heart rate.

I glared at it; Nolan chuckled at my reaction. Luckily, unless he'd learned to read minds during the past six years, he didn't know he was the cause of the momentarily faster beep.

"What are you . . . doing here?" I asked, my voice slurred and weak, as if it had been dragged over asphalt.

"Brandon called two days ago and told me you had been attacked and were in a coma. I came as soon as I could get a flight here."

My brain slowly processed the things he'd said, and I wasn't sure which left me with the most questions. I decided to go with the most pressing issue first. I'd worry later about the part where he'd come back to see me, especially after he'd abandoned me all those years ago and never bothered to return my calls or texts. "What do you . . . mean, I was . . . attacked?"

Nolan's eyebrows furrowed together. "Don't you remember what happened?"

I thought for a second or two, but that caused the pain in my brain to become more intense. For now, thinking was *not* my best friend. "I remember going to . . . work. That's the last thing I . . . remember."

The crevasse between his eyebrows deepened. "What day was that?"

"Monday."

"You were attacked Friday night. You don't remember anything at all about that night?"

"No," I whispered, and closed my eyes, letting the sweet floral scent wash over me.

The need to curl up and sleep staggered through me. The

world felt like . . . no, *I* felt like I was going in slow motion while my brain struggled to keep up.

A door swooshed open.

"She's awake," Nolan said. "But she doesn't remember anything since last Monday."

I peeled my eyes open again, curious to see whom he was talking to. Nolan rubbed the back of his neck as he studied me, as if by doing that he could answer his own questions.

A woman in her thirties, wearing blue scrubs, approached the bed. "Good afternoon, hon. How's the pain?"

"I hurt. All over."

Nolan laced his fingers with mine, like he used to whenever I got hurt playing soccer. Back when I'd first begun falling for him.

"How about your head?" the nurse asked.

"Especially my head."

"Let me adjust your pain meds."

"What about how she can't remember the attack or what happened for several days before it?" Nolan asked. I wasn't sure how I felt about the worry in his tone. He didn't have the right to be worried about me. He'd forfeited that right after giving me the silent treatment for years.

That was what I kept telling myself, but deep in my bones I knew that was a lie. He'd come back. For me. He hadn't forgotten about me after all.

I smiled inwardly and let my thoughts drift to how it would feel to kiss him again. To really kiss him. Despite the pain plaguing my body, a different kind of ache tormented me at the thought of that kiss.

"Sorry, the drugs won't help her there," the nurse said. "But the physician on call will be here soon to check her out." To me she said, "Is there anything else you need?"

"Water, please."

She grabbed the pitcher from the nightstand beside my bed

and went into what I guessed was the bathroom. She returned shortly after and filled the plastic glass next to where the pitcher had been. After adjusting my bed so I was partially sitting, she handed me the glass. I took the container with shaky hands and sipped the cold water through the straw. Nolan helped me hold the glass since my muscles weren't quite ready to do this alone.

Once I'd had enough, he placed it on the metal nightstand, the nurse long since gone. "Thanks."

He then lowered the side railing on the bed. Without asking me if it was okay, he sat on the small available space next to my legs. But he wasn't close enough, in my opinion, and I subtly shifted my leg so it touched his hip. Despite the bedding and his jeans between us, his warmth seeped into my leg, and I sighed, the sound too soft to be heard by him.

I closed my eyes, fighting the urge to go to sleep. "I feel lost," I mumbled. "What day is it?" I somehow managed to find the strength to open my eyes again.

"Tuesday. You've been in a coma since Friday."

It took me a moment to register his words. "Coma?" The word poured out slowly, like a foreign term I was trying to wrap my brain around. "Who . . . attacked me?"

"I don't know. The police don't know either. Can you think of any reason why you'd be in Westgate?"

I shuddered at the name. I only knew the place by reputation. It was the part of town good girls like me never went to. "Westgate? Why . . . why would I be there?" I said, more to myself than to Nolan. He clearly knew as little as I did. My gaze jerked back to him. "I still don't get why you're here, Nolan."

Pain flickered across his gorgeous face, but it vanished so quickly that maybe I'd imagined it. I kept staring at him, afraid that if I blinked, I'd wake up for real and he'd be gone.

Not that it mattered if he did disappear. It wasn't like he'd be sticking around. He had no need to. His life wasn't here. It was in L.A., with his band, and with his new girlfriend, Alyssa Graham. Those two were perfect together, as the media loved reminding me every chance they got.

"When Brandon told me you were in a coma," Nolan said, "I got scared. I was scared I'd never see you again."

I laughed, the sound a tinge bitter even if the attempt to laugh had been weak. Pain slashed my ribs at the movement, and I cringed. I'd been hurt plenty of times during soccer games, but I'd never hurt this much. And I was sure that if it hadn't been for the drugs pumping through my system, I'd be hurting a lot more than I currently did.

The frown was back on Nolan's face, the deep lines on his forehead peeking through his bangs. I craved to smooth away those lines and brush his hair out of his warm chocolate-brown eyes. A girl could get lost in those eyes, and many already had.

"Why would you be . . . scared you'd never . . . see me again?" I asked. "You haven't exactly . . . made a lot of effort to . . . see me as it is." The bitterness from my laugh now coated my words. I hadn't meant for them to come out that way. Guess the drugs were more powerful than I realized. The truth serum of emotions.

Well, if that was true, I'd have to work super hard at making sure Nolan didn't figure out how I really felt about him. That'd be the last thing he'd want to hear.

Nolan looked away, his gaze landing on the window. From my vantage point, all I could see was the crisp late-fall sky, blue and almost cloud free. I couldn't even tell if there was new snow on the ground. The last I remembered, it had been in the forecast.

"I'm sorry, Hailey." His gaze returned to me, and the sexy one-sided smile crept back onto his face. And once again the stupid heart rate monitor proudly announced the effect that his smile had on me. *Seriously, heart, don't you have something better to do?*

"I know I've been an asshole," Nolan continued, and no way was I arguing against that. "I should've at least answered your texts and let you know I was okay. I figured you were better off without me in your life, and as selfish as it sounds, I wanted a new start. I couldn't do that if I kept in contact with people here. I wanted to forget this town. I wanted to forget everything about it."

Part of that I could understand. And part of it was a lie. "You kept in contact with Brandon." If he claimed he only kept in contact with Brandon because Brandon was his best friend, I'd nail him on the side of his head with my pillow.

We'd been friends for too long for me not to know what he was thinking. Maybe I was a little rusty now at figuring him out, and maybe he had perfected the skill of masking his emotions while he was away being a rock star. But I could tell he was thinking the same thing as me when it came to Brandon and the best-friend excuse. He knew I'd call bullshit if he tried that one.

"I know," he said. "And I also figured you'd beat the info out of him if you wanted to know how I was doing."

Somehow I managed not to laugh at that and at the memory of when I had been twelve years old and wanted to be part of Nolan and Brandon's secret club. Only boys were allowed. That had been Brandon's idea. Nolan was all for me joining, and he explained to Brandon how I could benefit the club, most notably because I could sneak in cookies. It was only when I started hitting Brandon on the head with a pillow that he finally changed his mind.

"And I didn't exactly ignore you," Nolan added. "Brandon attended all your games back when you were playing on the collegiate team, and taped them for me."

My eyes widened. "He did?" I knew Brandon had been at the games, and I'd always thought that was a little odd. Unlike Nolan and me, Brandon had never been a soccer fan. Hockey and football were more his sports. And unlike Nolan and me, he'd never spent his childhood attending practices. He'd never stayed up late, practicing his footwork until he was doing it in his sleep.

"You didn't think I'd miss it, did you?" Nolan sounded almost horrified I would even believe that. "And by the way, congratulations on being voted MVP."

I blinked. "You knew?"

His sexy grin became a full-out beam. "Of course I knew you were named most valuable player. I might not have kept in direct contact with you, but you were still very much part of my life." He cleared his throat and shifted on my bed. "Now I sound like a creepy stalker."

If that made him a creepy stalker, then I was one too. As much I had first claimed I wouldn't go looking for info about him when his band first became popular, I hadn't been able to stop myself. When I read the fan sites about how amazing he was between the sheets, I knew I should quit punishing myself that way, but I still kept reading them. Although from the sound of it, beds usually weren't involved in the quick-and-dirty fuck sessions. Some girls practically wrote erotic novels in their enthusiasm to share about their shameless trysts with him.

When it came down to it, I'd believed I had somehow failed Nolan, but I'd wanted to make sure he was okay, even if he was no longer talking to me.

Now that he was back in my life, though, I knew I wouldn't survive once he left again—maybe this time forever.

All I could do was protect myself from falling even harder for him.

Only I didn't know how.

6

NOLAN

Shortly after I'd admitted to semi-stalking Hailey, the physician came into the room and asked me to leave while he examined her. So while I waited, I paced the hallway, pretending not to notice the nurses at the nurses' station watching me.

I was used to my life being splashed around the tabloids and by the media. It was part of the job. Okay, it wasn't exactly my real life that was talked about. Everything about it from before I met Jared was fiction. What little I chose to reveal, that is. I didn't have a cheat sheet in my pocket I could refer to, helping me remember details about the life I'd fabricated. I was still pretty elusive about my life prior to forming the band. I gave just enough details to satisfy most people's curiosity. But as lucky as I had been so far, I knew my secret wouldn't last forever. I knew eventually the media would find out the truth about my father. I was surprised they hadn't already.

Being pursued by fans and the media was commonplace for anyone in the spotlight. But admitting to Hailey that I had watched her soccer games from afar had felt awkward, and I was unsure if my actions had flattered or repulsed her. *Shocked* might have been a better word to describe her reaction. Brandon had done a good job keeping secret what I'd been up to when it came to Hailey.

I continued pacing the hallway, waiting to be allowed back in Hailey's room, waiting to find out how she was doing physically, and waiting to find out when her memory would return.

Right now an attacker was out there, and I had no idea why he had hurt Hailey. Nor did I have any idea if he would return to finish off the job. It could've been a random attack—Hailey might have been in the wrong place at the wrong time. But the attack also could have been planned. Maybe Hailey had found out something she shouldn't have. Maybe the attacker would try tracking her down to ensure she couldn't talk. Permanently.

I swallowed back the sour taste of irony. Both of us were dealing with amnesia. But while Hailey wanted to remember the past—*I* wanted her to remember her past—my memory was something that needed to stay buried in the three coffins where it belonged. Forgotten. By everyone.

Until Hailey remembered that night or remembered who might've wanted to hurt her, or until we knew if it had been a random attack or not, she wasn't safe. I had two options. The first one was to bring her back to L.A. Then I could work on songs with Jared for the upcoming album. But after we finished recording the album, there would be the promo blitz in anticipation of the release of the first single. Following that would be the exhaustive touring. I couldn't drag her along just to keep her safe. What was I even saying? No way would she agree to it. She had a life. She didn't need it to make it any more complicated than it already was by moving to L.A.

The second option was to stay with Hailey and see if I could help her jog her memory and be there for her while she recovered. Keep an eye on her as much as I could. But if she didn't remember what happened by the time I had to leave, then what?

"Hi." A female voice snapped me from my thoughts. Two girls in pink scrubs and with name tags identifying them as nursing students grinned at me.

"Aren't you Tyler Erickson?" the shorter girl squeaked. The second girl stared at me like someone had performed a tongue-ectomy on her.

"I am."

"Oh my God! We loooove your music. I didn't know you were doing a concert here tonight."

Every muscle fiber in my body stiffened. The last thing I wanted was to bump into fans while I was in town. Too many questions would start circulating, and the risk was always there that someone would remember who I really was and leak it to the media. "I'm not," I said, inwardly cursing myself for not having the foresight to wear my hat and sunglasses in the hallway.

"So why are you here?"

"What? In the hospital?" I asked. They nodded. I didn't want to talk about Hailey, or at least share about our past together. "I'm visiting a fan." It wouldn't be the first time since the band's debut album had climbed the charts that I had been asked to visit a fan in the hospital. So this lie was plausible.

"That's so sweet," the taller girl said, finally finding her voice. "Can we get your autograph?"

"Absolutely."

Both produced notebooks from their pockets for me to sign. I'd just finished signing for the second girl when a woman with a perma-frown approached. "Ladies, you're not here to harass patients and their visitors."

"But this is Tyler Erickson. The lead singer of Pushing Limits," the short girl gushed.

The scowl on the woman's face hardened. "I don't care who he is. But if you don't have enough work to do, I can find you some." Her tone made it clear that whatever she came up with would be far from pleasant.

Both girls hung their heads. "Yes, ma'am." Before she could respond, they scurried down the hall.

"Sorry about that," was all the woman said to me before following them, not giving me a chance to explain that it was all right, I hadn't minded.

I went back to pacing. By the time the physician poked his head out of Hailey's room, I'd worn a trench in the floor. "How's she doing?" I asked.

"Are you family?"

"I'm her fiancé." I hoped that wouldn't get back to her parents; if it did, I'd have some explaining to do. But I figured it would get me more answers than being just Hailey's friend.

He eyed me for a moment, almost causing me to squirm. I was positive he knew I'd lied, so I wasn't expecting it when he said, "She's doing well considering everything that has happened. I want to monitor her for a few days before I release her. And she'll be sore for a while."

"What about her memory? When will she get it back?"

"It's hard to say. It might never return." *Fuck.* That was not what I needed to hear. I thanked him and entered Hailey's room.

She was staring out the window, lost in thought, and not for the first time since she'd woken up, I wished I knew what she was thinking.

I used to be able to easily read her, but I was out of practice. I couldn't even tell if she was happy to see me. She hadn't exactly welcomed me with open arms. More like the opposite. I mean, other than the part about the kiss—although I doubted that she had even known it was me at the time.

But I couldn't blame her for her reaction after the shit-headed way I'd treated her. I'd intended to protect her, but all

I'd done was hurt her. I could spend the next ten years trying to make it up to her and I would always fall short.

I stepped closer to the bed. If she heard me approach, she didn't let on. She continued staring at the sky, as if she could find the missing memories spelled out in the clouds if she looked hard enough.

"What are you thinking?" I asked, desperate to break the tension.

"He said"—she gestured toward the door—"I might never remember the attack."

"I know. He told me. But there's a chance you will." Or that she would remember what had happened, but not enough for the police to arrest the asshole who'd attacked her. It was possible she hadn't even seen him, which would be great if the guy knew she couldn't identify him. But if he wasn't aware of that, Hailey could be in danger.

I sat back down next to her on the bed. I didn't know how to bring up my concerns without freaking her out. And no way would she *not* freak out. "I'm planning to stay in town until the police capture whoever did this to you."

"You can't do that," she blurted out. "Aren't you supposed to work on your next album or something?"

"I can work on the songs here."

"It's really not necessary, Nolan. I mean, what if I never get my memory back? You can't stay here indefinitely. Your life is in L.A."

I stared at her for a good ten seconds. It sounded like if she could've gotten out of bed, she would've escorted me to the door and wished me a good life before sending me on my way.

"Look, I'm concerned about your safety." I was one step from glaring at her to show her I meant business. "What if the attacker went after you specifically and knows where you live? You could have died. Maybe that was his intent but someone interrupted him and he didn't have a chance to kill you." *Way to go, Nolan, on sugarcoating it.*

Hailey rolled her eyes. Literally, fucking, rolled her eyes.

I folded my arms. "I'm serious. And I can stay with you until he's caught, or until I know you'll be safe."

She shook her head forcefully. "You don't have to worry about me. Besides, I . . . I have a boyfriend."

My heart punch-kicked my ribs, the pain reverberating inside me, and I tried to swallow back the air that solidified in my throat. "A boyfriend?"

"Yes, a boyfriend." She lifted her chin in the way that was totally Hailey. It was one of the things I loved about her. "So you can go back to L.A. and let him worry about my safety."

At the thought of just how much he'd done to protect her, anger clenched my gut in a tight fist. "Well, if it's true, you've got yourself one douchebag of a boyfriend."

She pressed her lips together, squeezing the blood from them until they were white. "He's not a douchebag. And what do you care, anyway?" Her voice cracked at the last part, and I inwardly threw numerous curses at myself. Brandon had mentioned at one point that she had a boyfriend, and it had almost killed me hearing that tidbit, so I'd never brought up the boyfriend question again.

"So where is this boyfriend? Why hasn't he been right here by your side every single day?"

"Because . . . because he was out of town."

"Was? So he's back now?"

She hesitated, her gaze going to the ceiling, and that was when I knew I had her. She didn't have a boyfriend. She just wanted to get rid of me. Well, to hell with that. It just made me want to stay put even more.

"He's due back today," she replied.

I patted her leg and kept my smirk in check. "Can't wait to meet him."

Hailey shifted on the bed, almost knocking me off the narrow space. "Maybe next time you're in town." Her eyes gave away what we both knew was true—that I wouldn't be returning to Northbridge after this.

A knock on the door interrupted our standoff. Before Hailey could say anything, a petite girl with long blond hair and curves that would drive most guys wild stepped into the room.

Hailey cursed under her breath.

7

NOLAN

Six Years Ago

The normally delicious smell of Mom's chicken casserole wasn't enough to hide the stench of fear and booze sitting heavy in the kitchen air. I grabbed a dinner plate from the cupboard. Dad expected me to serve him, just as he expected Mom to do the same. While I might not have cared if he was fed or not, I knew that if I didn't do it, Mom would ultimately pay for my recklessness.

I placed the plate full of food at his spot on the table.

"When's she coming home?" he asked, still leaning against the kitchen counter, whiskey bottle in hand. He made no move to sit. If I wanted to leave, I'd have to walk past him, dangerous glint in his eyes or not.

"She didn't say." *Never,* if Mom and Sarah were smart about it.

And maybe that was their plan.

Before I could do any form of rejoicing, a voice at the back of my head muttered, *As if that would ever happen.* Not as long as Mom believed that staying here was the only way she could provide for herself and her kids. It wasn't a big deal for me. I was eighteen and could leave anytime I wanted. But Sarah was only eleven.

I moved away from the table, ready to make my escape.

Dad grabbed my arm. "I'm not through talkin' to you."

I snatched my arm back and stalked to the kitchen door. "I need to do my homework."

As I reached to open the door, I heard a grunt behind me and instinctively spun around. That was the only warning I got. A blunt object hit my forehead, above my right eye. Whatever he'd thrown at my head shattered on contact with the stone-tiled floor.

I stood still, momentarily stunned, too dazed to fight back.

My father snatched the whiskey bottle from the counter and topped up his empty glass. His hand shook as he poured the brown liquid. It wasn't shaking because he'd hit me. He'd been drinking ever since he got home and found his wife and daughter gone. The note Mom had left said that her friend had suffered a stroke. There was no hint in it as to when they would return.

I blinked my senses back into place and walked out of the kitchen. Instead of heading to my room, I kept going, slamming the front door behind me. Adrenaline pumped through my body; all I wanted to do was run.

I sprinted down the front path, across the street, to the rear of Hailey's house. If it hadn't been for my sister and mother, I would have kept running and never looked back.

Blood dripped down the side of my face. I brushed my hand against my forehead. It stung like hell but somehow I managed not to flinch. Blood was smeared across my hand, warning me I couldn't hide the truth from Hailey.

As I contemplated turning around and walking to who knows where, Hailey's window opened.

"I'll be right down," she said through the screen. "Meet me out front."

She was already waiting for me in the doorway when I came up the pathway. Her short shorts revealed her toned, never-ending legs; her light purple tank top hinted at the lack of a bra. And I instantly forgot what had happened at home.

A frown scrunched between her eyes. She brushed my bangs across my forehead and inhaled sharply. "*Oh, God*, Nolan. What happened?" She inspected the wound. "You're gonna need stitches. It's pretty bad."

Her gaze dropped to mine, and her unanswered question shone in them, pleading for me to tell her what happened, giving away what she already suspected.

"I walked into the patio door. I wasn't paying attention and didn't realize it was closed." As much as I hated lying to her, I couldn't tell her the truth.

I couldn't risk my mother's life.

8

HAILEY

Present

For a moment Nolan looked dazed. Before I could ask him if he was okay, he shook his head, as if trying to clear his thoughts, and stared at my best friend. It was clear that she looked familiar to him but he couldn't figure out why.

Nothing about this should have made me feel jealous, but I would be lying if I said it didn't affect me. Sure, Kayla was the kind of girl guys normally drooled over. And sure, her curvy body and long blond hair were guy magnets. But she had a boyfriend whom she loved. And even if she was interested in Nolan, he wasn't mine, and never had been. He was free to stare at any girl he wanted to.

"Well, this explains the excitement at the nurses' station," Kayla said. "The prodigal rock star has returned." She hugged me hard, squeezing the air from my lungs. And I silently thanked the pain-med gods for my happy state of oblivion when it came to the pain I'd otherwise be feeling.

Kayla pulled away and whacked my arm. "Don't ever do that again. Promise me."

"Er, what exactly am I promising you?" For all I knew, she was referring to something that had happened during those five days missing from my memory.

She gestured at the hospital bed. "This. You being attacked. Getting yourself almost killed. It's the unspoken deal we made when we agreed to be best friends. Remember?"

I chuckled. "I do vaguely remember something about that." I looked at my other best friend, who was still watching Kayla, frowning. "Nolan, you remember Kayla, right?"

Kayla gasped in her fake melodramatic way, hand on her chest. "How could he not remember me? He and I were almost inseparable." She winked at him.

Inseparable was the last word I would've used to describe them.

Nolan's puzzled expression transformed into one of surprise, his eyebrows raised. "You look ... different."

"You mean I don't look fat anymore."

Nolan glanced at me for confirmation that he was standing in front of a live grenade. "Didn't say that."

"You're saying I still look fat?"

Some things never changed. Like when Nolan had put worms in Kayla's lunch in elementary school after she poured glue on his artwork project. She claimed she'd been helping him get an A. He thought different.

"No, you look great. You always did. What happened? You took Hailey up on her offer to run with you?"

Kayla ran her finger along the IV machine. "No, my mother died of a heart attack. I didn't want that to be me."

Silence weighed down the room at how much in common they shared.

"Sorry about your mom." Nolan's voice emerged like it had been dragged across a cheese grater. I longed to hug him and give him some sort of comfort. It couldn't have been easy for him to return to Northbridge with all the memories waiting to drown him.

"I know. And I'm sorry about what happened to your mom and sister. You left before I could tell you."

Nolan didn't respond. He walked stiffly to the windowsill, picked up the bouquet of pink roses, and read the card.

Kayla's expression was a mix of regret and sadness. Not because she was still thinking about her mom. She had long since moved past it, except for at certain times of the year. She realized, like I did, that Nolan hadn't pushed past his sister's and mother's deaths. He still hurt and would probably continue to feel that way for a long time. Murder wasn't something you could easily walk away from, especially given that he was there the night it happened. He might've even witnessed it. The last I'd heard from Brandon, Nolan had blocked out the memories of that night. He simply could not remember at all what had happened. Was that still the case?

Kayla's face brightened. That combined with the impish grin was the only warning I got before she blurted out, "So how long are you staying in town?"

"I'm not sure yet," he said. "I'm worried about what happened to Hailey. I want to make sure no one tries to hurt her again."

If I thought Kayla's face was bright before, that was nothing compared to now. Even the sun couldn't compare with it.

Which made me all the more nervous.

"If you're worried about her," she continued, avoiding eye contact with me, "you should stay at her place. I happen to know that her roommate is moving out, and Hailey hasn't replaced me yet."

While Nolan looked like he could kiss her, I was ready to hit her with a . . . with my pillow. That would be justified assault, right?

The stupid sexy smile that always did me in returned to Nolan's face. The equally stupid heart rate monitor failed to keep the always-did-me-in part a secret. I wasn't a hundred percent sure, though, if the rapid beeping was because of his smile or because, unless I talked him out of it, Nolan might be sleeping with me. Correction—he'd be sleeping under the same roof as me. But try telling that to my body and heart when they didn't give a damn about semantics.

"You think her boyfriend will be okay with me staying with her?" he asked, the smirk in his voice directed at me.

I attempted to send Kayla a silent message to go along with my original lie. But since she hadn't been around for it, that was hopeless.

"You don't have to worry about that," she said. "Hailey is as single as you can get."

Thanks, traitor.

I glared at her, but that was as useful as my mental message. "I don't need a babysitter," I grumbled. "And maybe I don't want a roommate. Maybe I'm happy to live on my own."

"Well, *I'd* feel happier if you didn't live on your own," Kayla said. "At least for now."

Nolan crossed his arms and waited for my next volley.

I bit back the urge to tell him that if he was so desperate to stay in Northbridge, he could stay at his parents' place. I might not be happy with the direction of the conversation, but I would never say anything so callous to him. "He can stay with Brandon."

Nolan shifted, and the sexy smirk was back. "Can't do that."

"Why not?"

"His roommate won't allow it. Has something against rock stars."

I snorted. Nolan was the never the type of person to refer to himself as a rock star, no matter how famous he became. A musician, yes. A singer, yes. A songwriter, absolutely. But never anything as ostentatious as a rock star. His down-to-earth attitude was another reason I loved him. That had never changed, even while he pretended to be someone he wasn't.

"Then it's settled," Kayla said, making herself at home on the only seat in the room. "You can crash in my old room while you're in town."

9

———

NOLAN

Northbridge had been my home from the day I was born until the day I turned my back on it. Over the years, I'd let my memories of the college town, with its beaches, the lake, and the surrounding deciduous forest, fade away.

The only memories that hadn't faded with time were of Hailey. And yes, she was just as beautiful and just as goddamn stubborn as I remembered.

The apartment door opened and Kayla gestured for me to enter. I still hadn't convinced Hailey to let me stay, but I had talked Kayla into letting me help move her stuff to her boyfriend's apartment. We hadn't been close before, but right now I needed her to be my ally when it came to Hailey.

"So what's the deal about Hailey's ex-boyfriend?" I hoped I sounded like an interested friend, instead of a jealous guy who still had a thing for his best friend.

I walked into the living room and stopped short. The place resembled any other apartment for someone who'd graduated from college two years ago. The forest-green couch had once belonged to Hailey's parents. The TV hadn't been theirs;

neither had the dark wood coffee table and the matching enter-tainment center. The small dinner table, with only two chairs, also hadn't belonged to her parents. They all looked new. Not expensive, like her parents would've bought, but new.

But that wasn't why I'd stopped short. That came from seeing the old foosball table in a prime location behind the couch. Her parents' old foosball table.

It was as if I'd never left.

My fingers and muscles twitched at the memory of playing against Hailey. My skin itched at the memories of sharing about our day, our dreams, our fears while we played the game. Foos-ball had been our version of therapy.

"I can't believe she still plays it." I twisted the white knob. The blue players kicked the air, searching for the ball.

"Technically, she doesn't." Kayla walked to the other side of the game, as if getting ready to play against me. That'd be a first. The Kayla I remembered hated the game.

"What do you mean?"

"Once you left, she didn't have anyone to play against anymore."

"So why is it here?"

Kayla's eyebrows raised in her familiar you've-gotta-be-kidding-me expression. It had been directed at me more times over the years than I cared to remember. "Why do you think it's here?"

I shrugged. Hell if I knew.

"Because it reminds Hailey of you." She ran her fingertip along the side wall of the game, along the smooth dark wood. "You guys were best friends for like forever. She was hurting when you left and never spoke to her again."

"I had my reasons, but I never meant to hurt her."

"I know, but you did." She narrowed her eyes at me. "Just don't do it again, okay?"

As much as I didn't want to hurt Hailey, it wasn't something

I could easily avoid. I could only reduce the risk of it happening. "You never answered my question about her ex-boyfriend. What was the deal between them?" That didn't make me sound like a jealous ass, right?

Kayla cocked her head to the side. "What's it to you?"

I sighed. She wasn't making this easy for me. But then what was new? "Hailey's still my friend and I still care about her. I get the idea the asshole hurt her." I had no idea if it was true or not, but figured Kayla would be more likely to answer my question if I turned *him* into the evil one.

She studied me for a moment before releasing a heavy breath. "She dated the jerk for two years and he ended up cheating on her. With several girls, apparently. Needless to say, they weren't too impressed he was jerking them around." She chuckled. "Rumor has it one keyed his car."

"Did she love him?"

"Well, she wasn't picking out their china pattern yet, but she did care about him." She pressed her teeth into her lower lip, once again studying me like I was a piece of artwork to be analyzed. "Hailey's not the same girl you left behind. Between you leaving and what he did, she's changed."

"Changed how?"

"Hailey used to be the kind of girl who believed in long-term relationships. She's not that girl anymore. She won't let guys get close to her. I mean, she'll let them get close, if you know what I mean. But all they are to her is mindless sex with no commitment."

So, pretty much how things were with me.

"How often was she . . . ?" The words clung at the back of my throat. I didn't want to know the truth but asked anyway. "How often does she have one-night stands?"

"At least once a week . . . when we go dancing."

"And they're all strangers?"

Kayla nodded, seemingly as thrilled with this as I was. This didn't sound like the Hailey I remembered. But the Hailey I remembered was the one from six years ago. We'd both changed since then. Though from the sound of it, we'd both changed in the same way.

"Does she go out with any of them after?"

"You mean date them? No. She's not interested in them after that. Or as she puts it, 'Once I've screwed them, what's the point of going out with them? I already know they're only interested in sex. I can get that from someone else without the drama.'" She nailed Hailey's voice.

The twinge of jealousy that had appeared at the thought of her ex kneed me in the nuts. Hard. In all the years I'd been living in Northbridge and had been in love with Hailey, I had fantasized about being her first—and about being the only guy she ever slept with. I'd woken up many a morning sporting a hard-on to rival all others because I'd been dreaming about making love to her. Even after I moved away and had been screwing a shitload of other women, some delusional, caveman part of me wanted to believe that Hailey would always remain a virgin. For me.

An alarming thought formed. "Were there any guys who wanted more from her after they fucked her? Maybe someone who tried to press his luck again?"

Deep creases formed between Kayla's eyebrows. "You think one of those guys hurt her?"

"It's possible." A possibility I wanted to slam my fist into the wall over. If I had stayed in Northbridge, none of this would've happened. Hailey would've been safe.

In my case, the one-night stands made sense. It was impossible to have a girlfriend when you were on the road all the time. But I wasn't a monk. I was a full-blooded male who happened to love sex.

In the beginning, I had used sex to chase away the loneliness and had pretended I was fucking Hailey . . . until I could no longer pretend. Those girls never felt like Hailey. Those girls never smelled like Hailey. Those girls never sounded like Hailey. Eventually I stopped pretending, and the loneliness continued to grow, never fully chased away whenever I fucked some random girl.

But it was different with Hailey. She wasn't on the road. She didn't need to fill the loneliness.

"Did anyone make her feel uncomfortable?" I asked. "Maybe he tried to have sex with her again? Or maybe he kept trying to talk to her and she brushed him off?"

The creases in Kayla's forehead deepened. "There was one guy. She told him a few times to leave her alone. He finally did when Dylan, my boyfriend, showed up and told him to take a hike."

"Did he ever bother her again?"

"No, but he watched her a lot whenever we were at the same club as him. We eventually went elsewhere because he was getting beyond creepy."

"Did you see him again after that?"

She shook her head.

"When was this?" Hailey hadn't mentioned this to me, but what did I expect? She had just woken from a coma. She was confused at what had happened to her and confused about why I was back in town.

"About two months ago," Kayla said.

"Did you tell the cops?"

"Yes, but since I couldn't really describe him and I didn't know his name, they couldn't do much about it."

"Would you recognize him if you saw him?"

"Maybe. I'm not sure. He wasn't the kind of guy who stood out in a crowd. And he definitely wasn't Hailey's usual type."

"What's her usual type?"

Kayla cringed, but instead of answering me, she picked up a brown moving box.

I put my hand on it, halting her progress to the door. "What's her usual type?"

The air in her lungs came out as a huff, and she placed the box on the floor. "It's more like two types. She tends to go for either the jock or the moody musician. Even better if the moody musician is tattooed."

Her gaze dropped to the tribal tiger tattoo on my arm, partly obscured by my T-shirt sleeve. My heart stilled momentarily, reading too much into her words. It didn't mean those guys had been a replacement for me. It just meant she had a thing for musicians. The jock type made more sense, though, since she was an athlete herself.

Kayla and I spent the next two hours moving her stuff into her boyfriend's apartment. We didn't mention Hailey for the rest of the time. But that didn't stop my thoughts from dwelling on her and on the possibility the guy from the nightclub was the attacker.

10

NOLAN

Hailey was forced to stay in the hospital for three more days, so when I picked her up in the morning, she was ready to do cartwheels down the hallway. Or she might have been if her body wasn't still sore from the attack. The bruises on her face had faded and were now a combination of purple and green. I couldn't imagine the bruises on her body were much different.

Her parents would've driven her back to her apartment, but I convinced them to let me do it. There was a good reason for that . . . and Hailey was about to discover what it was. I knew she wouldn't like it. No need to have her explode at the news in front of her parents. Or maybe, in retrospect, it might've been a better idea to let her find out about it in front of them. Better for me, anyway.

I removed her duffel bag from the trunk. Clouds obscured the sun, but it didn't look like it would snow. At least not in the next few hours.

"Where are you staying?" she asked as we walked to her building. This was the first time she'd mentioned it since I announced I couldn't stay with Brandon. I'd moved out of his apartment three days ago, the same day I helped Kayla move. Hailey hadn't agreed to my crashing in Kayla's old room, so her best friend and I had decided I shouldn't mention where I was staying until Hailey had been released from the hospital.

"Kayla told me about the guy at the nightclub who was harassing you," I said, stalling the inevitable. "Do you remember his name?"

A red car crawled toward us, the driver searching for an open spot. It stopped in the middle of the road, even though nothing was available nearby.

"The cops asked me the same question. I never asked him his name. I didn't care what it was." Hailey muttered the last part and looked away.

I stopped walking and brushed a stray strand of hair, which had fallen from her messy ponytail, behind her ear. My callused fingertips grazed her soft skin. "Hey, I'm not judging you."

Dropping her gaze, she nodded. I couldn't tell if she believed me or not.

"But I am wondering if he was involved in the attack." From the corner of my eye, I noticed the car move forward again. It continued past us, the driver a girl in her early twenties. "It might have nothing to do with him," I continued. "He might not have known you were in Westgate. But there's also a chance he followed you there."

In which case he'd been stalking her. But even if that was true, it didn't explain why she'd been in that part of town.

"It's possible." Hailey's eyes found mine. "Like I told the cops, I haven't seen him for about two months. Ever since Kayla and I stopped going to Trysting."

"Would you recognize him if you saw him?"

Again she nodded, and we resumed walking.

"Good. Then as soon as you're up to it, I think we should go dancing and see if we can find him. If he was the one who attacked you, it's possible that just seeing him might help you remember. It's worth a try."

She narrowed her eyes at me. "And what if I do recognize him, Nolan? What are you gonna do?"

Ouch. Guess I deserved that. Well, semi-deserved it. "Don't believe everything you read."

She frowned. "What does that mean?"

"Just that."

"So you're telling me you weren't involved in that bar fight in San Antonio?" Her words were like stubbing your bare toe on an amp, the intense pain lingering after the initial shock had passed. It shouldn't have bothered me that she even questioned what had happened, but it did.

"Not in the way the media reported it."

She huffed. "Either you were or you weren't. There's no in-between, Nolan."

Sometimes, there was. "The paparazzi ambushed us. One of the lowlifes had found dirt on Mason that could have destroyed him. At least it could have if the asshole had twisted it to benefit the story.

"Mason swung at him. I tried to stop it from turning into something nastier. The other paparazzi took objection to that and jumped on a story that wasn't true." I shrugged. "At least it distracted them from going after Mason."

Hailey nodded but didn't say anything more on the topic. She also didn't ask what the dirt on Mason was, which came as no surprise. Hailey was like that. She respected people's privacy. It was one of the things I loved about her, along with her own need to keep her life private. I never had to worry about her selling me out for a few minutes of fame when it came to my secrets.

The same couldn't be said for the other girls I'd been with. Which was one of the reasons I always kept my T-shirt on whenever I had sex with them. I never wanted them to see my scar. It would've only led to prying and speculations.

"If you do spot the guy at Trysting," I said, returning to the original topic, "we'll contact the cops and let them deal with it. But they can't determine his connection to the attack if they don't know who he is. And you might not be his only victim."

A young couple exited the building as we entered. Both gave me a double take. I'd been fooling myself by thinking no one would notice I was staying here. If I was lucky, they wouldn't broadcast my location on social media.

We rode the elevator to Hailey's floor. Even though I had a key to her apartment, thanks to Kayla, I let Hailey unlock the door.

Once inside, she took her bag from me and headed to her room. My bedroom door was closed, hiding my guitar and what little I had with me. While Hailey had been in the hospital, I'd hit the nearby mall to pick up some clothes. Nothing fancy. Just long-sleeved T-shirts, jeans, and boxer briefs. I'd also bought workout clothing. Even when I was busy writing songs or on tour, I always worked out. As sad as it was, looks were everything in this industry when it came to the female fans. It was part of the fantasy. Theirs, not mine. But working out helped me deal with my demons, so I didn't care either way.

"You never did mention where you're staying," Hailey said as I hung up my coat.

I gave her a look, the one that said, *Guess.*

"Sorry, not happening." She folded her arms across her chest. She was always willing to help people, even strangers, but as soon as she got an idea in her head, there was no swaying her—most of the time. Only, I knew her kryptonite.

"Tell you what." I glanced pointedly at the foosball table. "One game. If I win, I get to stay. If you win, I'll find somewhere else to stay."

The old Hailey would have jumped at that, since she

usually beat me. This time a hint of uncertainty clouded her eyes. If what Kayla had said was true, Hailey hadn't played foosball in a while. She was as rusty as I was. Maybe even more so.

And that was what I was counting on.

The competitive streak I loved so much in her came to my rescue. "Okay. You're on."

11

HAILEY

Before we'd left the hospital, a nurse checked up on me. Well, more like checked up on Nolan, who hadn't arrived yet to pick me up. She wanted to know more about Tyler and Alyssa's relationship.

I had no idea if she'd been asking because she was a member of the Tylyssa fan club (and yes, I thought the name was stupid, too) or because she hoped the rumors about the couple were false, which would give her an excellent chance of hooking up with him while he was in town.

Either way, it reminded me I didn't have a chance with Nolan. He was way out of my league. Maybe even more so because he'd once been my best friend. He knew all my quirks.

And this was why his staying in my apartment was a bad idea. That, and just knowing he was in the room next to mine, just knowing how much I wanted to kiss him, just knowing how much my body ached to have him touch me like I wanted to touch him . . . all of this would turn his stay into my own personal torture. The Spanish Inquisition had nothing on this.

I'd planned to stomp my foot like a petulant toddler if it meant I'd get my way. What I hadn't counted on, though I should've known better, was for Nolan to challenge me to a game of foosball.

He knew I couldn't say no. I should have, given I hadn't played the game in six years. But if I was out of practice, so was he.

"Okay. One game. I win and you're out of here." I wanted to add that he would be on the next plane back to L.A., but I didn't want to push my luck. I knew him well enough to be aware that, much like me, once he got an idea in his head he'd follow through on it. And if I was completely honest with myself, a large part of me was thrilled I still meant that much to him. He was putting his life and his girlfriend on hold to help me remember.

He might not have wanted to remember what happened the night his mother and sister were murdered, but I wanted to remember why I'd been in Westgate and figure out why I'd been attacked. Bonus points if the guy was caught and tossed in jail.

"What color do you wanna be?" he asked.

"Red." Why break tradition? Especially when tradition usually had me winning.

We got into position. It didn't take long for me to realize my original belief was way off center. I might have grown rusty at the game during the past six years, but clearly I was the only one to have suffered that fate.

"You've been practicing," I huffed as my player pelted the ball down the field.

Nolan's player incepted it and kicked it in the opposite direction. "Actually, I haven't."

Before I could react and block the ball, his player sent it flying into the goal.

To win the game.

The stupid sun picked that moment to peek from behind the clouds. Sunlight streamed into the room, highlighting

Nolan in its warm, muted glow. Even the angels were conspiring against me.

I silently cursed my goalie for its betrayal.

To his credit, Nolan didn't burst into a cheer at his win. His mouth, though, couldn't resist enjoying my moment of defeat. It jerked into that sexy smirk of his. The sexy smirk I wanted to slap off his face.

Or kiss off.

"How about best of three?" Hey, it was worth a try.

Nolan shook his head. "To echo what you said earlier: sorry, not happening." He laughed, and my traitorous body responded to the deep sexy sound. Only my brain agreed that having Nolan stay with me was a terrible idea.

"Fine." No one had ever accused me of being a sore loser. "I'm going back to work tomorrow. So you'll have the apartment to yourself for most of the day."

"Already? But you just got out of the hospital."

"I know, but maybe I'll remember something if I go back."

He couldn't argue with that.

"I'm coming with you."

I barely fought the urge to roll my eyes. "I don't need a babysitter, Nolan. It's not like anyone will attack me there. Not in broad daylight. I promise you, I'll be safe."

"I know you don't need a babysitter, and I'm not applying to be one. But it wouldn't hurt if I asked around, see if anyone knows anything that might help the cops."

"Don't you think they'd have already done that?"

"Maybe, but I'd feel better if I could at least talk to a few people there. Besides, I can't let my body turn to flab while I'm here." He patted the rock-hard abs that girls would pay thousands of dollars to lick. I kid you not. I'd read it on a fan page a few months earlier. A group of girls actually had bid for the honor to lick them, as if Nolan had consented to it. At least I didn't think he had.

And no, I hadn't thrown in a bid. Not for real, anyway.

"I can hit the weight room while I'm there," he added. "Maybe even the running track."

Since I didn't have a good reason for him not to come with me, I quit trying to dissuade him. Sometimes it was better to just accept defeat and move on.

"So . . ." The word was drawn out, filled less with curiosity than with the need to change topic. "I hear things are going well between you and Alyssa Graham." I almost patted my back at the lack of jealousy in my voice. At the very least, I deserved a reward for it.

Perhaps a gold medal.

"There's nothing going on between me and Alyssa. We're just friends." He said it with a straight face, like he'd practiced the line a hundred times to keep his feelings for her out of the words.

I snorted. "Sure you are."

"I'm telling you the truth." While I might have succeeded at keeping jealousy out of my voice, the same couldn't be said for Nolan and the impatience leaking in.

"You're not even friends with benefits?"

"Absolutely not."

"So you and she have never had sex?" I wanted to bang my head against the wall the moment those words came out. If he had had sex with her, I'd rather not know. It was hard enough reading about his erotic trysts with his lucky fans. At least those I could pretend were make-believe, nothing more than wishful thinking by those girls.

Before I could tell him to ignore the question because my vivid imagination was enough, thank you, he replied, "Not even once. Which also means any rumors you may have heard that I'm going to be a father next year are false."

"That you know of." My heart tugged hard at the possibility.

"I always use a condom." He studied my face, his head tilted to the side like a curious golden retriever. As if he wasn't already adorable enough.

My heart rate kicked up. On the bright side, I was no longer attached to a heart rate monitor.

"What about you? Any little Haileys running around?"

A smirk lifted the corner of my mouth. "Not that I know of. At least no guy so far has come forth claiming to be carrying my child, or to have fathered a child with me. Besides, like you, I always use a condom. And I've been tested. So I'm clean." No idea why the sudden need to share that with him.

His gaze dropped momentarily to my lips. "Me too."

"Is it . . . is it hard being known by a different name? I mean, doesn't it get confusing at times?" *Or have you forgotten who you used to be?*

"Do I wish I could be Nolan Kincaid instead of Tyler Erickson? Yes. Do I want everyone to know the truth about my former life?" He shook his head, the sadness in his eyes unmistakable.

And that's when I did the one thing I hadn't done since Nolan returned home—I hugged him. He didn't stiffen or pull away. He held on to me like I was the air he needed to breathe. I rested my head on his shoulder and let my own grief at what he had gone through smother me. I'd loved his mother and his sister. I still felt their loss every day.

And for the thousandth time since their deaths, I wished I'd done things differently. Maybe if I had, they would still be alive, and Nolan wouldn't be so torn apart.

"As much as I wish I could be Nolan," he murmured in my hair, "that's not who I am anymore."

"You're wrong," I said, my head still on his shoulder, his scent of lemons and sunshine soothing me. "It's exactly who you are. Even if the rest of the world doesn't realize it yet."

I wasn't sure what woke me up. The room was dark, other than the red numbers glowing on my alarm clock: 2:13 a.m. It was that irritating time of night where if you didn't get back to sleep in, say, the next thirty seconds, you could cross a good night's sleep off your list of daily accomplishments.

The air was still and eerily quiet. I felt oddly out of balance, and it had nothing to do with the time.

It was a feeling I recognized all too well.

I climbed out of bed, wearing my favorite worn-out tank top and sleep shorts, which were more about comfort than sex appeal. I slipped out of my room and walked the short distance to Nolan's room. A faint light crept from under the door. Without knocking, I opened it.

Nolan was pacing in the small confines of his room, his head down, the carpet muffling his footsteps. He was lost in his own world, oblivious to me in the doorway.

"Hey, you can't sleep?" I asked.

His head shot up, eyes wide. He visibly relaxed when he spotted me, although I couldn't say I felt the same. More like the opposite. Blame that on his half-naked body, every muscle in his torso strong and defined.

Ever since he'd become popular, I couldn't remember a time I'd seen pictures of him without a T-shirt on. Now I could see why. He didn't want anyone to see the thick, five-inch scar along his otherwise perfect abs, halfway between his ribs and the waist of his low-rise jeans. I was surprised none of his one-night stands had ever mentioned it on the social media sites. If they had, the news would have gone viral.

I stepped into the room and surveyed the area. The room was dimly lit, a lightbulb in the ceiling fixture burnt out. The floral bedding was a tangled mess, the casualty of heavy tossing and turning. Other than the bed and Nolan's acoustic guitar propped against the wall next to the head of the bed, the place was empty.

Nolan sighed and scrubbed his face with his hand. "Sorry. Didn't mean to wake you."

I plopped down on the edge of his bed. He joined me.

"You didn't." I suspected it was a lie, but I didn't want to tell him the truth and upset him. I didn't want him to feel worse than he already did. And maybe it was just dumb luck I'd woken up. "Why don't you play something?"

"You should go to bed. You need to rest."

I shook my head. "No, I'm pretty sure I need to listen to you play. Please." I gave him my most pleading look—the one he used to be unable to say no to when we were kids. Besides, now that I was awake, I doubted I could fall back to sleep anytime soon. Not when I knew how much he was hurting.

"Okay," he whispered, and leaned over me to retrieve his guitar. He started strumming the melody, and I instantly recognized it: "This One Moment." My favorite song. It had done well on the charts, but it should have gone much higher. It should have been number one.

The moment Nolan sang the first verse, I was done for. His rich, clear voice melted my insides like a marshmallow in hot chocolate. I loved listening to his album, and I loved hearing him in concert, but neither of those compared to listening to him sing and play the song unplugged.

I wasn't the only one the song affected, although I doubted Nolan's insides melted like mine. The knotted tension in his muscles seeped away, the way it had whenever he used to sneak off in the middle of the night and play in the backyard shed. When you saw him like this, it was easy to understand how important music was to him. It was his lifeline, the thing that gave his life meaning.

I smiled at him. My blood heated at the way he smiled back. It was a smile he had perfected over the years and used to his advantage. It wasn't a smile meant only for me.

Nolan reached over my legs and leaned his guitar against

the foot of the bed. But for some reason, as if drawn to him like a magnet, I shifted forward as he straightened. His hand accidentally brushed against the side of my breast and I froze.

I might have frozen, but my blood didn't. It heated to two hundred degrees as my heart hammered hard in my chest, risking a few broken ribs.

His hand remained in place even when I turned to face him. Almost as if his thumb had a mind of its own, it brushed against my nipple. I sucked in a hard breath but still didn't move, silently willing him to keep touching me this way.

Neither of us said anything. I was afraid to break the silence and have him realize what he was doing—to me—and how I was reacting.

My gaze returned to his lips, and once again I wondered what it would feel like if his mouth melded with mine, if his tongue explored mine.

And then I discovered exactly what it felt like to have his lips caress mine. I didn't know who moved first, him or me, but one moment I was thinking about kissing him and the next we really were kissing. Softly.

I closed my eyes and his familiar scent teased me the same way his mouth teased mine. I was losing myself in his tender kisses, and I didn't care.

His lips parted, and the tip of his tongue traced along the seam of my mouth. We weren't even kissing hard, but my breath was coming fast and eager and free of doubt. I open my mouth and let him in.

The jolt shooting through me as his tongue stroked mine was almost my undoing.

It was also the splash of cold water I needed.

What the hell was I doing? This was Nolan, the guy who had been my best friend for much of my life, until he moved away. This wasn't one of my one-night stands. I never felt anything for those guys, and that left the sex less than satisfying. I felt too much for Nolan, and that was dangerous. Because in the end, he could walk away unscathed.

Not so for me.

I pulled away, unable to look at him. "You can keep playing if you want."

I didn't wait for his response. Like the coward I was, I fled his room.

12

HAILEY

The next morning I woke up feeling like I'd played two soccer games back to back without a break. After fleeing Nolan's room, I'd slept a grand total of an hour, if that. And it had nothing to do with Nolan and his guitar. His playing had only continued for an hour after I left. The real culprit for my lack of sleep was Nolan's kiss. It had been everything I expected from him. Experience had taught him well.

Which meant the kiss was not so easily forgotten or dismissed.

I was doomed.

I walked past his bedroom on the way to the bathroom. Nolan's door was open a crack.

"I swear I've got this," he said, voice low. "Everything's gonna be all right. I promise."

Giving him privacy, I left to get ready for work. Mom had texted at some point this morning to check up on me.

> Me: I'm fine. I just need things to get back to
> normal, then everything will be great.

> Mom: Maybe Dad and I should cancel the
> Mexican cruise.

She was referring to the trip they were going on after Christmas. She'd been counting down the days before she could trade the cold for the heat. Who could blame her?

> Me: Don't you dare cancel!!!! Honestly, I'm
> fine.

> Mom: If you're certain . . .

> Me: Absolutely!

But in case she wasn't totally convinced, I'd speak with Dad later and make sure she couldn't talk him into canceling their plans on my behalf. They deserved this break together.

Nolan, wearing jeans and a T-shirt, was in the tiny kitchen when I emerged freshly showered a short while later. The shower helped a little, but not as much as the smell of coffee waiting for me.

Nolan handed me a steaming mug and I almost kissed him, but for a different reason than last night.

I sipped it, and a satisfied smile slipped onto my face. "You remembered how I like it." Nolan as my roommate came with definite perks. Although if I had any more sleepless nights like last night, I'd need a lot more than a simple mug of coffee.

His gaze scanned my body, and he frowned. "Why are you dressed like you're gonna play soccer?"

"Not soccer. Work." I worked in a sports training facility, thanks to my kinesiology degree. It was mostly to gain experience so I could apply to get into a physical therapy education program. Because of that, I had several part-time jobs there, including working with special-needs kids.

Nolan's frown deepened. "You sure you don't want to take a few more days off?"

"I'm fine. Really." I was still sore, but nothing that would cause me too much trouble at work. I just needed to get away for a bit from Nolan and my feelings for him. Returning to work was the best way to do this.

He gave me the patented cut-the-crap look he used to save for whenever I'd tried lying to him. "Great. Then I'm going with you."

"I already told you I don't need a babysitter."

"And I already told you I'm not signing up for the job. I'm going to work out. Remember? I need to keep in shape or else this all turns to flab." He patted his rock hard abs. "And flabby rock stars are not all the craze right now."

I snorted a laugh. "I don't think you have to worry about it while you're here. It's not like you'll be in Northbridge long enough to become flabby." I tried not to think about those abs, which I'd seen last night. I did my best—but failed.

After a quick breakfast, Nolan drove me to the sports center, even though I'd insisted I was fine enough to drive myself. Neither of us mentioned the kiss. In fact, Nolan acted as though we hadn't kissed at all. He kissed girls all the time. Kissing me was no big deal. It was just one of those rock-star perks that came with his job. He got to kiss whomever he wanted, whenever he wanted, the girl's feelings for him be damned.

I was nothing more than one of those girls.

The sports center lobby area was busy with the early morning crowd. Some individuals were hitting the gym before work. Others were in one of the intensive, sport-specific training programs offered here. The center catered to all levels of athletes, young and old.

And that's when it happened.

By "it," I meant the effect Nolan had on the female persuasion. With the celebrity alert system wired into their brains going berserk, a half dozen girls suddenly looked in our direction. They eyed him like he was a juicy steak they craved after a week of chowing down on nothing but lettuce leaves. I braced myself for the fangirl screams. It was far too early in the morning for that.

Who was I kidding? The only good time for that level of fan enthusiasm was . . . never.

Fortunately, we were spared from going deaf. They just stared at him as if he was a delusion brought on from not enough caffeine in their systems.

Recovering first, two high-fashion-model wannabes sashayed toward us, their moves graceful yet predatory. Neither girl seemed aware she had competition also stalking her prey. Like a lioness going in for the kill, each was focused on one thing and one thing only. I wasn't even sure they noticed me walking alongside Nolan. Which was just as well. I didn't want to be considered part of the equation, an element they were eager to eradicate.

Both were tall and gorgeous, with shiny blond hair cascading down their backs. They could've just stepped off the pages of *Vogue*. Next to these two, I was invisible. Cute, but invisible.

"Oh my God," Blonde #1 said. The only difference between her and Blonde #2 was their eye color. Blonde #1 had pale blue eyes; Blonde #2's eyes were amber. "You're Tyler Erickson."

"That's right." Nolan smiled at the two girls. It wasn't the same smile that had graced his lips last night. This smile was the polite smile you gave your fans . . . when you weren't seducing them out of their panties.

Blonde #1 read a different message in the smile—a message that apparently said, *Please stroke my chest and abs.*

Nolan stepped away, not a huge amount, but enough to break her contact with his body. I turned my head so she didn't catch me grinning.

"I love your music," Blonde #2 gushed, but the way her eyes stripped him naked suggested it was more than his music that she loved. "And I love your tattoo." Her gaze dropped to the tiger tattoo on his arm. At least she got the message and didn't try to touch him, although I didn't doubt she'd be all for touching him and exploring his body, given the chance.

Heck, who was I kidding? I'd be all for that too.

Heat rushed to my lower belly at the memory of his fingers brushing against my tank-top-covered nipple. Not inclined to miss out on the fun, my nipples tingled at the memory. It was all I could do to restrain the moan hovering at the back of my throat.

I was so busy mentally dousing the heat with cold water, I almost missed Blonde #1 scribble on a piece of paper and shove it in the pocket of Nolan's gym shorts.

"Call me," she said as Blonde #2 did the same, although I could've sworn Blonde #2's fingers stayed in his pockets for a few seconds longer.

I wanted to rip the offending fingers out and tell her where to go, but the need to not make a scene overruled that desire by a narrow margin. A very narrow margin.

Besides, wasn't this part of Nolan's job? Socializing with his fans went a long way toward selling albums, especially if the band wanted to do even better next time. The fans were the ones to put them there. And Nolan deserved that . . . even if it meant I had to watch these girls practically drool on him.

Just as I was about to leave him to his fans, a pair of masculine hands covered my eyes. My heart rate spiked until I remembered whom the hands belonged to, and then it settled back to its normal pace.

"Hey, Chris." I didn't have to look to know it was him. He did it every time he saw me.

He dropped his hands from my eyes, and I turned around to talk to the personal trainer, a former NFL player whose career had ended due to a knee injury. He was the guy Blonde #1 and Blonde #2 usually fawned over. Yes, rock stars and former football players were their men of choice.

"Didn't expect to see you back so soon." His gaze traveled over my body, but not in the same way the two girls had checked Nolan out. Chris was checking me over for broken bones and other visible injuries.

"You know me," I said. "I can never get enough of this place."

A muscle in his jaw twitched. "Shit, if I hadn't canceled on you at the last moment, you would have been with me and not in Westgate. Do the cops know who did it?"

I shook my head. "And it doesn't help that I can't remember what happened. I don't even remember you canceling." Heck, I didn't even remember we had planned to meet up.

"The moment you feel up to it, you're taking a self-defense class." He fisted his hands on his hips, going all alpha on me and daring me to defy him. The same way Dad had been when he called this morning to make sure I was okay and told me the exact same thing about the class.

"You mean a refresher course. I took a self-defense class two years ago." After a rash of campus rapes. I had no idea if it had helped me or not during the attack. I had no idea if I even remembered anything I'd learned during the class.

A high-pitched giggle rose up from Nolan's little group. Chris glanced at the groupies and Nolan. "Wow, that guy looks a lot like Tyler Erickson."

"That's because it is Tyler Erickson."

"No way. Wonder why he's here." Before I could reply, Chris walked to the group and introduced himself.

"I'm visiting a friend who lives in Northbridge." Nolan could've been describing either Brandon or me. More than likely he didn't want to admit to knowing more than one person here. That would only lead to more questions about his connection to the town.

A growing unease jabbed at me like a pin you couldn't see in your clothing, but it was there all the same. I was a private person, for the most part. Being linked to Nolan would be like open season on me. The last thing I wanted was for Blondes #1 and #2 to think I was Nolan's personal assistant and that hooking him up with fans was in my job description. They had already tried that stunt when it came to Chris. No way was I going there again with Nolan.

13

NOLAN

The first time I had performed onstage was a few weeks after I fled Minnesota for L.A. It was shortly after I joined three other guys, all with the goal of making it big.

Our first gig had been in a dive, as was usually the case when you're new to the scene with no experience and no fans. It'd been a chance to prove ourselves to a rowdy crowd who didn't give two fucks about us and our aspirations. It had been both exhilarating and scary.

That experience was nothing compared to how I felt now.

I paced the hallway outside Hailey's room, waiting for her to get ready so we could go to Trysting.

Her bedroom door finally opened. At the sight of her, my dick pressed hard against my zipper. This was a side of Hailey I'd never seen before. I was used to athletic Hailey, the one who never dressed sexy. She didn't have to. She was sexy no matter what she wore.

At least, that was what I used to think.

But seeing her like this changed my mind. Her fitted black dress revealed more than it covered, but on Hailey it looked classy. The short hem showed off her long, toned legs, which looked never-ending. The black stilettos added to the effect. This was a side of Hailey I was unfamiliar with. But it was a side I wouldn't have minded getting acquainted with.

For my sanity's sake (as well as my dick's), I tried not to imagine her legs wrapped around me while she was wearing only those shoes. I tried but failed.

The dress didn't help either. It was sleeveless and would have covered her breasts if it weren't for the cut-out in the front that pointed down, ending just below her cleavage.

Hailey turned around, and I sucked in a hard breath. The back of her dress cut away, so the skin from her shoulder blades to her lower back begged me to caress it. Her shiny brown hair flowed down her back, brushing her bare skin.

Shit, I was in serious trouble.

But who was I kidding? I'd been in serious trouble the moment my lips touched hers the night before last. I hadn't meant to kiss her. That didn't mean I hadn't wanted to. But Hailey wasn't interested in me, not that way.

Or so I'd once thought. But after the other night, I wasn't sure anymore what was true and what wasn't. She'd kissed me back. That much was true. Then she had pulled away and couldn't get out of my room fast enough. She could have thrust a flaming knife into my heart and it would've hurt far less.

Before that night, I had craved to touch her, to taste her. And after I did? The craving grew stronger, until it got to the point where it was all I could think about. On the plus side, I'd poured my emotions into a new song, and I had to admit it was damn good. Even Jared had agreed with me after I played it to him via Skype this afternoon.

"How do I look?" Hailey bit her lip and looked down at the dress.

Amazing. Hot. "Good."

"Kayla loaned it to me."

I was officially going to kill Kayla.

"Are you . . . ?" I wasn't sure how to finish the sentence and how she would react if I did. But the thought of her bringing home some random guy was too much to even think about. All I knew was if some guy hit on her, I was likely to punch him.

Which would make me no better than my old man.

"Am I what?" Hailey asked.

"Are you planning on hooking up with someone tonight?" My gaze lowered to her lips, and the craving to taste her again was a dropkick to the gut.

She shook her head, eyes locked on mine. The yellow and green bruises on her face from the attack were faint, mostly hidden by her makeup. "Are you?"

I barely heard her. I was too focused on the image in my head of making love to her. And once again my dick got excited at that possibility.

Brilliant going, dickhead. As if I wasn't already in enough trouble with Hailey dressed like this.

"No. The only person I'm going home with tonight is you." My voice came out low and sandpaper rough, and I silently cursed—again—my body's reaction to her. Hailey had already made it clear she was only interested in one-night stands. The last thing I wanted was to be another of her one-night losers.

She blinked and quickly looked away. "Are you ready?"

"Yep. Brandon texted that he's on his way. He should be here soon." Kayla and her boyfriend were meeting us at the club.

I waited while Hailey grabbed her coat and purse, then we headed down in the elevator to the main floor. The easygoing feeling that used to be between us had shifted. Now an odd tension blanketed us. Hailey stood several feet from me in the empty elevator, but that did nothing when it came to her sweet vanilla scent. Even in the stale air, her scent made it impossible to pretend she wasn't there.

Brandon's truck was waiting for us outside the building when we stepped out of the lobby. I opened the passenger door and waved for Hailey to get in. But given what she was wearing, it was nearly impossible for her to climb in without flashing her ass. And while I might have appreciated seeing her sweet ass and panties any other time, I didn't want anyone else to witness the view. Plus, seeing her this way would only make things more difficult for me. I was already in a shitload of trouble as far as Hailey was concerned, and I didn't need to make things worse.

I gripped her waist with both hands and hoisted her onto the seat. A faint blush swept across her cheeks, and I did my best not to chuckle at her response. Instead, I focused on the way Brandon was checking her out, and I frowned. Hailey's skirt had hiked up her thighs when she scooted over, leaving only a thin strip of skin covered.

Before I could say something we would all regret, Brandon turned his head to look out the driver's window. *Smart move, douchebag.* I wasn't sure if Brandon knew how I felt about her, but he'd never shown any interest in her before. But who was I kidding? Who wouldn't be interested in Hailey? She was too sweet and too hot for her own good.

Hailey readjusted her skirt, wiggling it down her thighs as I climbed in next to her. My leg pressed against hers, and I silently lamented wearing jeans, which prevented me from feeling her soft skin.

"Remember, if you see the guy," I said, "let me know. All right?" Brandon knew the real reason we were going to the club tonight, as did Kayla. While I trusted Brandon to be cool, I wasn't too thrilled that Kayla knew why we were there. She was just as protective of Hailey as I was. I was worried about what she would do if she saw the asshat. But I didn't have a choice. As soon as Hailey had told her what we were up to, Kayla insisted—correction, Kayla *demanded*—we take her with us.

"I will," Hailey said.

"And don't for any reason go off on your own. If you want to go somewhere, Brandon or I will go with you."

Hailey smirked. "And which of you fine gentlemen plans to accompany me to the bathroom?"

"That honor goes to Nolan, thanks." Brandon's smirk matched Hailey's.

"Don't girls usually travel to the bathroom in packs?" Either way, I'd be waiting outside until she came out.

Kayla snorted. "We're not wolves."

It would've made my life a helluva lot easier if they were. Then no guy would be idiot enough to touch them.

The nightclub was busy when we arrived, with people milling around outside. The bouncer checked my ID, not giving me a second glance. Either he didn't recognize me or he just didn't care.

Because I didn't want to draw an unnecessary crowd, I was wearing my baseball cap. I tugged it low enough so I wasn't as easy to recognize, unless you were really looking, but not low enough to prevent me from keeping an eye on everyone.

Half pretending to search for Kayla and her boyfriend, Hailey walked around the nightclub, scanning the crowd for the guy. All she could tell me was that he was maybe five foot eleven, medium build, with short brown hair. Which described quite a few guys here.

She surveyed the crowd, the light a mix of bright spotlights flashing in time to the beat and dark shadows. The contrast highlighted some faces while others remained easily hidden. I kept my eyes open for anyone fitting the description and whose gaze was fixated on her. I couldn't fault guys for checking her out, but there was a big difference between checking her out and studying her every move.

We found Kayla and her boyfriend on the other side of the bar.

"Is he here yet?" she asked Hailey.

Hailey shook her head.

"Do you remember anything from the last time you were here?" I held on to a sliver of hope that being here would trigger a memory for Hailey.

Again she shook her head, and the sliver crumbled away in the perfume-filled air.

"Tyler." Kayla overemphasized my name, as if to remind herself to use my stage name around anyone who didn't know who I really was—and that included her boyfriend. I'd been adamant about it. I didn't know him, which meant I didn't trust him. "This is my boyfriend, Dylan."

The guy held out his hand. "Good to meet you, man. I thought Kayla was shitting me when she said she knew you."

We chatted for a few minutes while I answered a multitude of questions about the band and what it was like touring. Kayla had never mentioned how big a fan he was. She'd only mentioned he liked my music.

"C'mon," I said to Hailey after Dylan paused his questioning long enough to take a sip of beer. "Let's get a drink and check out the rest of the place." I excused us.

Not far from us, a girl headed up the staircase tucked in the corner. A guy followed her, his hand on her lower back. Hailey started walking toward the bar. I grabbed her arm and gestured with my chin toward the stairs. "Where do those go?"

"The club's private party rooms."

My insides clenched at what she meant and at the possibility she'd used the rooms herself. That wasn't to say I hadn't been in a few, which was why I knew what could happen there. "Can you see the dance club from up there?"

She shrugged. "I don't know. I've never been up there." My insides partly unclenched.

I turned back to Kayla and Dylan. "Do you guys know if you can see the dance club from the private rooms upstairs?"

They both shrugged.

"Okay," I said to Hailey, "let's go." I nodded toward the bar.

We squeezed past the growing crowd. I kept my head down to avoid having anyone recognize me, which would make searching the nightclub impossible. Once we were at the bar, I asked her again if she'd seen him. She shook her head, disappointment sitting heavily on her shoulders. She wanted to find him tonight as much as I did, maybe even more.

I ordered our drinks. When the bartender returned with them, I asked him about the private rooms.

"The music from the club is piped into the rooms, but there are no windows in any of them. Other than the doors, they're cut off from the club." He quickly added, "But there's a bouncer at the top of the stairs to make sure nothing bad goes down." I wondered if he figured I was an undercover cop making sure no one could be sexually assaulted there. I nodded my thanks and turned back Hailey.

"At least we now know if he's here, he can't watch you from upstairs. If he shows up, we'll see him."

We returned to our friends. Keeping an eye on the area, I joined the conversation until the girls decided to dance. Since I didn't intend to let Hailey out of my sight, never mind letting her dance with another guy, I grabbed her hand and led her to the floor.

Figuring I'd be safe from people approaching me while I danced—the Tyler me, that is—I removed my hat. Hailey ran her fingers through my hair. Her fingertips stroked against my scalp. The skin tingled at her touch, and for several seconds I could only stare into her warm brown eyes, mesmerized by the gold flakes in them.

Her fingers remained in my hair and her lips parted. Around us, people moved to the fast beat, but we just stood there, uncertain what to do next. I felt myself lean down, my lips drawn to hers, craving her, the way it had been since our first kiss.

I paused inches from her lips. I barely heard the fast rock music pounding through the space. I barely noticed the people around us. All I could see was Hailey.

Someone knocked into her from behind and she stumbled into me. I wrapped my arms around her to steady her, our bodies touching. The music faded away, to be replaced by a slow song. I was about to ask her if she still wanted to dance when she whispered, "He's here."

I murmured in her ear, "Where?" I didn't want to alert him that I was looking for him, but I needed to know his location so I could tell Brandon.

"He's at your seven o'clock."

"Okay." I sent Brandon a text. "What's he wearing?"

Hailey's gaze darted briefly over my shoulder. "Light blue shirt. Jeans."

I fought the urge to turn around, and sent Brandon another text. The plan was for him to take a picture of the guy without him knowing, which was the hardest part given the lack of lighting. Brandon was then to contact the detective involved in Hailey's case. I had already told the cop what we were up to. He'd told me to get in touch with him as soon as Hailey spotted the guy, but under no circumstances were we to talk to him. To do so might've jeopardized the case.

I might not have been allowed to tell the asshole to fuck off when it came to Hailey, but no way would I let him believe he could watch her the way he had been.

I murmured in Hailey's ear, "I want him to think you're with me." I ran my stubbled jaw against her cheek. She sucked in a soft, shaky breath, and my body trembled slightly at her reaction. "I'm going to kiss you," I said, voice husky.

"Okay," she breathed, the puff of air warm against my cheek.

I closed my eyes for a millisecond to gain strength for what I was about to do. When it came to Hailey, a single kiss wasn't enough. But that was all I'd get. I traced my lips against her jaw, memorizing the soft feel of her skin, until I found her mouth.

The first kiss was tender. Hailey wrapped her arms around my neck and I enveloped her in my arms. We continued to kiss this way for the first part of the song, swaying to the music. But my craving for her became too much and I needed more.

I opened my mouth; Hailey did the same. Her tongue welcomed mine, and like a man savoring a fine meal, I explored her mouth. And just like when we had kissed in my room, I fell even deeper for her. She was everything I had imagined she would be when we were seventeen years old. Everything and more.

I had no idea how long we'd been kissing—though in my opinion it wasn't long enough—when Kayla said, "Hey, you two, get a room." She laughed as Hailey and I shot apart as though lightning had struck us. "God, it's about time you two kissed. The sexual tension between you was making me to want to jump one of you just to break it." She winked at Hailey.

"It's . . . it's not what you think," Hailey stuttered. "I saw the creepy guy. Nolan was just kissing me to send him a message. You know, like, 'Get lost. I'm not interested.'"

Her words were a rusty dagger to my heart, adding to the previous wound, although I shouldn't have been surprised. This wasn't news to me.

Kayla rolled her eyes. "Whatever."

"Is he still there?" I asked, needing to redirect the conversation. Right now the asshole was the priority, rather than how I felt about Hailey and how she didn't feel about me.

Her mouth traced the line of my jaw. "Yes."

"Is he watching you?"

"Yes."

The slow song ended. Even though the kissing was an act, I

wasn't ready to let Hailey leave yet. I removed her arm from around my neck and interlaced my fingers with hers. Kayla and Dylan followed us off the dance floor. We stood far enough from the guy so he didn't get suspicious, but near enough so I could keep an eye on him until the cops showed up.

Now that I no longer had my baseball cap on, people were beginning to recognize me. I could tell some were confused why my arms were around Hailey's hips, her back against my chest, when I was supposedly dating a Hollywood actress. Not that I cared what they thought. It was all a lie anyway. Much like me.

Brandon joined the four of us a minute later. "Detective Mathews is on his way."

"Thanks," I said.

"Anytime. Let's hope they can get the truth out of him so you can get back to L.A."

Hailey was busy talking to Kayla and Dylan, so I thought she hadn't heard my conversation with Brandon. I was wrong. She stiffened in my arms when Brandon mentioned L.A., which surprised me. Was she feeling something for me like what I felt for her? Or was that just wishful thinking? But whatever it was, we were facing a ticking clock. She knew it too.

I casually peered at the asshole. He was still watching Hailey, face red, lips flattened in a bitter line. I tightened my hold on her and brushed her hair away from her neck. My lips caressed the sensitive spot below her ear. She inhaled sharply. With her back against my chest, I didn't hear it as much as feel it.

I closed my eyes and breathed in her sweet scent. God, this time when I left town, it would feel as if someone had gutted me. Last time I'd had no idea what she tasted like, no idea what it felt like to kiss her. Now that I was aware of these things, my days were about to become emptier than last time. And no amount of screwing other girls would save me.

Even though I knew I should move away from Hailey to spare the last of my sanity, I kissed her neck again. But before I could do any more than that, a hand grabbed my arm and roughly yanked me away from Hailey.

I released my hold on my girl and swiveled around to see what douchebag had pulled me away from her.

The asshole who'd been watching her glared at me, nostrils flaring. Even though he was a good several inches shorter than me, the height difference didn't faze him. His face was practically in mine.

"Get away from her," he growled.

"What the fuck is your problem? I'm with her."

Brandon placed his hand on my shoulder—a subtle reminder of what was at stake here if I screwed up.

"You celebrities are all alike. You only care about yourselves."

I glared back at him. "You don't even know me."

The nearby crowd eyed us with interest, waiting for me to live up to my cocky, bad-ass reputation. *Shit.* Where the hell was the detective?

"I know your type. You plan to use her, then toss her aside like a three-day-old piece of luncheon meat."

I flinched at the truth behind the words, at least when it came to any girl besides Hailey. Contrary to how he'd put it, the girls I'd met while touring hadn't been interested in me beyond a satisfying fuck. And he was stepping well out of bounds when it came to Hailey. But as Tyler Erickson, I'd done nothing to prove the asshole wrong.

Hailey was watching me, her eyes wide. I had no idea if it was because the asshole had verbally attacked me in her defense or because she'd heard the truth in his words. Like him, how was she to know that he was wrong?

But I couldn't tell her that now. Not in front of him.

The asshole stepped in front of me and shoved me in the

chest with both hands. I stumbled back a step. "Touch her again and you'll regret it," he said, tone heated, voice a low growl.

His words caused me to pause, but not for the reason he expected. If this was the guy who'd attacked Hailey, why was he being overly protective of her? Was it because he felt guilty for what he had done or because he'd had nothing to do with that?

I didn't have time to contemplate it further. A man in a suit that screamed cop in a place like this approached Hailey. "Miss Wilkins, we received a report that the man who's been allegedly harassing you is here."

Hailey nodded, but before she could say anything, the asshole poked me in the chest. "Yes, this is him."

The cop looked at Hailey for confirmation.

"That's not him. He's my friend." She purposely avoided my name and pointed to the asshole. "That's the guy."

A deep frown formed on the asshole's forehead. "What the fuck are you talking about? I haven't been harassing you."

Detective Mathews stepped closer to the man. "How about we continue this conversation at the station?"

The frown remained. "Why? I haven't done anything wrong."

"Then you won't mind answering a few questions at the station."

The asshole glanced back and forth between the detective and Hailey. "What's going on?"

"At the station." It was no longer a suggestion.

"Fine," the asshole bit out.

14

HAILEY

Detective Mathews escorted the man out, and my heart rate slowly returned to normal. It had been going crazy ever since Nolan kissed me, but when I saw the man attack him, my heart came close to scrambling out of my chest.

Nolan turned back to me, frowning. "I don't think he's the attacker."

"Of course he is." Kayla's expression equaled Nolan's in the frown department.

"Why don't you think he did it?" I asked, curious why he would believe that. Deep down I suspected he was right.

"Did you see how he reacted when he thought I was using you?" Nolan said. "He acted like I would have if our places were reversed."

"But you're my friend. He's a stranger. And you've always been a tad overly protective." A side effect, no doubt, of having a father like his. Nolan had been the same way with his sister.

"But why would the guy attack you and then try to protect you from douchebags like Tyler?" Brandon slapped Nolan on the back, partly in jest.

They both had a point. Unless there was more to the story than we realized.

But for now I didn't want to think about it. "Can we go?" I just wanted to go to bed and forget about tonight, especially the part where the creepy guy had pointed out the truth. What had happened between Nolan and me on the dance floor hadn't been because Nolan felt the same way about me as I felt about him. He'd been protecting me. That was what Nolan did best.

I hugged Kayla goodbye. Before I could pull away, she whispered in my ear, "Be careful. Okay?" I had no idea if she was referring to what had happened between Nolan and me or was just telling me to be careful in general.

"It was nothing," I said, going with the first option. "It was just an act for the loser's benefit."

"Just make sure you guys are both on the same page, Hailey. I don't want to see you get hurt again."

My eyebrows jumped up my forehead. "I thought you wanted this. Weren't you the one who invited him to crash at my place while he's here?"

"That doesn't mean I want you to risk your heart again. You guys were best friends, and I know you still missed him."

"You don't have to worry. I won't get hurt this time. I'm not the girl I used to be."

A sad smile wavered on her face. "I know. That's what I'm afraid of."

I didn't have a chance to ask her what she meant, as Nolan was waiting to leave. I followed him and Brandon to Brandon's truck.

We didn't say much on the drive back home, all three of us lost in thought, but you couldn't miss the tension between Nolan and me. It was that thick. I didn't know, though, if the tension was because of what had happened between us on the dance floor or because of what happened afterward. The entire evening was a kaleidoscope of confusion in my head.

Brandon dropped us off at the main entrance to my building. We thanked him and climbed down from the truck. The tension between us increased tenfold, but it suddenly felt different compared to how it'd been in the vehicle.

Kayla's words repeated in my head: *Just make sure you guys are both on the same page, Hailey. I don't want to see you get hurt again.*

The elevator was on the main floor when we approached. We stepped in, and I pushed the button for my floor. The door had barely shut before I found myself in Nolan's arms. A heartbeat later, I was against the wall and Nolan was kissing me. Not the tender kisses of earlier, when we were on the dance floor. These kisses were rough, demanding, amazing. I moaned into his mouth.

My entire body felt like I'd stuck a damp finger in an electric socket, but in a good way. I'd never felt this alive before.

All too soon the door pinged open. There might've been some mental cursing on my part. The elevator would've been kinder if it had dumped a bucket of cold water on me instead. At least then my body wouldn't be in this supercharged state.

We separated long enough to make it to my apartment. Even then, barely any space existed between us as we walked down the hallway. But as soon as the apartment door shut behind us, we were once again devouring each other.

I slipped my fingers under the hem of Nolan's T-shirt. They explored the hard ridges of his abs, his skin hot against my fingertips.

In my eagerness to memorize every part of him, my fingers brushed against the scar slicing across his torso.

Nolan's lips froze against mine.

15

NOLAN

Six Years Ago

I pushed the ball through the hole in the side of the foosball table and sent it flying toward my players. "Truth or dare. You plan on waiting till you're married before losing your virginity?" I knew what Hailey's answer would be, but I was trying to figure out a way to tell her how I felt about her. Not that my lame-ass question helped me there.

"False."

Not quite what I'd expected, but good for me, I guessed.

She nailed the ball with her player and sent it toward my goal. "But I don't plan to lose my virginity to just anyone. I want to be in love with the guy and for him to love me."

The ball ended up near one of my players, and I accidentally sent it spinning directly to Hailey's player. "So you wanna test-drive him first?"

"Something like that. Maybe." Her player kicked the ball hard. It flew into my goal, but I was too distracted by our conversation to block it in time. "Yes!"

My dick got excited at the thought of her saying that exact

word with that much enthusiasm as it thrust into her. *Down, boy.*

"What about you?" Her body was tense as she prepared to attack the ball once I set it into play again. "Are you waiting for the right person before you do it for the first time?"

Brandon knew the answer to this question. We'd already discussed my first time, just like we had discussed his first time. Those girls had meant nothing to us. But even though I'd told one best friend about what happened, I couldn't tell the other one, because let's face it, it wasn't the kind of conversation you had with your female best friend. Even if you wanted tips on how to satisfy the opposite gender.

My phone rang, saving me from answering the question. I checked who was calling. Sarah.

"Hey, squirt," I said, answering the phone.

"Can you . . . pick me up?" Sarah said between sobs.

"Where are you?"

"Ballet lessons. Dad left but never came back."

Fuck. I shoved my fingers through my hair. Sarah's class had finished an hour ago. "Are you inside the building?"

Another sob. "No. Outside."

Still talking to my sister, I stormed up the basement stairs. "Go inside until I get there, okay?"

"I can't."

My heart pinched hard at how scared she sounded. "Why not?" I struggled to keep the anger out of my voice. I didn't need to upset Sarah any more than she already was.

"The place is closed. I can't get in."

"Okay, stay where you are. Can you do that for me, Sarah?" I reached my car, and for the first time realized Hailey was with me, standing expectantly on the passenger side. I'd been so focused on Sarah, I hadn't realized Hailey had followed me. I barely remembered leaving the house.

"Hailey's with me," I told my sister. "We're driving there now, but I want you to stay on the line with her."

"Okay."

Hailey and I quickly climbed into my car and I handed her my phone.

16

NOLAN

Present

I snapped out of the memory, the one that until now I had locked away. I knew there was more, and refused to go there.

I stepped away from Hailey. She flipped the hallway light on. Her gentle gaze searched my face as she tried to piece together what was going on. I'd just gone from hot to cold in a matter of seconds, and I could see the confusion on her face.

What I really wanted to do was run—run hard and run fast, and keep running until I was back in L.A. But a small part of me refused to do that while Hailey's life was in danger. I had let my mother and sister down. I had let so many people down. I couldn't do that to Hailey. Not again.

Instead I turned away from my best friend. "I'm sorry. But I can't." All I could think about was the last memory I had of my sister smiling. It was not from the night I was trying to keep locked away. It was from a happier time with Sarah and Hailey, when we'd gone out for ice cream. It felt like a lifetime ago.

Without a single word to Hailey, I walked to the bathroom

and locked the door. I slumped against it, the darkness closing in on me. But it wasn't enough to shut out the memory. Nothing would be enough.

I turned the bathroom light on. The bright light glared at me from above the mirror like an interrogation lamp. It wanted to know the truth as much as everyone else did. Everyone but me.

The lower corner of the mirror was chipped, something I hadn't noticed before. My gaze continued up the smudged surface and caught sight of my reflection. I was a mess. I mean, appearance-wise I looked fine. My shirt and jeans were clean and wrinkle free. But the guy who'd gone to the nightclub with his girl and best friend was not the same one staring back at me in the mirror. This guy looked exhausted, beaten. Forever scarred.

With my clothes still on, I climbed into the shower and turned the cold water on. I stood in the stream of water, doing my best to hold back the building sobs. Once I was soaked through, my body shivering to the point where I couldn't remain standing if I tried, I slid down the shower wall.

I wrapped my arms around my bent knees, rested my head against them, and silently cried. For my mom. For my sister. For the guy I used to be.

Through the hammering of water against the tub, I was vaguely aware of banging on the door.

"Nolan." Hailey's sweet voice broke through the fog in my head. "Are you okay?"

I turned the water off. "Yes." The word came out as a harsh croak.

She must not have believed me, because she was standing outside the door when I opened it a minute later.

"Oh, God, Nolan . . ." Several emotions I couldn't get a firm grip on filled her beautiful, warm brown eyes.

I used to be able to get lost in those eyes and nothing could bother me. But that had been a lifetime ago. I dropped my gaze from hers, not wanting her to see into the deepest recesses of my soul. I wanted to make some smart-ass comment, like how I'd forgotten to remove my clothes before getting into the shower. Anything to keep her from guessing the truth. But what I wanted to do and what I did were in opposite hemispheres.

Besides, this was Hailey. This wasn't a random chick I'd screwed around with after a show. Hailey knew me. She knew the real me. Even as kids, she'd had a knack for understanding what I was thinking and feeling.

Except for the part where I was in love with her. She'd never figured that out.

Hailey was the first to recover from the shock of what I'd done. She grabbed a towel from the towel rack and wrapped it around my shoulders. Then she led me to my room. Water dripped from my clothing onto the carpet, marking a damp trail down the hall.

In my room, she peeled the clothes off my body. A few minutes ago I would've been more than thrilled to have her do this while I removed her clothes. Now I could only stand there like a helpless child, too exhausted to stop her, too drained to care.

If this was how it would be with a sliver of the memory, what would I be like if I remembered everything? I couldn't afford that. I suspected it would destroy what little was left of me. That'd be great if I wanted to spend my musical career writing nothing but angst-filled songs. But that wasn't what Pushing Limits was. That wasn't what the fans wanted.

My boxer briefs clung to my body like a wet rag. The shivering that gripped me refused to ease up. I wasn't even sure anymore if it had anything to do with the impromptu cold shower, the temperature of the room, or something deeper. Or some combination of all three.

Hailey took hold of my hand and led me to my bed. The

warmth of her touch cut through the chill claiming my body for its own. Icy water dripped from my wet hair and down my face and back. Hailey picked up the towel from the ground and towel-dried my hair. Then she pulled back the bedcovers and indicated for me to climb under them. But they weren't enough to warm me up.

I closed my eyes. That was all I had the energy to do.

The mattress dipped under Hailey's weight as she climbed onto the bed. She wrapped her almost naked but toasty body around me and kissed my forehead and my cheek. Then her lips pressed gently against mine.

Before I could open my mouth and taste her, she pulled away. "I'll stay here, Nolan," she whispered, "for as long as you need." She snuggled against my body, her arm keeping me close.

That was the last thing I remembered before exhaustion dragged me down.

17

HAILEY

When Nolan and I were eleven years old, his family had owned the cutest little golden retriever puppy. For years he'd asked his parents for a dog. That and a guitar were all he ever wanted. His parents had eventually given in and gave him the puppy for his birthday. The dog meant the world to him.

He was Nolan's first and only pet.

Then one day after school we returned to his house to take the puppy for a walk together. Normally Lucky would bound to the front door as soon as he heard Nolan unlock it. Not so this time. We searched the place, becoming more worried as the seconds ticked by. After what had felt like an eternity, we found Lucky in the backyard. Lying on the ground. Not breathing.

For the longest time after Nolan fell asleep, I watched him. He looked so fragile, like he had the day we'd found his puppy dead. My heart broke seeing him this way.

I knew his tour had been grueling. Who wouldn't be exhausted after all the touring the band had done during the past year? Now that it was over and he had time to recover, he should've looked different. Refreshed. But instead he looked as though he still wasn't sleeping much.

I slipped out from under the covers. He didn't so much as stir. I picked up my clothing and returned to my room.

When I woke up several hours later, sunlight was streaming in through the blinds, and the smell of coffee perked me up a little. I grabbed an old sweatshirt that used to belong to Nolan. He'd left it at my house shortly before he disappeared to L.A. I also slipped on my yoga pants and trudged into the hallway in search of the beverage of the gods.

Nolan was in the kitchen, leaning back against the counter. Or rather, his body was in the kitchen but otherwise he looked to be a billion miles away. Next to him was the box of my favorite sugar-loaded cereal. The true breakfast of champions.

"Hey." I walked to the coffeemaker and filled my favorite mug, the one that said I'M SORRY FOR WHAT I SAID BEFORE I HAD MY COFFEE.

Nolan remained silent, the corners of his lips slightly curved down. I sipped my coffee, then placed the mug on the counter.

I wrapped my arms around his waist and rested my head on his shoulder. This was no different than in the past, when we used to be close. I would do this whenever something was bothering him. "Talk to me."

It took a few seconds before he finally enveloped me in his arms and kissed the top of my head. He still didn't say anything. I shifted in his arms and stroked his jaw with my thumb. The rough feel of his facial growth excited me, and I reached up and kissed the spot I'd touched. I couldn't help it. The constant craving to touch him was almost unbearable, like a chocolate addiction. But like with most addictions, I'd eventually have to walk away from it by going cold turkey.

Nolan turned his head ever so slightly and my mouth accidentally brushed against his. My lips parted, a silent invitation for him to deepen our kiss. His warm, coffee-scented breath caressed my face.

My cell phone played the song I'd programmed for general calls. If Nolan had planned to kiss me, I would never know. He pulled away. His rejection stung worse than a bee stinger dipped in battery acid.

I avoided looking at him and answered my phone.

"Hello, is this Hailey Wilkins?" a male voice asked.

"Yes."

"This is Detective Mathews."

I straightened at his name. "Hi. Did he say anything? Was he the one who attacked me?" The words came out in an unstoppable gush.

"I'm sorry, but it doesn't look like it. He has a strong alibi for that night. He did see you Friday morning where you work, getting into the passenger seat of a black car around eleven-fifteen a.m. That was the last he saw of you until you showed up at Trysting last night."

I had a billion questions based on what the detective had just told me. "Who was the driver?"

"Unfortunately, he couldn't see the person. He couldn't even tell me if it was a male or female. And he wasn't able to tell us the make of car, other than it was a sedan."

My throat clogged up at what he was telling me. "Has . . . has he been stalking me?" I could feel Nolan's gaze on me. I refused to acknowledge it.

"There isn't enough evidence to suggest he has been. Other than when he saw you regularly at Trysting a few months ago and then the day you were attacked, he hasn't seen you between those two times."

"But why was he watching me get into the vehicle if he wasn't stalking me?"

"He was meeting a friend at the sports center. They had a squash court booked. It checked out."

My mind stumbled over that statement. Something still didn't seem right. "What about how he watched me all those times when I hung out at Trysting?"

"He claimed he was worried about you. Every time he saw you there, you left with a different guy. He was upset you were leaving with guys he felt you didn't know very well and putting yourself at risk."

Even though he didn't say the words, the detective had indirectly judged and lectured me. Worse yet, now I looked like a slut because I liked sex and because I avoided relationships so as not to let a guy hurt me. Nothing wrong with that. The choice was mine. But it didn't mean I deserved to be attacked, and it didn't mean I'd been in Westgate because I was prostituting myself out.

"He promised he'd leave you alone and not watch you anymore," the detective continued. "So unless he does something else and you can prove he's stalking you, there's nothing I can do about it right now."

I nodded, forgetting he couldn't see me. "Okay."

We spoke for a few more minutes about the case, but he had no new information about that night. Nor did he have any new information about the days leading up to it.

I ended the call and let out a long breath. Why couldn't I remember anything? Why did my brain insist on keeping the truth from me? I could understand it with Nolan. He didn't want to remember. But I did.

I picked up my mug, ready to hurl it across the room. And I would have if Kayla hadn't given me the mug as a birthday present and if it hadn't still been full of coffee, albeit lukewarm coffee.

"What did he say?" With his chin, Nolan indicated the phone in my hand.

I filled him in on the call and everything the detective had told me, then I left to shower. When I stepped out of the steamy bathroom after taking longer than I needed to, Nolan was leaning against the opposite wall.

He pushed away from it. "I'm making you dinner tonight."

"I've never seen you cook before. I mean, other than macaroni and cheese." Which was not my favorite food. Not even close.

He smirked, and everything south of the equator heated up. Damn sexy smirk. "I've learned a trick or two since I was nineteen."

I didn't doubt it. "What are you making?"

He winked. "It's a surprise."

I snorted, remembering what we had, or rather didn't have, in the fridge. As did Nolan. He suggested we hit the store for groceries. As much as I wanted to talk about why he'd been showering in his clothes last night, I knew he didn't. And I didn't want him to put up any walls between us because of it.

As we wandered around the store, a girl my age rushed over to Nolan. "You're Tyler Erickson! Can I have your autograph?"

I glanced around, half expecting a horde of other fans to come screaming at us from both ends of the aisle, trampling me in their haste to touch Nolan.

"Sure," he said, "but I don't have a pen on me."

Before I could say I probably had one, the girl whipped out a Sharpie from her back pocket and handed it to Nolan. Seriously? Did she normally walk around with a Sharpie in her back pocket in case she saw a celebrity? I guessed so.

She yanked down her low-cut T-shirt, exposing her lacy bra—her *transparent* lacy bra, which left nothing to the imagination when it came to her large breasts and nipples.

I rolled my eyes and looked away.

Without paying much attention to what I was doing, I snatched up a package of bran-loaded cereal—the kind that would make you regular for a month with just one spoonful.

She didn't care about Nolan. She was only hoping to get laid. She didn't even notice how tired he looked.

But who was I to judge? How many of my one-night stands had I cared about? How many of them had I wanted to date after we screwed, and how many had I given fake phone numbers to when they asked for my number? The difference was I hadn't hooked up with any of them because of who they were. None were celebrities.

"Where are we going?" I'd asked, watching the passing scenery.

"It's a surprise," a man said, his voice familiar, comforting.

"Since when did you start eating this stuff?" Nolan asked, grinning like he was pleased with himself. I blinked. The fan was gone, as was the memory.

Nolan was standing next to our shopping cart, holding the box of cereal I'd grabbed off the shelf. And it looked like it wasn't the only one I had grabbed. Five other boxes mocked me from the cart.

"I . . . I . . ." I didn't want to lie and say I'd decided to try the stuff, because then he'd expect me to actually eat it for breakfast. No thanks. "I don't." I grabbed it from his hand, returned it and the rest of them to the shelf, and got the sugary brand I really wanted.

Without saying a word to him, I pushed the cart down the aisle, eager to escape him. The last thing I wanted was for him to see how much his groupies bothered me. They shouldn't have, but they did.

On the drive back to the apartment, I deliberated if I should mention the brief memory that had hit in the store. But really, what was there to tell? I didn't even know if it was related to the attack or if it had happened during one of the other days I didn't remember and so had nothing to do with what had left me in the coma.

Ahead of us, on the main road back to my apartment, a car

was pulled over on the side, its hazard lights flashing. An old woman was staring at the rear tire, which was clearly flat.

Nolan pulled up behind her and parked the car. He didn't get out, though. He just stared at the tire, and I instantly knew why.

18

———

NOLAN

Six Years Ago

As I drove to the dance studio where my asshole father had left my eleven-year-old sister, Hailey talked to her on the phone, reassuring her that we were on the way.

Several raindrops splattered on the window.

"Have you seen the new Disney movie yet?" Hailey asked. "Yes, that's the one. . . . It looks good. Do you wanna see it this weekend? . . . Then it's a date. Do you think Nolan wants to see it? . . . I think so too. He just doesn't want to admit it out loud."

The raindrops grew in intensity and a flash of lightning lit up the sky. *Shit*. Thunder rumbled not far in the distance.

"It's okay." Hailey's voice was soft, almost the calming tone of a lullaby. "We'll be there soon. . . . I know, sweetie."

I fought to keep my focus on the road. My sister hated storms. She told me once that they reminded her of our father when he got angry. Both were loud and threatening.

The healing wound on my forehead, the one that had required six stitches, suddenly throbbed, as if to remind me how threatening my father could be. But I didn't care what he did to me this time. I'd rip him a new one once I saw him. No way would my father make the mistake of abandoning my sister again. I'd make sure of that, even if I had to drive her to and from dance class myself.

The ride turned bumpy, and I realized a moment or two later that the problem wasn't the road surface. *Fuck.*

I pulled over to the curb and threw Hailey a look, telling her to keep talking to my sister. With the rain now pelting the ground, I climbed out of the car. Hailey joined me, the rain biting our skin as it turned to hail.

"Is there somewhere nearby you can go for shelter?" Hailey practically yelled into the phone.

An image of the building where the dance class was held shoved its way into my head. The stupid thing wasn't designed for staying dry if you were unfortunate enough to be out in the rain. And as far as I remembered, there was nothing near her that would protect her.

I had only two choices and neither of them was ideal, but at least one of them would keep my sister safe, even if I had to pay the price later.

Hailey kept talking to Sarah.

"Where's your phone?" I asked Hailey.

She shook her head, her eyes apologetic. She placed her finger over the receiver. "I didn't have time to grab it."

Shoving my hand through my hair, I paced back and forth. *What the fuck do I do now?*

19

NOLAN

Present

I blinked the world back into focus. The memory faded yet lingered with promises of more to come.

"Stay here." I needed to collect myself. I felt off balance, as if I were teetering on the edge of a precipice and I'd never get back up if I fell. Besides, I didn't want Hailey to know I'd remembered something about that day, or else she might've pushed me to remember more. "I won't be long."

I stepped out of the car and joined the old woman. "Do you need help?"

A gust of wind wrapped around us, warning of the approaching storm. She shuddered. "Thanks, but there's no need. My grandson's on his way."

"You can warm up in my car and I'll start changing your tire." He could be her hero when he got here. Fine by me.

"Are you sure?"

I nodded. She opened her trunk, and I removed the spare tire and jack. While she joined Hailey in my car, I jacked up her vehicle.

I'd barely finished doing that when a car door slammed shut. Hailey walked toward me, pushing against the bitter wind. "Do you need any help?" she asked.

I grinned up at her. "Couldn't handle her company, huh?"

Hailey snorted. "I think she's scheming to set me up with her grandson. He's all she can talk about. Apparently, according to her, he's great boyfriend material. Which means he's not."

I chuckled. "You never know. Maybe you're missing out on something great." I might have said that, but inside I hoped he'd be an arrogant ass. Definitely not Hailey's type.

But neither was I, thanks to my career. Any other time, any other career choice, I would've proved to her that I was her type and she should give me a chance. As it was, I'd chosen my career over the girl I loved. I didn't see how I could have both. At least not yet.

But just because I couldn't have her didn't mean I wanted Grandma hooking Hailey up with her grandson. I upped my pace so we could be out of here before he showed up. But before I had a chance to tighten the lug nuts, a black BMW pulled up ahead of the woman's car and parked. Right now even the paparazzi would have been preferable to her grandson. But not by much.

A good-looking man, dressed in a suit and long black coat, got out of the car and walked toward us. The back door of my vehicle opened and the old woman stepped out, beaming at him. Too bad he couldn't have been a random stranger wanting to help us.

The woman shuffled over to us across the snowy ground. "Hailey, this is my grandson, Craig." She patted the man's shoulder.

Craig held his hand out to Hailey. I narrowed my eyes at the offending limb. I'd punch his lights out if he was one of those sleazebags who kissed the back of a girl's hand.

Because Hailey was turned away from me, I couldn't tell if

she was interested in him. But the smile on his face warned he was interested in her.

The guy might actually be good for Hailey, a voice somewhere in my head pointed out. I gave the voice a mental whack with the wrench even though it had a point.

As Grandma explained to her grandson that Hailey wanted to be a physical therapist and help kids, I tighten the last nut and straightened. "There you go," I said. "Tire's changed."

Craig glanced down at the tire and disappointment landed briefly on his face. It had nothing to do with him wanting to be the one who changed the tire for his granny. To be her hero. He just wanted more time to steal my girl. Asswipe.

"Maybe you two would like to get together for coffee." Grandma looked between Hailey and Craig.

Craig lifted an eyebrow. "I'd like that if you're game."

Hailey glanced at me for a heartbeat before looking back at him. "Uh . . . sure."

What did I expect? Yes, we had kissed, but we both knew that couldn't go anywhere right now. I should be happy that she was ready to move on after what the douchebag of an ex-boyfriend had done to her.

While I put the flat tire and jack in his grandmother's trunk, he programmed Hailey's number into his phone. It took everything I had and then some not to slam the trunk shut harder than necessary.

He thanked me for helping his grandmother, the entire time eyeing me the way most people did when they recognized me but couldn't figure out where they knew me from. He wasn't a fan of the band. He'd just seen my picture a few times.

Hailey and I returned to my car and climbed in. "Are you really going out with him?" I asked as we drove away.

"I wouldn't say I'm going out with him. I'm meeting him for coffee. Big difference."

I remained silent the rest of the way home, stewing over

emotions I had no right feeling. Dying on the inside at what the woman's flat tire had cost me.

Once home, I brooded in my room and worked on the song I'd been writing for the past few days. I knew I needed to talk to Hailey, but I just couldn't deal with it all right now. I needed to get lost in my music first. I needed to finish the current song I was working on, which was almost ready to share with Jared.

By the time I'd fiddled with the final verse to the point where I was happy with it, the sun was low in the sky. I started playing it through once again but had only made it to the second verse when the opening strains of an Aerosmith song came from my phone. Jared.

I accepted the call. "Hey, man. I'm almost finished with the song."

"That's great." A pregnant pause fell between us, which was odd given that Jared had phoned *me*. "How're things going?"

"Great, but I still can't go back to L.A. yet. I have . . . things to deal with here first."

Another long pause. "I'm joining you. It's just too hard writing songs this way."

Fuck. "Look, give me another week. If I still can't return to L.A. next week, you can join me."

"Fine, you've got a week. But then it won't be just me joining you. The whole band will fly out. Otherwise there's no way we'll be ready in time."

Double fuck. Once they showed up, I wouldn't have time for Hailey anymore. But maybe it wouldn't be so bad having the band here. They'd be a distraction to keep me from remembering.

Only problem was, where the hell were we going to work?

20

HAILEY

While Nolan was in his room, talking on the phone, I started cooking dinner, even though he'd originally planned to make it. I needed to distract myself while he was busy. Something about him on the drive home had been off. It had been that way since we'd pulled over to help the woman with her flat tire . . . and I knew why. It wasn't because I'd told Craig I would go out with him for coffee. Nolan was returning to L.A. soon. We both knew that. Plus Nolan didn't feel the same way about me that I felt about him. No, Nolan was remembering. Despite his plans to do otherwise, he was beginning to remember the night his father killed Nolan's mother and sister. Maybe not everything, but enough to leave him off balance.

And that worried me.

By the time Nolan returned from his room, the seafood fettuccine was on the table. Cue candles and music, and it would have looked like a romantic dinner.

He sat down. "Wow, this looks great. But wasn't I going to cook?"

"You were busy and I was bored." I popped a garlicky

scallop in my mouth. It practically melted on contact with my tongue, thanks to Kayla having taught me a thing or two about cooking.

Nolan and I didn't say anything at first, the air around us off-kilter. I couldn't tell what Nolan was thinking, and it drove me nuts. It had never used to be like this between us. I used to always know what he was thinking. I used to know what to say to him to make him feel better.

"You're remembering, aren't you?" I didn't want to cause him more pain. I wanted to help him rip off the proverbial Band-Aid, but sometimes ripping it off wasn't the way to go. Sometimes you needed to gently peel it away to avoid leaving the individual raw and exposed. The trick was knowing which way was best at that particular moment.

He froze, his gaze fixed on his food, a slight tremble to his hand.

"It'll be okay, Nolan." *I'll be there for you. I'll never let you deal with this alone again. Not as long as you let me in like you used to.*

"How can you say that?" His words came out as a choked whisper, confirming my suspicions. He was remembering. As much as he didn't want to, he couldn't stop it, not unless he left Northbridge and returned to L.A. And maybe even then the memories would still come, unable to stop now the floodgate had been pried open. "I didn't stop it from happening, and . . . and maybe I'm just like him and I don't know it yet." The final words were no longer a whisper. They were harsh, bitter, intended to cause pain. Not to me; the pain was all his own, and that made the hurt inside me even stronger.

"You're not like him," I said. "You're nothing like him, Nolan, and you never will be."

Nolan slammed his fork on the plate, metal clinking against ceramic, and I jumped. "You don't know that." He pushed away from the table. "I don't want to talk about this." He stormed off.

I rushed after him and gently grabbed his arm. "I'm sorry. I didn't mean to upset you." When he still wouldn't look at me, I placed my hand on his face and guided it so he was forced to look at me. "You need to trust me. I only want to help you. You know that, right?"

He studied my eyes for a second, then nodded. "I do trust you. But I'm not ready to remember." He looked away. "I'm scared. I'm scared of remembering what I did or didn't do to save them. I'm scared of having to relive it again and again."

I brushed my lips against his cheek. "I know you're scared, Nolan. But I'm here for you. No matter what, I'm here for you."

He hugged me, body shaking, face buried in my hair, and whispered, "I know."

We stayed like this for several heartbeats before he finally pulled away. His wall was sliding back into place, even if there were now holes in it that hadn't been there before. He still wasn't ready to remember, but ready or not, it would happen. And there was nothing he could do to stop it.

"How about we finish dinner, then watch a movie?" My lips curled up on one side. "I'll even let you pick it."

Nolan snorted. "Yes, because I've been dying to watch a chick flick all day."

"Hey, I also have *Lord of the Rings*." I poked him in the side. "You can't say no to that."

He leaned down and brushed his lips against mine. "It's you I can't say no to."

My heart leapfrogged into my throat. Before I could respond or kiss him back, he returned to the table and ate like the last few minutes had never happened. Fine—if it made him feel better for now, who was I to argue?

After dinner, I snuggled against him to watch the movie. We'd done this a million times before, but this time it felt different. *We* felt different, and I didn't mean because we'd been kissing lately. I still hadn't figured out what that was all about. I knew I should ask him what was going on between us, but hello, this was Aragorn we were talking about. He was nice to look at, and I didn't have to figure out how he felt about me. He just went to work, killing orcs and making the girls watching the movie swoon.

At one point, as the wind and snow stormed outside the window, Nolan stiffened next to me—and I had a feeling it had nothing to do with the movie.

21

NOLAN

Six Years Ago

I paced back and forth on the wet sidewalk as Hailey did her best to soothe my sister on the phone over the sound of the storm. Single-story houses and tall trees stood on either side of the street, but I might as well be in the middle of nowhere as far as I was concerned.

I stopped my pacing long enough to glare at the flat tire. Too bad it wasn't my father; if it had been, I could've beaten his fucking ass.

I needed to use the phone, but I didn't want to take away the only lifeline Sarah had to knowing that help was coming. Once I hung up on her, she'd be alone.

But I didn't have a choice.

I indicated for Hailey to give me the phone. "Hey, squirt. Everything's going to be okay, but I need to hang up and call for help." I didn't want to tell her the truth, that I had a flat and wouldn't be there for a while yet. "I'll call you right back. Is that okay?"

"You promise?" my sister asked, her voice quiet against the

pummeling hail. My heart hurt hearing her like this. I was her big brother and I was doing a shitty job of protecting her.

"I promise."

"Okay." The word came out as a defeated whisper.

As much as it killed me doing so, I ended the call and dialed 911.

"Nine-one-one. State your emergency," a woman said on the other end. Several cars drove past, slowing down long enough for the drivers to check Hailey out.

I glared at them as I explained Sarah's situation to the woman. I kept the information as brief as possible, avoiding anything that would give away my family's situation. I told her something must have happened to my father. He should've been there by now. Who knew if I was making things worse for all of us, especially Mom. But I couldn't risk my sister's life because I was worried about that. Sarah came first.

"I'm sending someone to the address," the woman said. "Please stay on the line."

I shook my head even though she couldn't see me. "I can't. My sister's alone. I need to call her back to make sure she's okay. This is the only phone I have."

"All right."

I hung up and dialed Sarah's number. She answered on the first ring. "You okay, squirt?"

"Are you coming?" she asked, sobbing. Lightning lit up the sky, followed a second later by the loud rumble of thunder. Sarah shrieked, and I pictured her huddled against the wall, her knees to her chest as she made herself as small as possible.

"Sarah, it's going to be okay. You have to believe me. I'll be there as soon as I can. But the police will be there before me. I called them."

"I don't wanna go to jail," she said, her voice small.

"I swear you won't go to jail. But I have a flat tire and it will take me a while to get there. The police will keep you safe until then. But while you wait, you can talk to Hailey. That way I can change the tire and we'll be there as quickly as possible. Can you do that for me?"

"Yes," she breathed.

I passed Hailey the phone. She took it from me, body shaking. When we had rushed from her house, she'd only been wearing a flimsy tank top and shorts that revealed her long legs. And now every part of her was drenched and covered in goose bumps.

Needing to get Hailey warm and to get to Sarah as soon as possible, I worked quickly to change the tire. Hailey continued talking to my sister.

"The police are there," Hailey told me as I removed the tire.

"Tell Sarah I want to talk to them."

She relayed the message to my sister. I began tightening the lug nuts and was almost finished when Hailey handed me the phone. "Hello?" I said into it.

"Is this Nolan Kincaid?" a gruff voice asked.

"Yes. Is my sister okay?"

"She will be. I'm driving her home."

My gut tightened, and I was positive I was going to puke. "No one's home right now." Unless my father had returned, in which case there would be some serious shit flying soon. As far as the police knew, based on what I'd told the dispatcher, he could have been in an accident. That was the only explanation for why a normal, caring parent would be so late picking up his child from dance class.

"Where's her mother?"

"She had a meeting tonight with the hospital foundation." Dad allowed Mom to help them because it looked good, status-wise and all. And people might grow suspicious if she was never allowed to leave the house. "She won't be home for another hour."

"When do you expect to arrive home?"

"Not long. I'm almost finished changing my tire."

"We'll wait for you, then."

"Okay." I didn't know if it would be all right. I couldn't think that far ahead. For now, the main thing was my sister was finally safe.

22

HAILEY

Nolan was watching the TV, but I had a feeling he wasn't seeing anything on the screen.

I shifted around and cupped his face with my hand. "Hey, what's going on?"

Nolan blinked twice. "Sorry. I'm just tired." He closed his eyes and pinched the bridge of his nose. "I think I'll go to bed now."

He reopened his eyes, and his thoughts waged a battle in his mind as he deliberated for a moment. "Would . . . would you stay with me tonight?"

An excited thrill trembled through my body even though it shouldn't have. It had been over six years since we had slept together, and that had been innocent. That was before we had kissed. And I meant really kissed, not just a friendly peck between close friends.

He smirked, and the slight hint of humor eased my fears about what he was going through. "Just keep your hands to yourself. I have my virtue to protect."

I rolled my eyes. "Duly noted."

Once I was ready for bed, I joined him. Even though this

wasn't the first time we'd been in bed together, just like when we watched the movie, things between us felt different.

But unlike on the couch, an ocean of space now separated us. Yet an odd sense of intimacy crackled in the air between us. I felt torn as to what I should do, or if I should do anything at all.

Nolan turned around and switched off the bedside lamp. "Good night, Forget-Me-Not."

"Good night, rock star." I laughed at his mocked groan. I wasn't sleepy yet, so I listened to his breathing. Though he'd told me he was tired, it took forever before his breath became slow and even.

Light from the streetlights leaked into his room and rested gently on his face. I could see his old scar partially hidden behind his bangs, and bit back the temptation to trace my finger over it, somehow removing all his pain. A pain that had started way back, when his family first developed cracks in its once smooth surface.

Eventually my eyes drifted shut.

When I woke again, the room was still dark, other than the dim light from the streetlights. It didn't take much to discover what had woken me up: Nolan was moving restlessly on the bed.

He let out a soft whimper and my heart broke for him once again. At some point he had kicked the bedding off him, leaving his abs exposed. In the soft light, I could just make out the thick scar cutting across his skin.

"Nolan," I whispered. "You're having a nightmare."

He didn't respond. He kept tossing and turning, the covers becoming tangled with his legs. He mumbled what sounded like his sister's name, then whimpered again.

I rested my hand on his chest. His heart pounded hard against my palm. "Hey, Nolan, it's okay. You're just having a bad dream." I moved my hand to his far shoulder and gently shook him.

His eyes opened and for a moment he stared at me like he wasn't sure if I was real or not.

"Do you want to talk about it?" I asked, still partially leaning over him.

"No," he whispered. He no longer looked scared, like he had been during the nightmare. His eyes, dark from the dim room, focused on my eyes, then drifted to my lips.

My heart fluttered against my ribs, nudging me to follow through on what the rest of my body wanted me to do. Mistake or not, I leaned down, my chest pressing against Nolan's. Only difference was, I wasn't half naked like Nolan. I had my tank top on but my girls were braless.

At the warmth seeping from his body through the thin fabric of my top, my nipples tingled with want and egged me on, like perky cheerleaders. I lightly pressed my lips against his. Nolan didn't move. He didn't speak. He just watched me through hooded eyes. I gently nipped his lower lip between my teeth. He sucked in a soft breath.

I pulled away but didn't get far. His hand threaded through my hair and brought my mouth back to his. This time my kiss wasn't tentative. This time I completely lost myself in it. Tasting Nolan was pure heaven. His tongue stroking mine was pure heaven. I moaned and deepened the kiss.

His hand slipped away from my hair and skimmed down my back. It continued to drift to the side of my breast. He paused there, and I almost whimpered in frustration. I didn't know what we were to each other these days, and I didn't want to think about it right now. Even if it was just for one night, I wanted to make love to him. To let him know how I felt about him. To temporarily forget everything else.

While still kissing him, I shifted so his hand covered my breast. Hey, a girl's gotta do what a girl's gotta do. My new motto

—one I needed printed on my tank top. In reply, he brushed his thumb against my nipple. Desire cannonballed its way from my breast to between my legs. My body jerked slightly and I moaned again.

"Oh, God, Nolan," I murmured in his ear. "I want you so badly. I want you inside me so badly." I traced the tip of my tongue against the shell of his ear. *Please want me like I want you.*

Nolan paused teasing my nipple. Fear shot through me that maybe I'd misread the situation and he didn't want me the same way I wanted him.

"Are you sure, Forget-Me-Not? If we do this, everything will change between us. Is that what you want?"

I bit my lip to keep from saying things had already changed between us. They'd changed years ago. I knew what he meant, though. If we had sex, there'd be no going back to what we used to be, especially because there never could be a him and me. Our lives made that impossible. While we wouldn't exactly be a one-night stand, it would be close enough. Once he left for L.A., there would be no more us.

But I was willing to take the chance, no matter how much it hurt later on. And it would hurt. A lot.

"Yes," I said. "It's what I want . . . if it's what you want."

His hand on my breast moved to my face and his thumb caressed my cheek. The intensity in his eyes almost did me in, and I inhaled sharply. The sound was soft and slightly shaky.

"It's what I want too," he said. "More than you can ever realize."

I pulled away and yanked my tank top off over my head. In the dim light, I could just make out the slow rise and fall of his Adam's apple.

He reached up and cupped one of my breasts. My ribs were still bruised and slightly sore from the attack, but the discoloration had faded enough so it wasn't noticeable in this lighting. The last thing I wanted was for Nolan to change his mind about what I sensed we were going to do, worried he might hurt me.

Wonder lit his eyes, like he was gazing upon one of the Seven Wonders of the World. The expression made him even sexier—something I'd never thought possible until now. I bit my lip to keep from moaning out loud.

"Do you have condoms?" I didn't want to get all heated up only to realize he didn't have any in his room. I had some, but I needed to know if I should get them.

He cringed. "I wasn't planning to get lucky on the trip, so no."

"I'll be right back." I slid off the bed and practically ran to my room. I opened the drawer in my bedside table and removed the box of condoms. I dumped the contents on the bed. Three spilled out. I shook it again. Nothing else joined them. But really, did we need more than three? Unless we were going to be snowed in for the next two days and required steamy sex to stay warm, the answer was no.

But I wouldn't have complained if we were snowed in. The sacrifice, well worth it.

I grabbed the condoms and rushed back to Nolan's room. "I have three left."

Nolan was standing next to the bed. He grabbed my hips and pulled me to him. My breasts squished against his chest and made them very happy. Then his mouth was on mine again.

One of his hands traveled to my lower back and his thumb stroked lazy circles against my skin. My hands knotted in his hair as our kisses heated up.

But it wasn't enough. I wanted more. More of him. More of us.

I let my fingers explore his body, enjoying every ridge of the muscles on his stomach. Enjoying the smooth skin above the waistband of his boxer briefs.

I ran my fingertip above the stretch of fabric. His muscles tightened, then relaxed under my touch.

Nolan's hand moved down to squeeze my butt. It stayed there for a second, then drifted to the waistband of my cotton shorts. I wasn't the only one excited at what we were doing. His length strained against the fabric of his underwear.

A thrill trembled through me. Touching a guy this way wasn't new to me. But this was Nolan. The last thing I'd ever expected was to one day touch him so intimately.

Other than in my dreams.

I ran my fingers along the thick length of him, but it wasn't enough. I slipped them under the waistband of his underwear and wrapped them around him. I came close to purring at the velvety softness of his tip, and traced my thumb under the head.

"Oh, God, Hailey," Nolan breathed, and I couldn't help but smile at his reaction. "Unless you want this to end before we're started, I recommend you slow down."

My thumb found the sensitive spot below the head and I gently massaged it. "Maybe I don't want to slow down."

He let out a hiss of air, then his fingers tugged on the waistband of my shorts. He peeled them off ever so slowly. His touch, as it caressed my skin, tormented my super-sensitive body. The way he looked at me sent a warm flush over me, and I was positive if he didn't stop doing that soon, I'd combust.

Which, right now, sounded like a heavenly way to go.

His finger brushed the outside of my right ankle, against the six forget-me-not flowers tattooed there. Each one tiny, delicate, realistic. An old belief claimed if you had a forget-me-not tattoo, your lover wouldn't forget you. When I'd gotten it, Nolan had just moved to L.A., and I'd foolishly wanted to ensure he never forgot me—even though he wasn't my lover. But when he never called back or texted me, I'd known the old wives' tale was nothing more than a foolish belief.

"What's this?" he asked.

"They're forget-me-nots." I skipped on my reason for getting the tattoo. Let him believe I got it because I loved the flower (which was true) and not because of some misguided story.

He lifted my ankle, removed the shorts, and tossed them aside. He gently kissed the flowers. The sweet and simple action almost did me in.

Nolan lowered my foot back down.

With my shorts off, I was lying on the bed in nothing but my red cotton underwear. Okay, not the sexiest piece of underwear I owned. That honor went to the satin panties Kayla had given me for my birthday. Her motto: if I was going to get lucky, I'd better look sexy while it went down. To her, plain cotton underwear was a big no-no. It wasn't sexy enough. But the way Nolan looked at said underwear, he clearly didn't agree with her. Not even close.

I licked my lip, a slight nervousness at what we were about to do creeping in. I'd had sex plenty of times, enough to know what I was doing, yet for the first time since I'd lost my virginity, I was genuinely nervous. Things were different when you weren't about to screw some random guy you didn't care to see again after that night. It was different when you were about to have sex with someone you'd been secretly in love with for so long—and that scared me.

Nolan didn't give me a chance to dwell on it further. His mouth was on mine again. I pushed aside my fears at what was about to happen, and at what would happen once he returned to L.A. For one night I wanted to forget all that. I wanted to live in the moment. This moment.

His fingers, warm and callused, traced along the outside of my thigh. At my knee, he nudged my legs apart. His fingers resumed their journey up, up, up to torment me. Once he was midway, he paused and drew lazy circles on my skin.

My skin tingled in response, and the throbbing between my legs begged for those lazy circles to migrate closer. I might've even wiggled a little, encouraging Nolan's fingers to keep moving north.

And eventually they did.

While his mouth created music against mine—and holy mother of all things wonderful, did that man ever know how to kiss—his thumb brushed against my supercharged center. A jolt of electricity shot through my body, enough to power Northbridge if it ever experienced an outage. My lower body jerked in response.

Nolan wasn't the only one who knew how to please. I had my own tricks I was dying to try out on him. I tugged his boxer briefs past his hips, wrapped my fingers around his balls, and gave them a light squeeze. He groaned his satisfaction, and he might have muttered, "Holy shit."

I grinned. "Liked that, huh?"

He didn't answer. Instead, he pulled away from me and practically ripped his underwear off. It landed somewhere on the floor, presumably near mine.

His fingers returned to what they'd been doing earlier— making the ache between my legs a little happier, a little more demanding. And just when I thought it couldn't get better, he slipped a finger inside me and then another. He didn't move them. He just pressed against the lining. The promised combustion from earlier was nothing compared to now.

"Oh, God, Nolan," I somehow managed to say.

He chuckled. "Liked that, huh?" he replied, echoing my earlier words.

"Yes. I like."

He moved up the length of me, his fingers still inside me, and settled his mouth on one of my nipples. He sucked on it as he slowly pumped his fingers in and out. I guessed I shouldn't have been too shocked. He was both the singer and guitarist from Pushing Limits. That made him multitalented in my book.

I ran my fingernails roughly down his back and he groaned, further exciting the nipple in his mouth. I was so close to the edge, it wouldn't take much more to push me all the way.

"I need you. Inside me. Now." My voice was rough and standing-on-the-edge-of-a-volcano heated.

Grinning, he pulled away from my nipple and reached for a foil package on my nightstand. He carefully ripped it open and rolled it onto his thick length. Oddly enough, seeing him like this and remembering how we used to be as kids was enough to set my face on fire. He wasn't just another guy I had met and gone home with. This was the guy who had played 007 with me when we were ten and were chasing around the neighborhood on our bikes. The guy who had been there for me when I suffered through my first heartbreak at fourteen years old. The guy who had been there for me at every soccer game while we were growing up.

He positioned himself between my legs. I wrapped them around his hips and he slowly plunged inside me. My body stretched to accommodate his wide width. Those girls who'd written all the erotica about him on the fan sites turned out to have been right about a few details after all. Not that I planned to tell them.

"God, you're so fucking tight, Forget-Me-Not." Nolan's eyes flared with lust and desire. "So fucking tight and hot. I'm not going to last much longer."

That made two of us.

I expected him to begin pumping inside me. He didn't, though. He lowered himself so his chest lightly touched mine and he kissed me long and hard.

Before he started moving inside me, I caught a flash of

emotion in his eyes. It went further than lust and desire. What I saw in that moment was a reflection of what I felt for him: love.

But there wasn't enough time to register what it meant. The slow burn inside me, which had ignited when he first touched me, flared out and consumed me.

I cried out his name. And the sound of my name falling from his lips was the sweetest sound I'd ever heard.

Never until then had I loved my name more.

23

NOLAN

I could've easily stayed inside of Hailey all night. So it was with great reluctance that I pulled out of her and tossed the condom in the garbage. Outside, the wind howled, restless, the opposite to how I now felt.

But by the time I returned to the bed, Hailey was bailing on me.

Like hell if I'd let that happen.

I wrapped my arms around her and pulled her tight. "Where do you think you're going?" I murmured in her ear.

"My room." The vulnerability in her eyes almost brought me to my knees, and I took her face in my hands.

"What if I don't want you to go?" This was the first time I'd ever said that to a girl. With all the other girls I'd spent the last few years entertaining myself with, none had meant enough to me to want them to stay after we'd fucked.

"All right," she said hesitantly.

"Thank you." I brushed my lips against hers, then led her back to bed.

She cuddled up to me, her head on my chest, listening to

my satisfied heart. Listening to the heart that wondered how the hell I'd be able to leave her again.

Which was why I couldn't say the three words sitting on the tip of my tongue. As much as I loved Hailey, and because I did love her, I couldn't tell her the truth. I couldn't ask her to come with me to L.A. I couldn't introduce her to my world. I couldn't expect her to put her life on hold and come on the road with me. Everything about *my* life would destroy all that made her special.

So, instead, I traced lazy circles on the soft skin of her lower back, hoping that deep down she would hear the words I couldn't say.

After a few minutes, Hailey's breathing evened out, and for a few seconds I allowed myself to believe this was my new permanent. That every night and every morning for the rest of my life, Hailey would fall asleep and wake up in my arms.

But while my brain knew this was all only temporary, I wasn't so sure my heart was on the same page—or even in the same book.

Careful not to disturb Hailey, I moved from under her. She muttered in her sleep, then curled up under the covers. I grabbed my notebook from the nightstand. Using my cell phone to light the page, I scribbled down the lyrics that poured from my heart.

And like the last song I'd written since moving in with her, the words easily poured onto the page.

24

NOLAN

The first thing I noticed when I stirred from my sleep was the warm body pressed against me. The second thing I noticed (well, third after the raging hard-on) was Hailey's scent.

I smiled and lightly kissed the naked shoulder peeking from under the covers. Hailey stirred, pressing her hot ass against my cock.

"Mornin'," I murmured into her ear. I had no idea of the time, but judging from the sunlight streaming into the room, it had to be midmorning.

"Hmmm," she replied, which I took to be a positive sign.

My hand shifted under the cover and brushed against her full breast. This time she sucked air in sharply. I cupped the warm flesh and traced circles around her nipple. This was met by a moan from Hailey and her body jerking back against me.

From the bedside table, my phone played Jared's song. I ignored it and moved my hand down Hailey's stomach to between her legs. I palmed her heated pussy, which was already aroused and waiting for my touch. "God, Hailey. You're so fucking ready for me."

I interpreted her answering moan to be an agreement, then slipped a finger between her folds to tease her. My thumb brushed against her clit.

"Oh, God, Nolan," she called out.

Jared's song played again.

Again I ignored it.

With a little more pressure this time, I circled her clit, and I swear she was this close to coming.

The song played for the third time, and I was ready to hurl the damn phone against the wall.

"You should probably answer it." Hailey shifted away from me, not giving me much choice.

I reached for my phone. "Hey, what's up?" Lucky for him he couldn't read my mind.

"Who the hell are you?"

At his near shout, I yanked the phone from my ear. "What are you talking about? You know who I am."

"What they're saying about your name. Is it true?"

"What are they saying?" Not that I needed to ask. I had a painful suspicion I already knew.

"That your real name isn't Tyler Erickson. It's Nolan Kincaid."

Fuck! How the hell . . . ? Who the hell . . . ?

My head flopped forward and I shoved my hand through my hair. "It's true."

I smoothed my hand against the sheet, ironing out the creases. If only it had been as simple as that when it came to the mess of my life. If only it had been as simple as stripping the bedding from the bed and starting fresh.

"But why?" Jared said. "I don't mean why the name change, but why didn't you tell me? Why am I only finding out now?" The hurt in his voice almost gutted me. He was right. I should have told him. "I've told you things I've told no one else. Why? Because I trusted you, Tyler—or Nolan, or whatever your real name is."

"Nolan is my real name," I muttered.

Hailey moved to kneel behind me on the bed and held me close, sharing her strength. She tenderly kissed the bare skin on my shoulder.

I smiled at her, the movement small but genuine. "And I'm sorry," I told Jared, "but I had my reasons for keeping it a secret."

"Are you in trouble?" he asked.

"No, nothing like that. I needed to escape my past and couldn't do that with my old name." Since I had nothing to lose by telling him the truth, I told him about my family and how I couldn't remember that night. Better he found out from me than from the media.

"I'm sorry, Ty . . . Nolan."

"Once the police finished questioning me, I ran off to L.A. Where I've been ever since."

"But how come no one knew until now about your real identity?"

"My mom home-schooled me. So other than a few friends, who I trust with my life"—I glanced at Hailey—"no one remembered me by the time we signed with the record label." Same deal with the kids I used to play soccer with when I was younger. I'd changed enough over the years that they didn't recognize Tyler Erickson as the same lanky kid who'd been on their soccer team.

"So the record label doesn't even know?" he asked.

I cringed. "They know. They did a background check before they signed us. They couldn't find a single mention about my life. Nothing. They asked me about it and I told them."

"And they didn't have an issue with it?"

"It's not like I'm the first musician to use a different name from what they were born with. They just wanted to make sure I hadn't been involved in anything illegal. They understood my need to protect my privacy. And that I wanted to be known for my music, not because of what my father did."

"You could've told me. I would've understood and wouldn't have told anyone."

"I know." And I did. "But I'd kept it a secret for so long, I was used to being Tyler Erickson. As far as I was concerned, Nolan didn't exist anymore." I looked at Hailey, my gaze absorbing everything about her, including the part where we were still naked. "Or he didn't exist until recently."

She smiled softly at me, understanding what I meant.

"So what're you going to do?" Jared asked.

"Right now I have no idea. Other than writing songs for the album, my only concern is the reason I came here originally." And for the first time since coming to Northbridge, I told Jared the truth.

"I can't leave until I know she's safe," I finished.

"And what if the cops can't solve it before you're due back here? Then what?"

"I'll figure it out if it comes to that."

"Fine. Just make sure that whatever's going on down there, you don't get caught up in it, okay?" Jared said. "And don't do anything stupid . . ." He left the warning hanging, leaving me to fill in the blanks. *Don't get yourself into deeper trouble with the media than you're already in.*

Don't get yourself killed.

25

HAILEY

The best part of doing something meaningful to you is that it steals you away from all your problems. Even for just a few minutes a day, it fills you with a joy that can't be found anywhere else, and gives you a passion to keep going when you feel like the world is conspiring against you.

Or in my case, my feelings for Nolan were conspiring against me.

I walked out of the gym where I'd been helping the physical therapist with the kids with special needs. The more I worked with them, the more I knew this was the area I wanted to specialize in when I became a therapist. It might not mean the same as music meant to Nolan, but it came pretty darn close.

Dad had sent me a text to check if Nolan and I were okay now that the news about Tyler Erickson's true identity was out. He'd been skillfully fielding questions at the hospital, where he worked as a surgeon, ever since Nolan had been spotted coming out of my room. In many ways, Dad had always been more of a father to Nolan than Nolan's own father had been.

"Oh my God, isn't that Tyler Erickson?" a female voice shrieked from behind me as I was about to respond to my father's text, the sound rivaling that of a cat whose tail had been stepped on. Cringing, I glanced over my shoulder.

Everyone around us stopped walking, searching for their golden rock star. Once they spotted him, a handful of squealing college-age girls rushed him. A few other girls showed a little more restraint, but they too joined the small crowd fangirling over Nolan.

As I approached the group, Lindsey, who worked in the sports center part-time, looked at her phone and then over my shoulder. Her eyes narrowed.

I turned to see what she was looking at. A tall, good-looking man strode toward us, and for a moment I thought it was Nolan's father. The similarities between the two were so overwhelming that I shuddered unexpectedly.

But this wasn't Nolan's father. He was dead.

"Who is that?" I asked her.

"My stepfather . . . I've gotta go." She hurried over to him.

I watched them walk away. He said a few words and she laughed. I would be hard pressed to remember a time when Nolan had laughed at something his father said.

"How was work?" Nolan asked. His fans hung on his every word. I swore a couple even sighed. But none melted into a puddle like I tended to do whenever I heard his voice, their hearts not as screwed up as mine. Lucky them.

"Good," I told him, and walked away from the group, not caring if Nolan followed me or not. I needed to get away from his fans. They had nothing to do with me.

Nolan reached for my hand and stopped me. "Hey, where're you going?"

"Home." I glanced back at his fans, some of whom still watched him, debating whether they should trail after him.

Nolan peered over his shoulder. "Do they bother you?"

I cringed that he knew me so well and how petty it would sound if I said yes. "No. Not really. Your fans are important to you." Without them, Pushing Limits wouldn't be as big as they were. Without them, the band wouldn't have a chance of being bigger for the next album.

He brushed his thumb against my cheek. "But you're important to me too."

I gave him a small smile. "But you won't always be here for me. You know that, right?"

"I know that. But while I am in Northbridge, I want to make sure you're safe."

"I can't stop my life because of what happened. Just like you didn't let what happened to you and your family stop you from going after what you wanted."

He leaned into me, mere inches separating our mouths. His warm breath against my lips sent a delicious heat wave to my core. I barely kept from squirming against him.

"Except I did . . ." He didn't finish the thought. His lips found mine.

The kiss wasn't heated like last night. This kiss was something deeper. It was a part of us opening up and sharing a vulnerability inside us. But instead of making us weaker, it would ultimately make us stronger. Braver.

Or so I hoped.

Not that I understood what was going on between us. We were former best friends who were now fucking until he left. The advanced version of fuck buddies. As far as I could tell, Nolan didn't do the girlfriend thing, other than in the eyes of the media.

He pulled away, breath heavy, and looked around us. "You and I need to talk."

"I thought we were."

He chuckled. "That's not what I mean. I was referring to last night. About you and me. And—"

And then I got it. He meant about what happened last

night. He was already regretting it. Except his arms were still around me. If his goal was to confuse me, he'd succeeded.

"And how you'll be leaving soon." I smiled even though it was the last thing I felt like doing. "Don't worry, I get it. What happened between us was nothing more than a fling." I almost said "meaningless fling," but I couldn't get the words out. It might've been meaningless for Nolan, but it was far from that for me.

He frowned. "A fling?"

"Okay, more like a . . ." A what? A one-night stand? A mistake? The best night of my life? Even though I wanted to, I couldn't say the last one either.

"A one-night stand? Is that what you were going to say?" He pulled away. "Or was it just a pity fuck, Hailey? You felt bad for me and decided to fuck me to help me get over it?"

He might as well have stabbed me in the chest with a blunt knife, except his accusation hurt worse.

I took a step back, needing to maintain distance between us. Fortunately, his fans had moved on. No one was listening to our conversation. "Is that all you think I'm capable of? That I'm nothing more than an empty shell who only does one-night stands?" I tried to sound pissed but sounded hurt instead.

I turned and stalked off. Last night's storm had been nothing compared to how I felt after Nolan's accusations.

I made it as far as the main entrance before Nolan grabbed my arm. A group of moms with young kids turned to see what was going on.

"I'm sorry, Forget-Me-Not. I didn't mean for it to come out that way," he said softly, doing his best to keep the conversation between us private. But it was a waste of time. Maybe if I was talking to someone who wasn't a celebrity, no one would've paid attention to us. But at this point I was too angry to care either way.

"How did you plan for it to come out?" I asked.

He glanced away briefly. When he turned back to me, the battlefield of emotions was still etched on his otherwise perfect face. "I don't want what happened last night to be nothing more than a meaningless one-night stand. I can get those anytime."

"So you want us to be fuck buddies?" It spilled out harsher than I'd meant for it to sound, and I earned a few angry glares from the moms. I was too pissed to care.

"That's not what I'm saying at all." His face softened. "I want to be with you, Hailey. I want to go to sleep with you curled against me. I want to wake up and the first thing I see is you. I know I don't have the right to say this because I'm leaving soon, but it's how I feel."

If ice had filled my insides, his words would have caused it to melt. What he was offering wouldn't last forever, but I was willing to take as much as he'd give me, while I could.

"I want that too," I finally said, biting back the three words I yearned to say. The three words I couldn't tell him because it would change everything. And right now what we had between us was too fragile for me to open up that way.

26

NOLAN

I'd meant every word when I told Hailey that I wanted to go to sleep with her curled up against me. For her to be the first thing I saw when I woke up.

But what I didn't say but meant was that I wanted this for the rest of my life. Only it wasn't possible with the career I had signed up for. At least not for now.

"I want that too," she said, the words almost a whisper.

Temporarily forgetting where we were standing, I closed the distance between us and kissed her forehead, the tip of her nose, her lips.

She parted them, and I plunged my tongue into her mouth. I flicked it against hers, a tease of what was still to come, then pulled away. "Maybe we should continue this *discussion* at home."

She grinned, understanding what I really meant. The only thing I planned to discuss when we got home was which room she wanted to fuck in.

I threaded my fingers with hers. Her smirk faded to a sad smile. "Have you been to their graves yet?" she asked.

I tugged on my hand, needing to get away from her and this question. But she only held on tighter.

"You should really go there, Nolan."

"I can't." The words came out as a whisper, and I closed my eyes, squeezing the picture of their funeral from my brain.

"I know, but I'll be there with you. It might help you deal with the nightmares."

My eyelids flew open and I stared at her. "How did you . . . ?"

"How did I know? I've heard you tossing and turning. I've heard you call out during the night." She ran her thumb under my eye. "And it's obvious you're not sleeping much. You looked tired when I woke up from the coma, but that was nothing compared to now. Now you look exhausted half the time." She swallowed. "You weren't having nightmares in L.A., were you?" When I didn't answer, she continued, "It's why you need to either go back to L.A. or face your ghosts. You need to visit your mom and your sister."

I wanted to make a joke, lighten things, change the direction of the conversation, but a nagging voice told me she was right. I owed it to them. I might have tried to move on with my life, but I'd never forgotten them.

"Okay," I said. "I'll go to the cemetery." I tightened my hold on her hand. "But you promise you'll come with me?" I looked into her warm brown eyes and saw my pain reflected back at me. "I don't think I can do this on my own."

"I promise. As long as you want me, Nolan, you won't be alone."

I didn't know if she meant I wouldn't be alone when it came to the cemetery or if she meant more than that. Fearing it was the former when I wished for the latter, I didn't ask.

Despite the heat in the car, cold gripped my body as Hailey pulled into the cemetery parking lot and found a spot. With the engine still running, she wrapped her warm hand around my shaky fist.

"It's going to be okay, Nolan. No matter what happens in there"—her gaze flicked to the cemetery entrance—"it will be okay."

I took in the ornate black metal fence, the tall stone columns on either side of the entrance, and the thick blanket of white beyond that. The memory of my sister and mother being lowered into the ground flashed in my head, and it was like being kneed hard in the gut.

But no matter how much it hurt, no matter how much I'd rather be somewhere else, Hailey was right. I needed to do this.

I nodded, more to myself than to her, and opened the car door. A cold wind chilled me to the core. While I waited for Hailey to join me, I stood frozen, staring at the entrance. I closed my eyes against the memories of my last time here.

At the feel of Hailey's fingers weaving with mine, I opened my eyes. No rays of sunlight streamed down from the heavens, guiding me to their final resting spot. No signs whispered to me that my mom and sister were happy I'd come back to visit. All that greeted me was the heavy gray sky. "I don't even remember where they are."

"I do," she said.

Guilt wrapped around me tightly, squeezing the air out of me. Hailey had been here at least once since the funeral, while I'd stayed away like a coward.

She led the way to the two graves. My father wasn't buried here. After what he had done, after all those years of abuse and secrets, I'd refused to have his remains anywhere near theirs. I had no idea where he was buried and I didn't care. All I knew was that his parents had claimed his body. He wasn't sharing the same sacred grounds with the people I loved.

A fresh bouquet of red and white flowers rested against a tombstone. Christmas colors. My sister's favorite time of year.

My steps faltered. "I don't even have flowers."

"They won't care about that."

I nodded and let Hailey lead me to their final resting place.

In the days leading up to the funeral, I had been numb. Hailey's parents stepped in to help with the arrangements. I didn't even remember what Mom's and Sarah's gravestones looked like.

Releasing Hailey's hand, I dropped to my knees in front of the two shiny black granite gravestones, sitting side by side. A million things that I wanted to say to Mom and Sarah jostled around in my head, but the boulder-sized lump in my throat blocked the heartfelt words.

Hailey knelt next to me. And for the first time in forever, I didn't feel so alone. For the first time, the loneliness that had consumed me all these years curled up in the corner and gave me some space.

I could finally take a breath.

"I'm so sorry," I whispered, looking between the two gravestones, doing my best to keep the memories at bay.

27

NOLAN

Six Years Ago

The cop car was sitting outside my house when we arrived, my sister in the back like a common criminal. Except she wasn't the one who had done anything wrong. That honor went to my asshole father.

None of the street-facing windows were lit up. So unless my father was in another room not visible from the street or was in the dark, he wasn't home. Relief rushed over me, both bitter and sweet.

A voice in the back of my head whispered for me to turn around and drive. Drive as far and as fast as possible and never look back. But I couldn't leave my sister. I was fucking nineteen years old and had my whole life ahead of me, but I had to stay until I was better able to protect my family—or until my father kicked me out.

Doing my best to hide the anger stewing inside me, I parked my car in the driveway and raced to the cop car. The storm had since passed, the last rays of the sun peering through the clouds. The officer opened the back door of his vehicle and

Sarah hurled herself at me, knocking me back a step. I wrapped my arms around her, her clothes wet like my own.

"I was so scared, Nolan," she said, her body shaking, and she started crying again. I couldn't tell if it was because of what happened or because she was relieved to be home. More likely a combination of both.

"It's gonna be okay." I almost choked on the lie. "Thanks for bringing her home."

The cop nodded. "Any word yet from your father?" He sounded concerned, which made my lie seem much worse. He wasn't concerned that my father had disappeared to get drunk. He was concerned something bad had happened to him.

He was the only one to share that sentiment.

I shook my head, unwilling to add another layer to the lie. At least my reply was the truth.

I peered at the neighboring houses. Until now my family had never caused as much as a raised eyebrow. My father would shit bricks if he thought we were the cause of neighborhood gossip. But maybe he should have thought of that before ditching Sarah.

"Have you tried calling him?" the cop asked.

"Why don't I take Sarah inside and get her warmed up?" Hailey broke in, handing my phone to me. I mouthed "thank you" before unlocking the front door and letting them in.

"No. I didn't have a chance to," I told the cop. "Other than when I called 911, I was on the phone with my sister the entire time. I mean, other than while I was driving or changing the flat tire, and then my best friend"—I gestured to the house— "was talking to Sarah."

"Fair enough."

I got the hint and called Dad's number. I wasn't sure if I wanted him to answer or not. If he did answer, chances were good I'd have to lie to the cop about where my father was. He'd probably driven to the bar to pass time while Sarah was in her dance class and had lost track of the hours. It was too much to hope for that tragedy had struck him down and we'd be permanently free of his torment.

After several rings the phoned transferred to voicemail. "Hey, Dad, where are you?" *There's a cop here, and I've got to sound like I'm worried about you instead of ready to kill you.* "If you're looking for Sarah, I've got her." *You know, in case you forgot all about her and need a not-so-subtle remainder of your parenting responsibilities.*

I ended the call. "He's not answering." I tried to sound worried. I'm sure I came a hundred miles short of it.

"What is your father's name?" the cop asked. "I can check if he's been involved in an accident."

I told him, and he called in to see if any accidents had recently been reported.

"Do you want me to file a missing-person report?"

Did I? "Don't you have to wait forty-eight hours?"

"Not if there is suspicious activity involved in the individual's disappearance."

Shit. What kind of suspicious activity was he thinking about? While I was positive nothing suspicious had happened to my father, I didn't want the cop to become suspicious about the whole situation.

"Does your father have a medical or mental condition I should be aware of?"

"Not that I know of." Regret for contacting the police began suffocating me. How the hell was I going to talk my way out of this so he would leave before my mom or dad returned?

Realizing I didn't have a choice, I invited the cop into the house and gave him the information for the report, just to get rid of him.

After he finally left, I went upstairs to find Hailey and Sarah. Before heading to my sister's room, I quickly ducked into mine, changed into dry jeans and a T-shirt, and grabbed a hoodie.

My sister was snuggled under the bedcovers, cuddling her stuffed tiger, when I entered her room. Hailey was sitting on the bed, her wet clothes still clinging to her body.

"Hey, squirt. You okay now?" I handed the hoodie to Hailey and sat behind her as she put it on. This wasn't the first time I'd seen her in my clothing, and the effect on my body hadn't changed. A tingling longing tormented me, telling me to pull my best friend into my arms and hug her for everything she was doing for me and for Sarah.

Sarah nodded at my question, then yawned.

Hailey ruffled her hair and pushed herself off the bed. "See you later. Don't forget our date for this weekend."

I didn't want Hailey to leave. I wanted her to stay a while longer. But I could tell she wanted to give Sarah and me some privacy so we could talk, and so I could reassure my sister again that she would never have to worry about a repeat of what happened tonight.

I would make sure of that.

I gave Hailey a smile that said a million things: *Thank you. God, you're beautiful. I want you to be with me forever.* Based on her sad expression, she'd seen none of that in my smile.

Once Hailey had left the room, I picked up Sarah's stuffed tiger. I'd given it to her when she was six years old. She'd been suffering from nightmares that a monster was going to hurt her. I told her the tiger would keep her safe.

I was doing a crappy job of keeping my promise.

"I'm sorry about tonight." I handed her back the tiger. She clutched it to her chest. "But I promise you it won't happen again."

She nodded, but this time a slight frown marred her otherwise innocent face. "Why doesn't Daddy love me anymore?"

My heart cracked at her words. "It's not that Dad doesn't

love you anymore. He just . . ." *Shit.* "He just doesn't know how to show it." I kissed her forehead and made a show of tucking her and her tiger in. "Good night. See you tomorrow." I walked to the door.

"I love you, Nolan."

I turned back to her and I smiled softly. "I love you too, squirt."

As I walked downstairs, Mom's and Hailey's voices rose to greet me. I couldn't hear what they were saying; the words were too quiet. I couldn't even determine if Hailey was telling my mom what had happened.

As I continued down the stairs, their words became clearer.

"I don't understand why you don't leave him." Hailey.

"I know," my mom said, her voice almost the whisper of a breeze. "But love is complicated."

What the fuck?

I paused on the final step.

"How can you say that?" Hailey said. "This isn't love. Not even close to it."

I quietly entered the kitchen. She was glaring at my mom, her body tense, my mother face's pale.

That's when they must have sensed me. They both turned around and the guilt and confusion on my mom's face almost knocked me back a step. But I knew what had happened tonight wouldn't be enough for Mom to leave my father. It would have to be bigger, something just short of him killing her.

At the sound of the garage door opening, my heart pounded loud in my chest, sending Morse-code messages to anyone within a ten-mile radius. I grabbed hold of Hailey's hand and tried tugging her toward the front door. She stood firmly in place and yanked her hand away. Shit, what was she up to?

"Look, Hailey, I have to get you out of here."

"Why? Is your father going to bully me like he bullies you? Is he going to hurt me like he hurts you?"

The door to the garage clicked open. Footsteps thumped from the laundry room, their sound uneven. My father was drunk enough that he stumbled as he walked.

I grabbed Hailey's hand again, and this time she didn't resist me. But it was too late. Before we could make it to the front door, my father stepped from the laundry room.

Fuck.

28

NOLAN

Present

uck. Fuck. Fuck. The unexpected memory tore down the dam of emotions I'd been successful so far in holding back.

A sob broke free. I buried my face in my hands.

Somewhere in the back of my mind, I heard the distinct clicking of a camera but ignored it. I stared at the blurry words on the gravestones, still unable to talk beyond telling my mom and Sarah I was sorry.

Those few simple words might not have sounded like much, but they represented everything I wanted to tell them yet couldn't.

"Don't you have any decency?" Hailey said, her voice low but fierce. She was no longer kneeling next to me. She was standing in front of a man several yards away. Based on the massive telephoto lens on his camera, he wasn't here visiting with a dearly departed.

Hailey looked ready to introduce his face to her fist or to

snatch the camera away from him and hurl it against a grave-stone. Most sane guys would've backed away, not wanting to experience her wrath. But when it came to the paparazzi, their level of sanity was questionable to begin with.

"This is a public place," the douchebag said, leering at her. "Which means I have the right to take photos if I want."

I scrambled up from the snowy ground and, before the situation could escalate, placed my body between Hailey and the asshole.

"What the hell are you doing here?" I recognized him and was positive he was responsible for the photos that had shoved Alyssa and me into the spotlight as a romantic couple. Just one more reason for me to want to slam him against a gravestone and tell him where the hell he and his sleazy lies could go. But I knew better. Experience was a bitch.

The leer on his face transformed into an ugly smirk. "Does Alyssa know about you cheating on her?"

"There's nothing going on between Alyssa and me," I ground out, purposely avoiding the question about Hailey. I didn't want to drag her into his twisted lies.

Before I could stop myself, I launched my body at him. But he was quicker and eager for the lawsuit shot. He lifted his camera and before I had a chance to yank it away, he snapped photo after photo.

Hailey threw herself between us. It was too late. Unless I was willing to destroy his camera and memory card, there was nothing I could do—other than make things worse for Hailey. She didn't need me dragging her into this, destroying her career along with mine. My career would bounce back. Hers might not. The media would always be in her face and business, rarely giving her a moment of privacy, constantly putting her and those she worked with on guard, disrupting her life.

"Does Alyssa know you're the son of a mass murderer?" the

asshole taunted. "Does she fear for her own safety when she's with you?"

As much as I wanted to pound on him, I kept silent and turned away, doing my best not to react to his questions.

Does she fear for her own safety when she's with you? His words echoed in my head, twisting with my own fears.

"Hailey, is your recent attack linked to what happened to Tyler's family?" he called out.

I froze at his comment for many reasons. First, the asshole knew her name and knew what had happened to her. Second, was it possible the two events were linked? Third, I wasn't sure what game he was playing by using my fake name, but I had a feeling it wasn't good. This was his way of telling me he was content with the idea of destroying my career and the life I'd built for myself since moving to L.A.

The asshole must have gotten everything he'd come for. He didn't follow us. Hailey was so pale and visibly shaken, I wanted to hug her and tell her it would be okay. But I also didn't want to risk that he was still lurking around, taking photos of us, so I kept my arms plastered to my sides.

"How did he know my name?" Hailey asked as we drove away, her voice bordering on panic.

I gripped the steering wheel, imagining it was the scumbag's neck. "You'd be surprised at what these guys discover. Nothing is sacred to them."

"But how did he even know where to find you?"

"I have no idea. But don't underestimate these guys. Their hunting skills put the CIA to shame. I'm sorry you got dragged into this, Forget-Me-Not."

She shook her head. "He hasn't done anything to me. I'll be fine."

"It's not that simple. Based on his reaction back there, I wouldn't be surprised if he plans to use you to drive a wedge between Alyssa and me."

"But . . . but I thought you said there was nothing going on between you two."

"There isn't. But because of assholes like him, it will look like I cheated on her with you." I checked the rearview mirror to make sure we weren't being followed.

"Me? Why? Because I was with you in the cemetery? That's crazy."

"Doesn't matter. And I wouldn't be surprised if those weren't the only photos he took of us today." I quickly glanced at her to see if she was putting it all together.

Her eyes widened. "Oh, God! He saw us kissing at the sports center?"

"There's a chance he didn't." A fairly nonexistent chance. "Or he might just focus the story on my father and leave you out of it."

"But you don't think he will, do you?"

"I think he'll find an angle to twist both together. I don't know how he'll do it, but by the time he's finished, it will be as far from the truth as possible, yet at the same time very believable."

"But if you're not dating Alyssa, his story will fall apart. No one will believe it."

"I wish that was true. But the reason tabloids are still around is because their readers do believe everything they read." But maybe now Alyssa would finally issue a statement confirming what I'd been saying all this time—she and I weren't romantically involved and never had been.

"Why do you even put up with it?" Hailey asked.

"There's not much you can do about it. It's part of the business. All I can do is ignore it. In a week's time, someone else's news will upstage mine, and the lies about me will be forgotten."

"So what are we going to do?"

"I'll talk to the record label." And see what they could do . . . after they killed me for screwing up.

But that was if my bandmates didn't kill me first for fucking things up for them.

29

___

HAILEY

I knew things had changed for me the moment the reporter insinuated I was nothing more than a hussy bent on destroying Tyler and Alyssa's golden relationship. I wouldn't be surprised if I was blamed for her losing the fictitious baby that was supposedly Nolan's. What then? Would the world turn on me even though none of the rumors were true? Would fans of their relationship hunt me down like the paparazzi and try to hurt me? Or would Alyssa finally issue a statement and set the record straight about their relationship?

But while I was nervous about what might happen if an upset fan confronted me, I was even more nervous about my future. To get into the physical therapy program, I needed a reference from the therapist I worked with in the playgroup for kids with special needs. Without it, my chances of getting into the education program were much lower. But a scandal like this might hurt me when it came to the reference.

We rode the rest of the way home in silence, both of us lost in thought over what this could mean for us. And by us, I meant our careers. Nothing had really changed when it came to what Nolan and I had between us. He hadn't indicated if there could be a him and me if I moved to L.A. Nor had he indicated he wanted me to move there. As far as I could tell, what we had between us was only short-term.

I almost expected to see photographers gathering outside my building when we pulled up. When I didn't spot any, I let out a relieved breath. The one at the cemetery had been bad enough. I couldn't imagine having to deal with more than that.

But as much as I didn't want to imagine it, I wasn't deluding myself into believing no one else was interested in Nolan's real past. He already had the bad-boy reputation, so why walk away from the possibility of even juicier secrets in his past? And once his story hit the tabloids, it was guaranteed to be the end of my privacy, at least until the next news story broke about another celebrity.

Nolan was still tense when we walked into the building. He held my hand the way he had in the cemetery. But unlike then, his grip was tighter. I didn't think he realized just how tense he was. He'd never be able to write lyrics in his current state.

I needed to help him relax and forget everything. If his label didn't dump him because of all the controversy that would soon suck him into its vortex, it certainly would if he wasn't ready in time to record the band's album.

I let us into the apartment. Before I could say anything, he stormed into his bedroom and slammed the door. Less than a minute later, I heard him talking to someone on the phone. The conversation lasted a few seconds and was followed by a long silence.

The muffled sound of him pacing slipped from under his door. He was so tightly wound from what happened at the cemetery, he couldn't focus on his work. This wasn't the Nolan I knew.

It was all my fault. I had insisted that Nolan visit his sister's and mother's graves so that he could take a step toward healing. As long as he kept away from their final resting place, he'd never move on. He'd never live the life they would've wanted him to have.

I knocked on his door but didn't wait for him to answer. I opened it. As expected, he was pacing back and forth. Not an easy feat in the room's small confines, even with the lack of furniture.

"Have you told the record label what happened?" I figured that was whom he'd been talking to on the phone.

"I left a message with the band's PR person. It's the weekend, so she gets to have a break from me and my stupidity." His jaw tightened. He really did believe this was all his fault.

I entered the room, my movements slow and cautious. "This isn't your fault, Nolan. None of it's your fault. And the people at the record label are idiots if they believe otherwise."

"But if I'd stayed in L.A. to work on the songs like I was supposed to," he said, "none of this would've happened."

I tried to block the sting in my heart from his words. I hoped he didn't mean it. I hoped the words had been said in the heat of the moment and not because he regretted coming here when I was in a coma. And not because he regretted what was happening between us.

I must have failed to keep the pain from his words off my face. One second I was staring at him, doing my best to blink away the burning tears, and the next I was in his arms.

"I'm sorry, Forget-Me-Not. That didn't come out right." He kissed the top of my head and tightened his hold on me. "I don't for a second regret coming back here for you. I couldn't have worked on the album not knowing how you were doing. I needed to be here for you."

"I know, but maybe it's time you return to L.A." The sting in my heart shifted to a dull burn. I did my best to ignore it, and pushed on with what I needed to say to convince him to return home, for all our sakes. "I'm no longer in a coma, and whoever attacked me hasn't tried to hurt me again. It was just a random attack. You don't need to be here anymore. And as long as you are here, the media will constantly hound us. All they want is a story. As long as you stay in Northbridge, they'll have one. And they won't stop there. They'll keep digging into your old life here, hunting for secrets to damage your reputation."

They'd be wasting their time. There were no more secrets. But who knew what other people would say about him, all for their fifteen seconds of fame.

"I'm not going back yet," he said, his tone the same stubborn one I remembered from years of being his best friend. "And even if I did return to L.A., nothing would change. Then the media would wonder what I was running from and would still dig deep." He scrubbed his hand over his face. "Fuck. All I wanted was for people to hear my music and not think about my past. I wanted to keep the two separate. And I didn't want them questioning whether some part of my father was also part of me. I should have known better. You really can't escape your past."

I didn't want to talk about this anymore. He needed to forget what had happened this afternoon, and I needed to help him so he could go back to what was important to him—his music.

Without saying a word, I grabbed hold of his hand and pulled him out of the bedroom. He didn't ask where I was taking him and he didn't resist. His eyebrow did jerk up when I led him into the bathroom. A hint of a smirk touched his lips. I turned the shower on, needing to wash away the ugliness of what happened in the cemetery. Steam quickly filled the bathroom.

Next I pushed my hands under his T-shirt, appreciating the

valleys and smooth muscle. I peered at him through hooded eyes, my heart beating an eager rhythm. "I want you," I whispered. I didn't just mean I wanted him now. I meant I wanted a forever with him. But if this was all I could get of him, then I'd make the most of it.

I slipped the button free on his jeans. My hand purposely brushed against his thickening length. He groaned.

Needing to see him without his T-shirt on, I pushed the hem up, exposing his tight abs. Being the wise man that he was, he got my not-so-subtle hint. A moment later, the T-shirt was making nice with the floor.

The corner of his mouth jerked up. "Am I the only one who's getting naked here? Or are you planning to join me?"

A shy smile slipped onto my face. "You want me naked?" I asked, voice husky.

"Fuck, yeah. I want to see your beautiful tits." He leaned in and said, voice low and with just the right amount of huskiness to make me melt inside, "And I want to see your beautiful pussy." His warm breath teased my cheek.

It wasn't as if I'd never heard a guy I'd had sex with say "tits" and "pussy," but somehow hearing them from Nolan, and the way he said them, set every nerve in my body on fire. Moaning, I leaned back against the bathroom counter. My T-shirt joined Nolan's a second later.

I slowly unhooked the back of my bra. Doing my best not to laugh, I performed a slow sensual dance, my hips swaying side to side, and peeled the plain white bra from my body. An exotic dancer I was not. My bra wasn't the sexiest of bras either. But wearing my sexy underwear while working with young kids just seemed wrong.

Nolan didn't care that my underwear wasn't satin or lace. From the way his gaze consumed me, none of that was important.

The bathroom grew steamier, the mirror foggy. Moments

later, the rest of our clothes joined the party on the floor, and I opened the shower door.

I stepped into the small space. Delicious hot water rained on my body. Nolan watched me, a hungry expression on his face.

I crooked my finger, indicating for him to join me.

He did exactly that, and his lips were instantly on mine. Our kiss deepened as I heated both inside and out.

My fingers brushed against the light growth on his jaw. Usually he went for the clean-shaven look, but he hadn't bothered to shave this morning. It looked good on him, and it felt great against my skin.

I moaned at just how great it felt against my skin.

His lips left mine and moved along my jaw and down my neck. Unconsciously I let my head drop to the side, opening up the area for him to explore. I could never get enough of this, from Nolan. All the guys in my past paled in comparison, and all the guys in my future would fail to compare, too. I already knew that much. Sucked to be me.

My hands wanted to do their own exploring. They traveled his body, mapping out my favorite parts, memorizing them so I could remember this moment once he returned to L.A.

My fingers caressed his jutting length, and I bit back a giggle. Nolan and I might have changed a lot since he'd moved away, but he was still the same guy who used to be my best friend. Even though I felt slightly awkward intimately touching the guy I used to share my deepest secrets with, it also felt natural. Like this was the way it was meant to be.

Nolan made a low, guttural noise as my fingers teased the most sensitive parts of him. He was definitely relaxed now, his thoughts about this afternoon long since forgotten.

Wanting to give him something new to focus on, I knelt in front of him and slipped my lips over his tip. I wasn't big on going down on a guy. I'd only done it once before with my ex, which might be why he'd cheated on me. He was big on being the recipient of blow jobs. The gifter? Not so much.

I took in as much of Nolan as I dared while my hand worked the rest of him. To his credit, Nolan didn't force me to take in more. Using my tongue and my hand, I entertained myself, grinning at the erotic sounds coming from Nolan's mouth. Those same sounds boosted my own aroused state. He didn't need to touch me, and I was certain if he did at this point, I'd come in three seconds flat.

The fingers of my free hand reached for his nuts and gently squeezed them. "Oh, God," Nolan moaned.

Before I could do anything else, he wrapped his hands around my biceps and tugged me up. "I want to be inside you."

I stood, my hair wet from the water that had found its way around Nolan's body as he shielded me from it. His mouth was on mine again and our kiss deepened, the time for talk long since forgotten.

Just as I was wondering how we were going to do this, Nolan squatted slightly, hooked my thigh with his hand, and moved my leg to wrap around his hip. The tip of his cock rubbed against the most sensitive part of me and the aching throb between my legs screamed, *Yes, please.*

Then my legs were around him and he was inside me, thrusting hard, driving our bodies wild with desire. My back pressed against the cool bathroom tiles and I jerked forward, taking him in deep.

The moment before I came was like rushing over the rapids—that singular moment when it was too late to turn back. All I could do was hold on tight and enjoy the ride.

And as my scream joined Nolan's satisfied grunt, I was sure my neighbors didn't doubt for a second that he and I both enjoyed the ride.

Later I'd be mortified at just how noisy we'd been. Later I'd be mortified when my neighbors realized I'd fucked Tyler Erickson—like the tabloids would confirm.

But for now, I wanted to enjoy what we'd shared. For now, I wanted to hold on to him for as long as I could, before I had to let him go.

Before I had to walk away.

30

NOLAN

When Pushing Limits had first signed with LS Records, we were told what was expected of us to ensure the band's success. "Keep out of trouble" might've been stressed a few dozen times. And each time they'd straightened out another one of my screw-ups, we were given the same lecture. I swear those four words played on repeat mode in my head during my dreams and my nightmare. But that still didn't change anything.

All those times, I'd been the fall guy. The guy who protected those I cared about, most notably the other members of the band.

This time was different.

This time the fault was all mine.

My phone played the opening of Bon Jovi's "Living on a Prayer" from the nightstand. Hailey was in the bathroom, drying her hair. I answered the phone instead of letting it go to voicemail, which would've been the preferred option given what I was about to tell the label's PR person. "Hello?"

"Nolan, this is Jennifer Stephens. I got the message you needed to speak with me."

I told her what had happened at the cemetery. "He might have stalked me from Hailey's apartment, and I wouldn't be surprised if he took pictures of us kissing."

"Is she your girlfriend?" She wasn't asking because she was curious. Her tone was calm and calculating.

"She's a friend." *Who I wish was my girlfriend.* "But the paparazzi asshole figured I was cheating on Alyssa Graham with Hailey. I wouldn't be surprised if that makes front-page news in the tabloids." By this time tomorrow, it would be trending entertainment news all over the Internet. "You need to make sure it's clear that I'm not dating and never have been dating Alyssa. Neither of us needs this crap right now."

"Is there anything else?"

"He discovered what happened to my mother and sister. He also found out Hailey was attacked and asked if the two were linked. So right now he's got enough story angles to keep the tabloids fucking happy for a while."

The long, slow breath of someone doing her best to stay calm when the entire manure patch was hitting the fan whispered from the phone. "You're not to talk to anyone, Nolan. And I need you back in L.A. so I can manage the damage better."

"I'm not leaving here yet. I need another week. Plus the band's flying out next week so we can work on the album together."

"Fine," she sighed heavily. "I'll discuss it with Mr. Remar, but you will have to do what I tell you so I can minimize the fallout. Are we clear on that?"

"As long as you can keep Hailey out of this, then I'll do whatever you want. I mean, other than going home on the next flight." I highly doubted the cops would've solved Hailey's attack by next week, and I was beginning to doubt they ever would. I was simply buying more time with her.

"I'm not sure I'll be able to do that if there are photos of you kissing her. They will only complicate things. But if they don't exist, we can have Alyssa confirm she knows about your friendship with Hailey and she completely trusts you."

Huh? "What difference does it make if Alyssa trusts me? I am not her boyfriend!" Pictures or no pictures.

"I'm not sure if you're aware of this, Nolan, but this relationship between you and Alyssa that the media fabricated has been the ideal opportunity for you. Her clean-cut image and the fact she was willing to give you a chance to turn the bad-boy reputation around has earned you more respect in the industry."

This was fucking unbelievable. How had the real me become this fabricated persona? Even as Tyler, I'd planned to be the same person deep down that I was as Nolan. How had things gotten so screwed up? "So what are you saying?"

"Alyssa has always been favorable to aligning herself with you." Which explained why she had never denied the rumors we were together. "Right now we have to wait to see what angle the media will take. We don't want to waste time extinguishing fires that were never an issue."

I glared at the abandoned thumbtack in the stretch of white wall in front of me. "Lemme guess. You're not issuing a statement confirming that the only relationship I have with Alyssa is purely professional, because she's the spokesperson for the emergency women's shelter in L.A.?" One of the reasons she had such a favorable reputation.

"That's correct. We're going to let people continue to believe you two are romantically involved. And in the meantime, you're to keep out of the spotlight. Don't leave that apartment for any reason, and don't get into any more trouble."

"And what about what happened to my sister and mother? What's going to happen once it's made public?"

"You'll have a lot of experts pointing out that the root of your bad-boy reputation stems from what happened to your father and your family." Her tone was cold and impassive. I had no idea why. I also couldn't tell if she believed her own words. "I won't lie and tell you it will be easy. Far from it. Those who've never liked you will have a field day. But we can also use it to our advantage when it comes to your relationship with Alyssa. You've been donating to the emergency shelter for the past few years. Alyssa can talk about how she fell for your compassion toward those women in need, and that's how the two of you became romantically involved."

I could almost hear the wheels turning in her head, and I could tell there was no point reminding her once again that Alyssa and I weren't romantically involved.

And if the photos of Hailey and I kissing were leaked, where would this all leave Hailey? She'd be labeled as the bitch who'd stolen me away from the selfless Alyssa. No one would see Hailey for the beautiful and equally selfless woman that she was.

And in the end, only Hailey would be hurt.

31

HAILEY

The moment Nolan walked into my room, I knew the news wasn't good. He'd been relaxed, satisfied after the shower. But now the corners of his lips curved down and he couldn't even look at me when he entered the room.

"What happened?" I asked, walking the short distance to him.

"I just spoke with the label's PR person."

My insides clenched into a tight fist, and I felt more raw and bruised than I had after the attack. "And you don't have good news?" Maybe they should redefine the term *PR* as meaning "personal ruin." That sounded more fitting, given the bad news I sensed coming.

"They're still figuring out what to do about the paparazzi situation, since we have no idea what kind of story will be leaked. They don't want to put out fires that don't exist."

"That makes sense."

He glanced at my bed, his expression a twist of pain and uncertainty. "But while they don't want to waste time extinguishing nonexistent fires, they want to be proactive about what it could mean for my reputation."

I frowned. "What do you mean?"

He shifted and finally made eye contact. "They want to make the most of the lie that Alyssa and I are romantically involved. They believe that her association with the women's emergency shelter I've been donating to for the past few years could help me. Because I was doing it anonymously, it means I wasn't trying to benefit from it and it will look good for my image."

A voice in my head repeated his words, *They want to make the most of the lie that Alyssa and I are romantically involved,* and my heart crumpled. "They want you to go back to L.A., don't they?"

"It was suggested that I return now, but I'm not ready to leave yet." He moved closer to me and ran his thumb along my cheek.

"Why's that?" I said, voice little more than a whisper. I'd known that what we had between us couldn't last forever, that I only had mere weeks with him anyway, but the record label's request for him to return sooner made it feel more real, more final.

His thumb brushed against my lips. "I missed you after I left the first time. More than I thought would be possible. You're my heart and soul, Hailey."

I was too stunned to say anything, which was just as well. His mouth captured mine and we were kissing. While I might have been unable to respond to his words with my own, I more than made up for it with my kiss.

He was my heart and soul, too.

I don't know long we were kissing before we finally pulled apart. He rested his forehead against mine and we stayed this way while we regained our breath. But as the fog in my head began to dissipate, those words from earlier came back. Nolan might have told me I was his heart and soul, but that wasn't what the record label wanted. They wanted him linked with Alyssa.

What would that mean for Nolan and me? Did the record label expect the pair to fake their relationship in public, so people believed what they had between them was real? Or did they expect Nolan and Alyssa to fall in love? Rumor was she wanted to record an album, since she was also a talented singer. Was this romance nothing more than marketing to benefit both their careers?

"I'm going to the store." I needed to temporarily get away from everything circling me like soul-sucking vultures. "Do you need anything?"

"I'll come with you."

I shook my head. A run-in with another of his ardent admirers was not what I needed right now. "It's better if you stay here. I won't be long." I gave him a quick kiss and left before he could argue otherwise.

The grocery store wasn't busy when I arrived. I wandered up and down the aisles, delaying the inevitable trip home. Dwelling on how Nolan had said I was his heart and soul. Doing my best not to think about anything else.

As I inspected a red pepper, the subtle, spicy scent of someone's aftershave taunted me.

"What the fuck did you bring her here for?" a low, rough male voice said, as if sharing a secret.

I opened my eyes to see what was going on but was met by the fierce glare of a flashlight.

Something bumped into my side, jerking me from my memory.

"Sweetie, I told you to be careful with the shopping cart," a mom gently admonished her four-year-old. The little girl barely reached the handlebar and looked perturbed that I'd been in her way.

I flashed her an apologetic smile, then scanned the area, searching for the source of my memory. The only people nearby were mothers and a male grocery clerk who didn't look familiar.

"Oh my God, it's her," a female voice shrieked.

My head jerked up at the sound. A seventeen-year-old girl was glaring at me as if I'd stolen her boyfriend and she wanted to scratch my eyes out.

Her friend glanced between us, as confused by the girl's outburst as I was. "Her who?"

"She's the woman trying to steal Tyler Erickson away from Alyssa Graham."

I'm not sure what made me cringe more, the way she screamed it or that the lies and my picture had already hit the Internet.

The friend looked me over, not thoroughly convinced I was capable of stealing Nolan from anyone who looked like Alyssa. Especially given the way I currently looked, with my hair in a messy post-sex-in-the-shower ponytail, barely any makeup, and clothes sitting on this side of comfy. Alyssa's hair was always perfect. Her makeup was always perfect. Her outfits were always perfect. The paparazzi had yet to shoot a bad picture of her.

"Are you sure?" The friend scanned the vegetable section, possibly searching for Nolan.

"I don't know why you're wasting your time with him," the shrieker yelled as I started to walk away, not wanting to be part of this conversation. "He'll never leave Alyssa. She's much better than you'll ever be."

Even though I shouldn't have let it bother me, her comment still cut deep. She didn't even know me, yet she was already judging me.

I hurried to the checkout, not daring to stay in the store longer than necessary, in case the shrieker decided to pelt me with cans of vegetables—the jumbo cans, which would do more than just bruise.

What I didn't get was why the girl blamed me for trying to steal Tyler away from Alyssa. Didn't it take two to cheat?

Or had the photo portrayed Nolan as the innocent party in the kiss? Had it made it seem as though I'd attacked him with my lips?

I knew I shouldn't look, but I couldn't help it. As soon as I got into my car, I Googled Tyler's name on my phone and found the picture the shrieker must have seen. All I could tell from the photo was that a woman was kissing him. You couldn't tell if he was kissing back or if he'd been surprised by the kiss —and you couldn't tell it was me.

I searched through the other photos. None were of us in the cemetery, although I expected they would surface soon. The other leaked pictures had been taken at the sports center. You could see us clearly in them, and you could see I was the same woman who was kissing him in the other photo.

The entire trip home I debated whether or not I should check what exactly had been said about Tyler and me. At least then I'd be prepared for the next person who brought up the article.

Kayla's song played on my phone. I let it go to voicemail. A moment later it played again. And as I pulled into my parking spot outside the apartment building, it played a third time.

Knowing that Kayla wouldn't quit phoning me until I answered, I accepted the call.

"Finally!" she practically screamed, forcing me to pull the phone away from my ear. "I've been trying to get hold of you."

"Sorry, I was driving."

"Have you seen the article and pictures yet? The ones of you and Nolan? They're all over the Internet."

"I saw two photos of us," I said, opening the car door. "But I haven't read anything yet. Is it as bad as I think it is?" I winced.

Of course it was, if the shrieker's reaction had been any indication.

"Depends on what you consider bad. The article claims you've been spotted getting cozy with Tyler."

I told her what had happened in the store.

"You're kidding," Kayla exclaimed, and once again I pulled the phone a safe distance from my ear. "Nolan's caught cheating on his supposed girlfriend and you're the guilty party? What about Tyler? Why didn't she attack him for cheating on his *girl-friend*?" She practically spat the last word.

I opened the trunk of my car. The cold wind slapped my cheeks and nose as if it too was angry at me. "Welcome to the wonderful world of double standards. But I'm not so sure everyone will react the same way. The only one who will get everyone's pity is Alyssa, and she's not even dating him." That was the most frustrating part of all of it. Meanwhile, Nolan and I would suffer the fallout.

It was no wonder the record label wanted to fuel the perception that Tyler and Alyssa were still an item. Anything to save the band and their upcoming album. Never mind that Nolan was a gifted singer, guitarist, and songwriter. Those should've been enough to stand on their own.

"So what are you going to do?" Kayla asked.

"About what?"

"About you and Nolan?"

"There is no me and Nolan." I grabbed a couple of grocery bags from the car with one hand and, with the phone sand-wiched between my ear and shoulder, closed the trunk.

"Right. That's not what it looks like from the photos."

"It was no big deal. We just kissed." And had sex. Several times. Great sex. Several times. "He's returning to L.A. next week anyway. So whatever we had between us will be over." *Being his heart and soul will be over.*

"Are you sure about that?"

"Positive."

Kayla believed everyone deserved a happily-ever-after. And maybe it was true. But Nolan and I wouldn't be getting ours. Not together, at least.

Not if it put his music career in jeopardy.

32

NOLAN

After Hailey left to go shopping, I sat on the couch and began phoning around. I needed to find a space to rent for when the guys showed up next week. We couldn't stay here. There wasn't enough space and the walls were too thin. The last thing Hailey needed was for us to piss off her neighbors with our loud music.

Forty minutes later, and no closer to finding us a place to work in, I hit speed dial on my phone.

"Hey, what's up?" Brandon asked.

I told him what I needed. "Any suggestions?"

"Sorry, can't help you there. I mean other than . . ." His final words faded away, his unspoken suggestion all too clear.

"No! No way in hell I'm going back there. I've already told you that."

"I know, but you have admit it's perfect."

I shook my head. Visiting the cemetery had been hard enough. Returning to the house where it all happened would be a thousand times worse.

I just couldn't do it.

"He's dead, Nolan," Brandon said after a long silence. "He can't hurt you anymore."

Tell me something I don't already know. "That doesn't matter."

"You really want to be in the dark about what happened?" I could hear the frown in his voice, along with *When did you become such a pussy?*

Or maybe that was just the voice in my own head. "What's the point of me remembering? It won't bring back the dead."

He sighed heavily, the sound reverberating through the phone. "You're right. It won't."

Since I had him on the phone and he would find out soon enough, I filled him in on what had happened earlier. I also filled him in on what the label wanted me to do about the situation.

"What exactly is going on with you and Hailey?" His words were slow, questioning. He wasn't questioning me about what she and I were doing together. He was questioning my motives and where I thought this would all end up.

"You mean other than I still love her?"

"Shit, you had sex with her, didn't you?"

"Maybe." I cringed at his groan.

"You sure know how to complicate things." Epic understatement of the year. "Have you told her how you feel about her?"

I squirmed on the couch. "Kind of."

"I take that as a no. You need to tell her the truth, Nolan. With all the other lies circulating about you, you need to tell her the truth."

"And then what? We have a long-distance relationship? It would never work."

"Why not? You'll never know if you don't give it a chance."

I swore aliens had abducted my best friend. Since when did the king of going-nowhere relationships dole out relationship advice? "It doesn't matter, not with the label pushing for this fictitious romance between me and Alyssa. I can't do that to

Hailey. She deserves better than to be hidden away like some dirty secret. But that's exactly what will happen."

Brandon released a defeated sigh but didn't say more on the topic. We ended the call and I went back to fiddling around with a new song I'd been working on.

But as much as I tried to block it from my mind, the image of my parents' home sneaked into my thoughts. And with it came the promise of a new memory of that night.

33

NOLAN

Six Years Ago

I entered my house and flipped the light on. Instead of the usual warm glow, the light was cold and harsh. But that wasn't what filled my body with icy dread.

Blood drops on the beige carpet formed a trail to the kitchen.

I strained to hear a sound, but my ears were met with nothing but silence. Darkness seeped from the room, and I walked toward it, my gaze glued to the bloody trail. A strong, unpleasant odor sat heavy in the air, and my stomach turned.

Ignoring the five alarms in my head telling me to get out of the house, I stepped into the kitchen and turned on the light. My hand recoiled at the sticky wetness on the light switch and I glanced down to see what it was.

And wished I hadn't.

Smeared bloody handprints stained the walls.

34

NOLAN

Present

I snapped out of the memory and rested my head on the back of the couch, body trembling. I closed my eyes and tried to focus on other things. Like Hailey. Naked.

It took several minutes for the trembling to finally subside. With a hard breath, I pushed myself off the couch and grabbed a beer from the fridge. I opened it and downed half of the cold beverage. Maybe this was the answer to surviving this town while I was here.

I returned to my room, grabbed my guitar from the case by my bed, and played the melody for the ballad I'd been working on. The music soaked into every part of my body, reminding me just how important it was to me. Like oxygen to fire.

But as much as I wanted it, I couldn't have everything. I couldn't have the music *and* Hailey *and* the oblivion from my memories. I had to choose.

The apartment door clicked open. I continued playing the guitar. When it became obvious Hailey wasn't going to check on me, I placed the guitar against the bed and went to find her.

Full grocery bags littered the floor in the hallway outside her bedroom door. It wasn't like her to just dump her groceries there and go off to do something else.

I walked into the living room. Hailey was on the couch, laptop on her lap. She looked nothing like the woman I'd made love to earlier in the shower. She didn't even look like the woman who'd left to go shopping. She looked hollow. Broken.

I joined her on the couch. "What happened?"

"The pictures of us are all over the Internet."

"Already?" Not that this surprised me.

"And it would seem people aren't too impressed with me. I'm the bitch who's trying to steal you from Alyssa."

"No one thinks that." My words were nothing more than a lie, but I couldn't stop myself from saying them. To give her some small amount of hope, no matter how tiny it might have been.

"Really?" She turned the laptop so I could read the comments on the band's unofficial fan site. "And it's not just here. A girl at the store recognized me and made her opinion about me quite clear. . . . Oh, and to top it off, I remembered something there that might have to do with what happened to me, but I can't be sure." Her words came out fast, tripping over themselves.

"What did you remember?"

She continued staring at the computer screen. "Nothing much, really. A man asked why the fuck the other person had brought me there. I was lying down and my eyes were closed. When I opened them, I couldn't see anything."

"Nothing at all?"

"It was dark and they were shining a flashlight in my face."

"Did you recognize the voice?"

She shook her head and slouched forward. "I just want to remember. I'm tired of having this gap in my life and not knowing what happened."

I placed the laptop on the coffee table and pulled her into my arms. "I know." But I didn't. Had it been in my power, I would have done anything to switch places with her. For Hailey to be the one who remembered what happened and for me to stay oblivious to my own private hell.

She rested her head against my shoulder and started crying. I held her tighter, as useless as that was. I had a feeling she wasn't crying because she was mourning her missing memories. It was a combination of that and the hate oozing from the fan sites because of the lies. Beyond holding her, I didn't know what to do. About anything.

My cell phone pinged. I ignored it, not wanting to let go of Hailey just yet.

Hailey's phone pinged. As did mine, again. And if that wasn't enough, they both started playing music to let us know we had calls.

Realizing something big was going down, I picked up my phone as she answered hers.

"What's up?" I asked Brandon.

"Have you seen the press conference with Alyssa Graham?"

I frowned, an expression reflected on Hailey's face. "What press conference?"

He told me what site to find it on. Whoever Hailey was talking to must have told her the same thing. She was already pulling it up.

"I'm watching it now. I'll call you right back." I ended the call and we watched the video footage.

Alyssa was standing outside, the sun shining behind her, lighting up her blond hair and giving her an angelic appearance. Even though I couldn't see the person, I knew her handler was within arm's reach, ready to end the press conference if necessary. "Thank you everyone for coming. I'm going to issue a statement first on behalf of myself and Tyler Erickson, and then I'll try to answer your questions."

I glanced at Hailey. Her face was free of emotion. I had no idea if that was a bad thing or not.

"First, Tyler and I thank everyone for the support you have shown us over the past few months. As you may have recently heard, his mother and sister were victims of domestic abuse when he was a teen. It was that tragedy that brought us together. For a number of years I've been involved with the emergency women's shelter in L.A., and through the generosity of people like Tyler, the shelter has been able to make a difference in the lives of those women who are survivors of abuse.

"Tyler has been donating to the shelter for several years, and that's how we met. Because of what we have in common in our own lives, we've grown close during the past few months. He recently returned to his hometown to help out a friend.

"Members of the media tracked him down there and pried into his personal life. Tyler chose to go by a pseudonym because he didn't want what happened to his family to overshadow the hard work he's done to prove himself. He wanted his talent to speak for itself.

"I am aware the paparazzi stalked Tyler and photographed him with another woman while he was dealing with his grief. I can promise you that he and I are still together. The photo misrepresented the situation, which, as we all know, is typical of the paparazzi. Only a few weeks ago they were proclaiming I was pregnant with Tyler's love child. But as you can clearly see, that is not the case." She rubbed her hand over her flat stomach to emphasize her point. Several reporters chuckled. "Questions?"

"How can you be so sure there is nothing going on between them?" a reporter offscreen asked. "The photos that went viral suggest otherwise."

"Because I trust Tyler when he says nothing is going on between them. And he's never given me a reason not to trust him."

"Aren't you worried that Nolan Kincaid might end up harming you like his father did to Nolan's mother and sister?" a female voice asked. "Research shows that children of abusers often go on to become abusers themselves."

"Research also shows that some children from abusive homes become victims themselves when in a romantic relationship," Alyssa said. "And other children are perfectly well adjusted despite the abuse. There has been no indication, other than some misguided reports, that Tyler is anything but the kind and generous man I know he is."

There were a few more questions, but nothing Alyssa couldn't smoothly handle. But despite what she had told the reporters, and subsequently the world, I had a feeling no one would completely buy her story about Hailey's involvement. If anything, it made Alyssa come off as naive when it came to our "relationship." Some people might've scoffed at her naivety. Some would frown at my involvement in the affair (given that I was the one supposedly cheating on her). But ultimately, Hailey would be the one paying the price.

The press conference ended, and Hailey and I sat quietly for a minute, all kinds of thoughts rushing through my mind. The most important one was what this meant for Hailey and me.

"I guess that's it, then," Hailey finally said. The skin on my body tightened at the real meaning behind her last three words —*that's it, then.*

35

HAILEY

When I was a little girl, I used to stay up late, waiting for my father to come home from the hospital, where he worked as a surgeon. To me, he was this godlike man who saved lives. He was invincible.

Years later I realized that wasn't true. He couldn't save everyone. And with each patient who died under his care, he had to gracefully accept defeat. He moved on and didn't let the loss paralyze him.

I hit Kayla's number on speed dial as I walked down the steps to retrieve the rest of the stuff from the car.

She answered the phone before it rang a second time. "Did you watch it?"

"I did."

"And?"

"And what?" The stale air in the stairwell closed in on me, making it hard to breathe. Much like what seeing the video had done to me. I picked up my pace.

"Is it true they're an item?"

I sighed. "The record label is pressuring them to do this." Although I had a tough time believing they needed to apply much pressure when it came to convincing Alyssa. How could she not want to be with him?

"I'm sorry, Hailey. I really am. I thought for sure you guys would make this work between you."

I laughed, but even though I'd meant for it to be full of humor, it came out flat. "It never would have worked," I said, repeating what I'd already told myself a million times. Although deep down I wasn't sure if I truly believed it. If I really had wanted things to work between Nolan and myself, I could've made the effort.

I guessed that in the end I was afraid. Afraid to give us a chance and risk getting hurt. Afraid of him leaving me again, like he'd done before, like my ex-boyfriend had done to me.

I didn't tell Kayla that, though. She'd never understand. I told her I'd talk to her later and ended the call.

Mom had sent me a text, asking if I knew the latest news about Nolan trending on the Internet. *It's not what it sounds like,* I texted back. *We're just friends. The reporter got it all wrong.*

That's too bad, she replied almost immediately. *I always thought you and Nolan were good together. You brought out the best in each other.*

During our senior year of high school, I had suspected Mom secretly wished I had been dating Nolan. I never would've expected her to still feel the same way given his career and his reputation. But then, she was one of the few people who knew the real Nolan and had never put much stock in the tabloids. She knew him as the same great guy I knew him to be.

Nolan was in his room, strumming a melody he'd been working on for the past day or two. Needing to get out of here and go for a run, I rushed to change into my workout gear and sneaked out the apartment door. Nolan didn't have an issue with me going to the store on my own, but I had a feeling he'd want to come running with me to make sure I was safe. Awesome if I wanted company. But this time I needed to run on my own. I needed to think about what to do with this whole Nolan situation.

The road wasn't busy as I ran down the street. The occasional vehicle drove past. I hadn't been for a hard run since the attack. My body felt a little stiff but otherwise cheered me on.

Once I arrived at the lake, I ran along the snowy path. The route wasn't busy, thanks to the colder temperatures. Only the die-hard runners would be outside. Everyone else would be pounding away mile after mile on a treadmill. But since I spent my days working in a sports center, I preferred running outside as much as possible, cold or no cold.

The only sounds greeting me were the ragged panting of my breath and the muffled thuds of my sneakers against the snow. I felt more at peace out here than I had in a while.

A bird cawed loudly not far from me and I startled, my breath tumbling out as a gasp. Then with a flap of its wings, the crow took to the sky.

A crisp snap of a branch echoed through the wooded area. I inhaled sharply the chilled air and surveyed my surroundings. I couldn't see anything.

Another crack of a twig.

Again I scanned the area. I still couldn't see anything, but unease spread through me. The kind of unease you get when someone you can't see is watching you. But who'd be watching me?

I didn't stick around to find out. I turned around and ran toward the snow-covered beach. But my energy stores started to drain from the near sprint. Even with the adrenaline rush, I couldn't maintain the pace.

A heavy breath was the only warning I got before a large man hurled himself at me and shoved me to the ground. A scream escaped my lungs, but the impact of my body against the hardened snow cut it short.

Momentarily stunned, I fought to regain the breath

knocked from me. But that couple of seconds was all he needed. He grabbed hold of my arm and yanked me to my feet.

"Where ya think you're goin', bitch?" a deep male voice said behind me.

I whipped around, but before I could fight back, I was slammed into the brick wall next to me. My head whacked against the hard surface, and the dark alley temporarily tilted in front of me. I closed my eyes.

Screaming, I kicked and squirmed and did everything I could to get away from the guy who had attacked me in Westgate. He was even wearing the same dark blue ski jacket he'd worn that night.

But he was too strong, and he half dragged, half pushed me to the steep ledge. With the rocks at the bottom, I'd never survive if I went over.

I dug my heels into the snow, resisting the forward movement, but he easily outweighed me. I continued struggling, twisting my body, trying to break free of his grip. He lost hold of my hand and I lunged at his face with my fingernails, clawing at his flesh. But I was wearing thin knit gloves. The attack on him was nothing more than a joke.

"Fuckin' bitch," he growled, even though I'd done zero damage to his face. Far less than he planned to inflict on me.

He shoved me backward. By some small miracle, I stopped my momentum, barely, the ledge mere inches behind me.

Then without warning, the ground under my feet gave way and I screamed. All I had time to do was grab hold of a root sticking out from the cliff. Nothing else existed between me and the boulders below.

My gloves weren't designed for this kind of abuse, and the knit fabric slipped against the root. I tightened my hold on it, praying it would be enough, knowing deep down it wasn't.

My hands and shoulders ached at the desperate attempt to keep from falling. My feet searched for anything that could help me. I couldn't even find the tiniest hint of a ledge to reduce the strain on my upper body.

Not deterred from his original goal, the attacker tried to pry my fingers from the root. I tightened my grip, but I couldn't hold on much longer. My hands, arms, and shoulders were rapidly fatiguing.

Pain burned in my shoulder muscles, and I cried out. Like it or not, I was going to die.

And then the worst thing that could possibly happen did. He pried the fingers of one hand off the root, leaving me dangling precariously with the other hand. I screamed and frantically flailed my free hand around, trying to grasp hold of the root again. But it was now out of reach and there was nothing nearby to hold on to.

Grunts came from somewhere above, but I couldn't see what was going on. I opened my mouth to call out for help, but was stunned into silence when the attacker stumbled to the edge. His momentum was too great, and before he could recover himself, he tumbled off the cliff a few feet from where I was dangling. Unlike where the ground had given way under my feet, there was nothing for him to grab hold of, even if he'd had the chance.

I didn't dare look down to see what happened to him. I didn't want to know. My fingers were sliding free of the root.

I screamed what would be my last scream.

A hand grabbed hold of my wrist, and Nolan's concerned face looked down at me over the ledge, his body flat on the ground. "I've got you." But he didn't. My jacket slipped in his grip. I gasped. "Hailey, give me your other hand."

I tried but couldn't reach that far. "I can't," I sobbed.

"Yes, you can, Forget-Me-Not. You can do it." He shifted his body further forward.

With what little strength I had left, I reached up. Nolan grasped my wrist and readjusted his hold on the other one. He pulled me up, inch by slow inch, until I was far enough that I could wriggle my body back onto the ledge.

Nolan pulled me back so I was solidly on the ground and threw his arms around me. He held me so tight I could barely get air into my lungs, but I didn't care.

I was alive. Shaky. In pain. But alive. We were both alive and trembling.

"Is he . . . is he dead?" The hoarse words scraped against my raw throat and I winced.

"Yes," Nolan said, his breath warm against the top of my head. He pulled away slightly, face pale. "Do you have any idea who that was?"

I nodded, the movement slow, my head heavy. "It was the guy from Westgate who put me in the coma." I shuddered, the truth of what had just happened gripping me tighter than Nolan. "What are you doing here? Not that I'm ungrateful."

"I heard you leave, and when I realized you'd gone for a run, I came looking for you." He frowned. "Why the hell were you running on your own? You should've asked me to come with you."

"I needed to be alone, and you were busy." And while I'd known the paparazzi might have been an issue, I'd figured whoever had attacked me had long since moved on. That in the end, it had been nothing more than a random attack. Well, the joke was on me. Nolan had been right all along.

But I wasn't about to admit that out loud.

Nolan didn't look thrilled with my answer but let it go for now. He started pacing back and forth, shoving his hand through his disheveled hair. Cursing. Muttering something about being no better than his old man.

Panic gripped me at how close he was from the edge. It added another layer to the thickening lump in my throat. "Please, Nolan. Don't go so close to the edge." It could give way at any second.

He startled at my strangled voice, glanced at the ledge where only a few minutes ago I'd been clinging for dear life, and stepped toward me.

I opened my mouth to remind him that he was nothing like his old man, but a dog barked not far from us and the sound of footsteps approached. My body went on instant high alert and my mouth slammed shut.

A golden retriever burst through the undergrowth and bounded toward us, panting, happy to see us.

His owner wasn't far behind.

Sorrow filled Nolan's eyes at seeing the dog. If Lucky, Nolan's old puppy, hadn't died from an unexplained broken neck, he would have looked like this dog.

Nolan grabbed my hand and led me to the woman in her early twenties. She recognized him and her eyes widened.

"Do you have a cell phone?" he asked. She removed the earbuds from her ears. "I need to call 911." I could see he didn't want to tell her about the dead body. And he certainly didn't want to let on that he was responsible for the man falling. That was the last thing Nolan needed leaked to the press.

Still star-struck, she handed him her phone. More than anything, she looked like she wanted to ask him to sign it . . . or her breasts. *Oh, please, not the breasts again.* I wasn't in the mood to witness another fan flaunt her girls at him. One was more than enough, thank you very much.

Nolan walked off a few yards with the phone. Neither the woman nor I could hear what he was saying. I don't even know if she noticed me. She was too busy staring at his backside. As long as she wasn't shrieking at me or throwing stones at me for stealing him from Alyssa, she could stare at it all she wanted.

Nolan returned a few minutes later and handed her back her phone. "Thanks." To me he said, "They're on their way."

I expected now that she had her phone back, the fan would leave. She didn't. She kept staring at Nolan.

Her dog, who'd been sniffing around the ground, wandered to the ledge, where the attacker had fallen, and barked. This broke his owner's attention away from Nolan. Barely.

She turned and took a step toward her dog.

"Well, thanks for your help," I said.

She didn't get the hint. She walked toward the edge. I threw Nolan a nervous glance. He eyed her, body tense. Both of us knew this wouldn't end well if she saw the body.

The dog barked again. Sirens wailed in the distance. The woman screamed.

"Is . . . is he okay?" she asked after the last echoes of her scream had faded.

I glanced at Nolan. I still hadn't seen the guy. Maybe he wasn't dead. Maybe he was unconscious.

The look Nolan gave her suggested otherwise.

She continued staring at the body, waiting for him to move, but didn't say anything else. Nolan pulled my shaky body into his arms. The adrenaline overload had already faded away and I relaxed slightly, the feeling of being safe battling against my fears. I wouldn't feel completely safe until we'd spoken to the cops, until this truly was over.

I ran my thumb across his cheek. "You saved my life, Nolan. That makes you nothing like your father. That makes you a hero." The words were soft so the woman couldn't hear them.

He gave me a small nod, but I wasn't thoroughly convinced he believed me. I pulled a blank as to what else to say to change that.

It didn't take long before deep male voices cut through the air, and two cops traipsed toward us through the wooded area. "Are you the one who reported the fall?" one of them asked Nolan.

"Yes. He's over there." Nolan pointed to where the woman and dog stood. She was still peeking over the ledge, as if she expected the man to get up and walk away.

The cop and his partner strode to the spot and peered down. One spoke into the mic on his shoulder and indicated where to find the body.

The younger cop asked the woman questions about what happened. The taller, bulkier cop, with an intimidation factor of one hundred, stalked over to us.

"We have some questions to ask you." He jerked his chin toward his partner. He wouldn't be interviewing us together. We'd be questioned separately.

My body trembled, again. Nolan kept his arms around me until the younger cop joined us, then the bulkier cop indicated for Nolan to follow him.

"You going to be okay?" Nolan asked.

I nodded, temporarily unable to speak.

He followed the officer until they were far enough away so I couldn't overhear them.

"Can you tell me what happened?" the younger cop asked me. I told him about being chased through the woods, about how I'd remembered the man was the person who'd attacked me a few weeks ago. I explained how I'd lost my footing and how Nolan had saved me.

As Nolan and his cop returned to us, my body started shaking again, but this time for a different reason. I believed Nolan was a hero for saving me. He hadn't meant for the guy to die. That was an accident. But would the cops see it that way? Would they detain him further because there was a death involved? Would tomorrow's headlines declare Nolan a killer, just like his father?

"Are you staying in town?" the cop asked Nolan.

Nolan glanced at me for a brief second before looking back at him. He let out a heavy breath as if his world was about to crumble. "I have to return to L.A. tomorrow morning."

My heart splintered in two. I pushed the pieces aside. I had known this was coming. Or at least my brain had accepted it. My heart wasn't so quick on the uptake, it would seem.

Nolan returned his gaze to me. "The president of the record label called earlier. . . . He demanded that I be on the next plane to L.A." So the band could prepare for the upcoming recording session. So he and Alyssa could begin work on repairing his image.

So he and she could become lovers in everyone's eyes— which could possibly develop into the real thing.

Ignoring our pain and Nolan's comment to me, the cop asked, "We might need to be in touch with you. Is there a number you can be reached at?"

After Nolan gave him the information and the scary cop suggested I go to the hospital to be checked over—which I refused to do—we were allowed to leave. Still concerned about me, Nolan pulled me against him. I sank into his warm, strong body. All I wanted was for him to take me home, hold me, and never let me go. At least I'd get the first two. The last one would remain a dream.

The younger cop drove us back to my apartment. Once inside my room, I grabbed my yoga pants, favorite T-shirt, and underwear, and headed to the bathroom. Nolan came with me. The memory of what happened last time we were in the bathroom came back to me, and my body heated.

"I just want to hold you," he said, reading my mind, his voice gentle. "I don't think you should be alone."

I nodded, removed my clothes, and turned on the water. Nolan stripped off his clothes too, and we entered the enclosed space.

I stepped under the water, closed my eyes, and let the heat soak into me. Nolan moved behind me and wrapped his arms around me. The water was hot, but that didn't stop the trembling that upgraded to earthquake-sized shakes. I tried to stop, but the harder I tried, the harder my body shook.

And then I was sobbing.

Nolan turned me around in his arms. He didn't tell me everything would be all right. He knew it wasn't over yet. I didn't have to fear that man again, just as Nolan didn't have to fear his father anymore. Now I had to deal with the emotional trauma from everything that had happened. But unlike with Nolan, I wasn't going to pretend it had never happened. I wouldn't let it bury me alive.

I'd get help.

The tears eventually slowed to a hiccup, and I remained under the water while Nolan gently washed my body. The sensation was both sweet and erotic. If I'd had the strength after everything I'd just gone through, I would have made love to him in the shower. Again.

Instead, I kissed him. As far as I was concerned, that was okay. The world might believe he was involved with Alyssa, but they weren't in the real sense of the word.

Even though our naked bodies were touching, the kisses remained sweet and unassuming, and they soothed my battered emotions. We gently swayed to the imagined music in our heads. The one I was hearing, of course, was the first song he'd written, the first of his songs I'd fallen in love with.

Eventually we turned off the water and dressed. The day's events had drained me, but I didn't want to go to bed yet. I just wanted to curl up with Nolan and watch a movie. To let it distract me.

"If you want," he said as I combed my wet hair, "I can order pizza."

"Mediterranean?"

He grinned. "Of course."

While we waited for the pizza to be delivered, I phoned my parents and Kayla to tell them the guy who had put me in the coma had been found. I didn't tell them about the attack or that he was dead. I didn't feel like talking about that now. I simply told them the police had him. Close enough.

We found a movie to watch and cuddled together on the couch. Even though it wasn't normally his top choice of genres, Nolan had suggested a romantic comedy. Okay, maybe not the best choice, since our romance wouldn't have a happily-ever-after ending, but at least it made us laugh.

Well, made *me* laugh.

I shifted to face him. "What's wrong?" There were so many possible answers, it was just easier asking than guessing.

He gave a bitter laugh. "What's right? I killed a man today, accident or not. And now I have to fly back to L.A. and deal with the repercussions of the shit storm that's hit since I got here."

I threaded my fingers with his. I didn't know what else to say when it came to what had happened today. I hoped that in time he would realize it wasn't his fault. "You've got to do what you have to do. You've worked too hard for this not to." I swallowed back the pain and tears. "When do you leave?"

"Early tomorrow morning."

Tonight would be our last night together. "I know you don't want to, but before you return to L.A., you should visit your parents' house. It'll give you the closure you need."

He shook his head, eyes full of heartbreaking sorrow that made you want to hug him and never let go. "But I don't want to remember," he whispered.

I glanced back at the foosball table. "Tell you what—if I win, you visit your parents' house." I squeezed his hand. "I'll be with you the entire time, like at the cemetery."

"And if I win?"

"I'll never bring it up again."

36

HAILEY

I rubbed my hands together, preparing to win the game. Since he'd moved into the apartment, we had played the game almost nightly. While we might both have been rusty at first, we'd quickly regained our form. It was almost like we'd never stopped playing, except Nolan was better at the game than he used to be.

Which meant this game could go either way.

We got into position and I popped the ball through the hole. Desperation hovered in the air, both of us wanting to win more than we'd ever wanted it before. Never had the stakes been so high.

Nolan's player kicked the ball down the field, but I blocked it in time. I attempted to shoot it toward his goal and almost succeeded, but his player regained ownership of it.

The game continued like this—just as one of us was about to score, the other one blocked the shot and stole the ball. We battled for what felt like half the night, but the score was tied at 2–2. The next goal would win the game. I'd never seen him look so determined and so intense as he did now.

I tossed the ball through the small hole in the side of the

table and immediately moved my nearest player to kick it. Only I nicked it, and the ball careened toward Nolan's line of players. I frantically tried to block it but I wasn't fast enough.

Nolan scored.

And angels wept. Or more likely, their tears turned to snow. Small flakes started falling from the sky and clung to the living room window.

But from the way Nolan cheered, you'd have thought he'd won the World Cup. Which meant not only was he not going to his parents' tonight—and never would—I couldn't bring it up again. If there was an again. I had no idea if this would be the last time I'd ever seen him.

Somehow I had a feeling it was.

As if thinking the same, Nolan let his cheering die away and he reached for me. He pulled me close and his lips found mine. Unlike when we were in the shower, these kisses weren't sweet and unassuming. They were knotted with both desire and an unspoken fear we would never see each other again. Not like this.

The kisses grew hungrier and more intense. I'm not sure how it happened, but one minute we were in the living room kissing, and the next we were in my room, our clothes on the floor.

The intensity of the kisses shifted. They were still passion-ate, but our caresses became tender as we worshiped each other's body, worshiped each other's soul.

I memorized his sounds, his smells, the feel of his skin against my mine. When he finally entered me, I memorized how he felt inside me, how he filled me, how he made me come, crying out his name. And as I came back down to earth next to him on the bed, I memorized the sound of his heart-beat, my head resting on his chest.

He enveloped me in his arms and drew soothing circles on my back. I fought against sleep for the longest time, neither of us speaking, both of us soaking in these last precious moments together.

Outside, the wind howled through the hibernating trees, warning of a coming storm. If I was lucky, it meant Nolan's flight would be canceled, and he'd be stranded in Northbridge for a few more days.

By slow degrees, my exhaustion from everything that had happened today became too powerful for me to hold back, and I drifted off to sleep.

WHEN I WOKE UP, THE EARLY MORNING RAYS OF SUNLIGHT LEAKED through the gaps in the curtains. Last night's storm had long since moved on. That was the first thing I noticed. The second was that Nolan's arms were no longer wrapped around me and my head was no longer on his chest.

Even before I reached out to his side of the bed and touched the empty sheets, an ache filled every cell in my body.

Filled down to my soul.

My fingers searched for a sign that he had recently been here, but the warmth from his body had long since faded. I didn't have to leave my room to know that he was on his flight back to L.A.

Blinking away the tears, I hugged his pillow and inhaled his scent still clinging to it. But this failed to dull the ache. If anything, it only intensified it. As did the knowledge that eventually the scent would disappear, like the warmth on his side. And then I'd be left with nothing to remember him.

Clearly a glutton for punishment, I relived the memory of last night, of the last time I would make love with him.

And I relived the memory of his lips against my forget-me-not tattoo. When I'd gotten it, I'd half hoped the old belief was true and that my lover would never forget me. But back then,

Nolan hadn't been my lover. Whether the belief was true or not hadn't mattered. Now it mattered more than I cared to admit. I never wanted Nolan to forget what I meant to him, but that was nothing more than a foolish wish. The wish of someone who deep down wanted to believe in happily-ever-afters.

As much as I wanted to, I couldn't stay in bed all day and dwell on those last moments. I had to go to work. I had to move on.

If I was lucky, no one at the sports center paid attention to the fan sites. But based on the reaction I'd seen when Nolan showed up there, I doubted I would get that lucky.

Still a little sore from yesterday's attack, and maybe a little apprehensive of being stalked while running again, I decided to skip my run this morning. I grabbed my work clothes and hopped in the shower.

After I finished getting ready, I entered the tiny kitchen to make a quick breakfast. At the sight of the folded piece of paper on the table, my heart tripped over itself to read it.

Forget-Me-Not,

You looked so peaceful when I left this morning, I couldn't bear waking you up to say goodbye. While I regret everything in the past twenty-four hours that has done nothing but hurt you, I don't regret a single second I've spent with you.

I'll never stop loving you.

Stay safe.

Nolan

My breath sucked at his second-to-last line, my vision growing blurry. I'd never told him I loved him, and he'd never said it to me, either. Yes, he'd told me I was his heart and soul, but neither of us had actually laid out what that meant.

Not that it mattered anymore. It was time for me to move on. For us both to move on.

But even after acknowledging that, I couldn't find it in me to throw away the letter. Instead, I refolded it and hid it in my underwear drawer. If I ever had the courage to open my heart to another guy, I'd make sure he never saw the letter. But for now, it and the memories from the past few weeks Nolan and I had spent together were all I had left of him.

And I already knew it wouldn't be enough.

37

HAILEY

I hurried along the recently cleared path to the sports center. The brisk wind nipped my exposed skin and found its way through my winter coat and jeans.

"Hey, you're early," Chris called out behind me. I turned to him, giving him a beat to catch up with me.

"I figured now that I'm healed, I should register for the self-defense class for this weekend, if there's still room. Though I think by now I've had my lifetime quota for attacks."

He winced at the truth of it, even though he didn't know about the latest one. The police hadn't yet identified the body and hadn't yet disclosed to the media the connection between the attack in Westgate and the man's death. They wanted to rule out first if he had been working with an accomplice the night he attacked me in Westgate—a detail I'd neglected to tell Nolan, since he already had enough to worry about with recording the band's upcoming album. As it was, I still had no idea why I had been in Westgate and why the guy had tried to kill me.

"I don't think that makes a difference, Hailey," Chris told me.

I shrugged. "A girl can always hope."

"Well, ya know, when in doubt, go for the nuts. That will buy you time." He flashed me a pained look to prove his point and opened the door for me.

Blondes #1 and #2 must have sensed his presence. We'd barely stepped into the building before they converged on us.

Expecting them to do their usual flirting with Chris, I walked toward the registration desk to check on the class.

I didn't get that far. Blonde #1 stepped in front of me. "You're not dating Tyler Erickson anymore, are you?"

"I wasn't dating him." That much was true. "We're just friends." Who had sex together, but she didn't need to know that.

"Is he coming back here?" Blonde #2 asked.

A loud bang startled me.

The sound of metal hitting metal slammed through my brain. I cracked open my eyelids but was met by darkness. From my cramped position in the enclosed space, I couldn't tell where I was. My head hurt. That was all I knew.

The world swayed around me.

Someone placed an arm around my lower back, steadying me. "I've got you," a man said.

I blinked him into focus. Blondes #1 and #2 were eyeing me like I was a dye job gone wrong.

"What was that noise?" I asked the man, whom I'd seen a few times in the sports center, working out or talking to his stepdaughter, who had a part-time job there.

"Someone accidentally knocked a chair over," Lindsey's stepfather said.

"You look like you've seen a ghost," Blonde #1 pointed out.

I shook my head. "It's nothing. I just remembered something."

"You remembered something that scared you? What the

hell was it?" Chris placed a plastic chair from the nearby waiting area next to me. "Sit."

"I'm fine. Really."

Blondes #1 and #2 looked more interested in pumping additional info out of me about Nolan than finding out why I'd been suddenly dizzy. Given I didn't want to discuss him with them or anyone, I added, "I keep remembering things about when I was attacked."

Chris's eyes widened. "Do you know who it was?"

"No. Not yet. I just keep remembering bits and pieces of that night."

"Other than that, how are you doing?" Lindsey's stepfather asked, his gaze sweeping over my body. But not in a sleazy, checking-me-out kind of way. "Sorry, hazard of the job," he explained. "I'm a firefighter."

Seeing that I was okay, he excused himself and headed for the main entrance without giving her a second glance.

"So, are you and Tyler still together?" Blonde #1 asked, returning to the original inquisition.

I let out a long exasperated breath. "Nothing's going on between Tyler and me." I didn't wait for her to ask me another question. I told Chris I would talk to him later and walked off to ask about the class.

The guy working the registration desk checked his computer. "That class is full. But there's space in the one after that."

"When is it?"

"January fifteenth."

"That's fine." Even thought I hadn't told Kayla my plans, I registered her in the class too. She could thank me later.

As if sensing I was thinking about her, she sent me a text.

Kayla: Dylan's got a work Christmas party
Thursday night. You want me to bring over
the popcorn?

That was Kayla's way of asking me if I wanted her to come over to watch a movie that night.

Me: Sounds great.

38

NOLAN

The final notes of the song we'd been working on faded away, and I nodded. The energy electrifying Mason's studio loft was at an all-time high since my return two days ago. For the past six hours, the band had been creating the arrangement to the song. No one had mentioned the lies I'd been feeding them all these years.

I figured Jared had something to do with that.

From the moment we'd walked through the front door, we were all business. We had just over a week to pull everything together before hitting the studio. And for the first time I realized how much I'd fucked things up for these guys. I'd been so focused on Hailey and how much I loved her, I'd forgotten how much the music meant to them. Being a recording artist wasn't just my dream. It was theirs too, and I'd put it in jeopardy.

No one mentioned that either.

We were working on the song Hailey loved. It was a ballad, and the moment I'd begun singing it, the guys' eyes had lit with a level of excitement I hadn't seen in a while.

"I think that's it," Jared said at last, grinning. The guys

nodded in agreement. But as much as we wanted to celebrate, we still needed to create the music for five more songs and the lyrics and music to two others. While I'd been away, Jared and I had written eleven songs in total. Some we'd collaborated on via the phone and Skype. Others we'd written on our own. He'd presented them to the band, and they had already arranged the music and tweaked the lyrics to six songs by the time I'd left Northbridge.

Mason ordered pizza and we took a quick break to check our phones. Disappointment kicked me in the gut that Hailey hadn't texted or called me. Since returning to L.A., I'd received one text from her, thanking me for letting her know I'd arrived safely. All my other attempts to contact her went ignored.

Alyssa was a different matter. Now that I had returned and the media were talking about our relationship (from what I'd heard), she sent me regular texts. I'd already warned her the band and I were in hiding while we worked on the album. So other than her movie premiere tomorrow night, which the label insisted I attend with her, I wouldn't be in contact with the outside world until the album was completed.

What she didn't know was that Hailey was the exception. If Hailey went back to acknowledging my existence, I'd be on the phone faster than you could say foosball champion.

While my phone had been turned off, Brandon had texted me.

Brandon: Call me ASAP. Important.

I called him. My heart pounded something fierce, each rapid beat spreading fear through my body like poison.

He answered on the second ring. "Hailey's fine," he said before I could say anything, "but I figured you'd want to know that someone she works with was found murdered yesterday."

"Who?"

"Chris Witterholm."

I could barely breathe. I remembered chatting with him a few times. He was a good guy. Why the hell would someone want to kill him?

"The police haven't released any details," Brandon continued, "other than he was in Westgate when he was shot."

My body turned to ice at his words. "Did it have anything to do with Hailey?"

"I have no idea. All I know is what I've told you."

"Let me know if you hear anything else."

"Will do."

We ended the call, and I began typing Hailey a text.

> Me: Heard about Chris. I'm sorry. Call me. I love you.

I deleted the final three words before hitting send. Given the situation with Alyssa, those three words would only screw things up more than they already were. I didn't want a long-distance relationship. I wanted Hailey in L.A. with me.

I contacted the detective who'd been assigned to Hailey's case. "All I can tell you," he said, "is that we're looking into the possibility they're linked." His tone was all business, and nothing I said would convince him to reveal anything more, especially to someone who was constantly in the media spotlight.

After getting nowhere with that, I returned to the guys, who were eating the pizza as if it were their final meal, especially Mason. I grabbed a couple of slices before he could devour them all. We quickly finished up, then went back to work.

But as much as I tried to concentrate on the music and lyrics, memories of my last time with Hailey crept into my head. It didn't help she'd been the inspiration for my songs. A bit of Hailey was in all of them. The loneliness that had kept itself at bay while I was with her returned with a vengeance.

An hour later, after I'd screwed up on my part for the tenth time, Mason exploded, "Fuck, Tyler—or Nolan, or whatever your freakin' name is. Are you gonna get with the fucking program or not?"

Jared tensed, ready to throw himself between me and Mason if necessary. Kirk and Aaron glanced between us. Unlike Jared, I couldn't see either of them jumping in front of the bulky drummer, any more than they would have jumped in front of a speeding semi.

"Hey, look, I'm sorry." Though I meant what I said, exhaustion, frustration, and anger pushed through to my words. "I never claimed I was perfect. I'm pretty screwed up, actually. Have been for years thanks to my craptastic dad."

Mason's features softened at the reminder of what I'd been through. He nodded, indicating we should get back to work.

"No," Jared said, "we need to talk about this."

We all threw him a look that clearly said, *What the fuck are you talking about, you pussy?* Guys didn't talk about their emotions. We drank beer and got laid. Which would be great if the woman I wanted to have sex with lived in the same city as me. After being with Hailey, no one else would do.

"Yeah, I get it," Jared said. "We're cavemen assholes who are only capable of grunting at each other."

Kirk chuckled. "But at least they're musical grunts." He threw me a glance that was part amusement, part frustration. "Most of the time."

"Shit, you're not gonna make us hug, are you?" Mason's arms were folded, emphasizing his huge, tattooed biceps. "Otherwise I'm gonna need some serious therapy."

Aaron smirked. "Given that you won't even hug a woman, I'd say you need serious therapy either way."

That earned Aaron a harsh glare. Aaron shrugged it off.

"Can we just play the song again?" I said. "I promise I'll do better."

"You better," Mason huffed.

Kirk chuckled. "Someone needs to get laid."

"Damn straight I do. But until you ladies get your act together, I'm going all monk," Mason said with a frown. I had a feeling the monk part wasn't by choice. Jared had probably something to do with it, demanding there was no getting laid until the album was finished.

"All right. Before Mas starts reciting religious scriptures," I said, "let's get back to work." Anything to avoid talking about all the shit going on with me, and about my fears for Hailey after what had happened to her colleague.

Jared and Kirk grabbed their instruments. Mason returned to his drums, and Aaron switched his keyboards back on. This time when I sang the song, I pretended I was singing it to Hailey. By the time we were finished, all four men were nodding their approval.

We continued well into the night. To save time, we'd planned to crash at Mason's until the songs were all written. Like the past few nights, we slept only two or three hours before starting up again. Coffee became our food of choice.

Before crashing on Mason's couch, I checked my phone. Hailey had finally replied to one of my texts.

> Hailey: I'm fine, thanks. Have fun tomorrow night.

At first my sleep-deprived brain had no idea what she was talking about with the last part, but then I remembered: Alyssa's movie premiere. Hailey must have seen it on the entertainment news. To her, I was moving on with my life. That's why she hadn't responded to my messages. It was her way of saying she understood.

I deliberated for a minute whether I should respond. What I wanted to say was, *I wish it were you,* but that would only hurt her more. And her message was quite clear. She was brushing me off. She wasn't fine about Chris's death. That much I knew.

I hurled the phone against the wall. Mason's drywall survived the assault.

My phone didn't.

39

NOLAN

The limo pulled up to the security post of Alyssa's gated community. After a brief word with the guard, we were waved in. The record label had arranged for the limo. They wanted to ensure we showed up at the movie premiere together, since I was there as her boyfriend.

My mouth dropped open as we drove past houses that were better described as estates. My parents' home was large, but it was nothing compared to these.

The limo turned in at the driveway of a house that belonged in a fairy tale. Hailey would have loved it. Sighing, I pushed away thoughts of her. This was Alyssa's big night. The last thing she needed was for me to be moody and ruin it for her.

I waited for the driver to open my door, then I walked to the house and rang the doorbell. A moment later the front door swung open.

Alyssa's painted pink lips curled up in a smile, and all I could do was wonder why she was wasting time with me. She should've been going to the premiere with someone who wanted to be there with her. She shouldn't have been going with someone who'd been coerced into being her date.

Alyssa was normally gorgeous, but in her silver gown she was stunning. The cleavage-revealing dress was fitted to midthigh, then cascaded to the floor. Her hair was knotted in a bun, adding to her elegance.

"You look great," I said.

"You don't look so bad yourself." Her gaze traveled down the tux that I felt like an idiot in. The record label had arranged it, too.

"Are you ready?" *To leave. To stand in front of hundreds of fans. To deal with the media storm.*

I offered her my arm and I escorted her to the awaiting limo. The driver opened the door and I helped Alyssa in, then joined her. She patted the black leather seat next to her. I took the one across from her.

She giggled. "I'm not going to bite, if that's what you're worried about."

"I know, but I'm happy here."

"Okay." She moved to sit next to me. I wasn't sure if it was intentional, but she practically sat in my lap.

And that's when I smelled the booze on her breath. *Shit.* She rested her hand on my knee and gave it a light squeeze as the limo pulled away from her house.

"Alyssa, you're a nice girl, but I don't feel that way about you." My voice was cautious, quiet, like how you'd talk to an animal you don't want to spook. I didn't want to upset her when we were attending the premiere, but I needed to ensure she understood this wasn't real.

"Why? Because of the girl in the pictures?"

"Yes."

"But she lives in Minnesota and you live in L.A. Are you really planning to have a long-distance relationship?" Her lips pressed together into a slight pout.

"We're not having a long-distance relationship."

"She's moving here?" The pout disappeared and the corners of her mouth dipped down.

I shifted my knee, subtly removing her hand from it. "No. We're not together."

It took a moment for it to sink in. Her eyes widened. "You're … you're in love with her, aren't you?"

I nodded.

"Does she feel the same way?"

I shrugged. "I'm not sure." And I wasn't. I'd seen her love for me in her eyes, but she hadn't actually said the words I'd longed to hear.

Alyssa scooted back, leaving more than a foot of space between us. "What do you mean, you're not sure?"

"Just that. I have no idea if she loves me."

"Well, what did she say when you told her you love her?" When I didn't answer, she said, "You did tell her you love her, right?"

"Not exactly."

Fine lines crossed her forehead. "What do you mean, 'not exactly'? You either told her or you didn't."

"I told her she was my heart and soul."

Alyssa nodded what I could only guess was her approval. "That's not bad. And what did she say?"

"Nothing. We were too busy kissing." I felt like I had back in high school, when Hailey used to give me advice about dating and girls. Or at least she did until our senior year. Then the advice suddenly stopped.

"Okay, so what did she say when you asked her to move to L.A.?"

Now it was my turn to frown. "I didn't. I mean, I didn't ask her to move to L.A. She wants to study physical therapy and get into the program back home. I figured she wouldn't want to move here."

"But you didn't give her the choice to decide if she wanted to move here with you."

"Sure I did."

Alyssa shook her head as if I was an idiot, and maybe I was. "No, you didn't. You decided she wouldn't want to move here because of her goals. You never asked her. Maybe she wasn't sure if you wanted her to come here to be with you."

She had a point. I'd just assumed Hailey wouldn't want to move to L.A. But she had never indicated she would want to or that she would be fine with my constant touring.

I pointed this out to Alyssa.

"What was she supposed to do?" Alyssa replied. "Your record label and my agent decided we'd both benefit from this fictitious relationship they dreamed up. And with our fans so enamored by the idea of the clichéd good girl taming the bad-boy rocker, why would she risk everything when it was already determined you two can't be together?"

She had a good point. "So what should I do?"

"Ask her if she wants to live with you. She doesn't have to physically live with you if she's not comfortable with that. But at least she could live in the same city as you."

"And what about the record label?"

"Couples break up all the time. If I want to break up with you, there's nothing stopping me."

"Except for the recording contract they offered you."

"I don't think they'll change their minds because of that. Tell you what. Why don't we take one step at a time? We'll attend this premiere as a couple. Give the audience what they want. Then the first chance you get—sooner rather than later —you go back home and ask Hailey if she wants to move here. And then we'll see what happens." She tilted her head to the side. "Does that sound like a plan?"

I wasn't sure if I was making a mistake or if I was about to cause myself more heartache, but Alyssa's plan had merit, except . . .

"How's this going to help my reputation? If anything, it will only make things worse. I'll be labeled as a cheating asshole." And it wouldn't score Hailey any brownie points, either.

Alyssa patted my knee. "It's going to be okay, Nolan. You just have to have faith. Let people get to know the real you, and everything will be all right. And I'd love to meet Hailey. If I accept her as someone important in your life, the fans will too."

I hoped she was right.

Once we arrived at the location of the premiere, the traffic surrounding the theater slowed the limo's progress. As the occupants of each limo in front of us climbed out to greet the crowds lining either side of the theater entrance, my leg bounced with restless energy. But it had nothing to do with the screaming fans.

It was due to Alyssa's advice. If I could, I would've hailed a cab and rushed to the airport to catch the next flight to Northbridge. But as much as I wanted to do that, I couldn't let the band down again. I needed to stay in L.A. until the record was finished. Or at least until the band's part in recording the album was completed. Only then could I return to Northbridge and show Hailey how much I loved her and how I wanted to spend the rest of my life with her.

I hoped she felt the same way about me.

The limo pulled up to the red carpet. Camera flashes lit the area as fans waited with abated breath to see which celebrity had just arrived. The limo door opened and security helped Alyssa from the vehicle. Adoring screams filled the night sky as the fans caught sight of her. The woman I recognized as her assistant was instantly by her side and spoke to her while I stepped out of the limo.

You'd have thought that I, too, was starring in the movie,

from the way the crowd reacted at seeing me. Feeling a little sheepish at the attention when I was nothing more than Alyssa's escort for the night, I waved. Alyssa stepped up to me, wrapped her arm around my waist, and cuddled close. I knew it was nothing more than an act, but that didn't stop me from stiffening.

Flashes of light burst in front of us as fans and the media captured this fake moment. Inwardly I groaned. This wouldn't help my case with Hailey, especially if she saw the photos and video footage. If I was lucky, she would be avoiding anything to do with Alyssa and me and would never see any of this.

A production assistant indicated for us to keep moving toward the theater. But that didn't mean we got to escape to the safety of the building. We still had to deal with the various entertainment reporters.

Alyssa held my arm, like the adoring couple we pretended to be. It was easy for her. She was an actress. I was just a singer and songwriter. That didn't require me to act beyond what was needed for the band's music videos. Even my years of pretending to be someone else were pretty useless right now.

We approached the first reporter and her camera operator.

"Hi, Alyssa," the tall redhead gushed in that overzealous way common among entertainment reporters, which often left me inwardly rolling my eyes. "Megan Keyes with *We Talk*. You look absolutely gorgeous. As always."

Alyssa smiled graciously, her reaction no doubt genuine. "Thank you, Megan."

"And you . . ." Megan looked momentarily thrown as to what to call me. Which wasn't surprising. I hadn't really decided myself what name I wanted to use career-wise.

Alyssa gave my arm a light squeeze, reminding me what she had told me in the limo: *Let people get to know the real you, and everything will be all right.*

"You can call me Nolan."

Alyssa beamed at me, but not for the same reason Megan

assumed. I smiled back, even though it would only further cement everyone's belief we were a couple.

"Nolan," Megan said, "you look particularly yummy." To Alyssa she added, "You have very good taste." She then asked a few quick questions about the film before we were hustled to the next reporter. She barely had enough to time add "Congratulations, you two" before we were gone.

Alyssa waved to a group of teenage girls screaming at her and waving banners that proclaimed NOLYSSA, WE LOVE YOU and NOLYSSA FOREVER!

"Nolyssa?" I said under my breath.

"Nolan and Alyssa," she explained. "That's what our fans have been calling us." She directed her smile at me. "They've accepted you as Nolan. They want to get to know the real you, too."

"How long has this been going on? With the joint name, I mean."

She looked at me, slightly taken aback. "They were referring to us as Tylyssa for a while before this. The name changed after the paparazzi leaked your real name."

No wonder fans reacted the way they had when it looked like Hailey had been trying to seduce me away from Alyssa. But what would happen when Alyssa and I ended our fake relationship? How would these die-hard Nolyssa fans react?

I hoped that if Hailey agreed to move to L.A. to be with me, the fans would realize that she was the right woman for me. But in the end, it didn't really matter if they agreed or not, as long as they left her alone and moved their attention to another celebrity couple.

"Kiss her!" a girl called out. Before I could react, Alyssa leaned in and kissed my cheek. Camera flashes went crazy.

I scowled at her. "Why did you do that?" I said, a little more forcefully than was warranted.

She smiled sweetly. I didn't know if that was for my benefit or for the benefit of those watching us. "Because if I didn't, they'd keep hounding you to kiss me. This way they're semi-appeased. At least I didn't kiss you on the lips."

She was right, but it didn't make me feel any better about the situation.

Alyssa and I endured being interviewed by two more entertainment reporters before we could finally enter the grand theater. And like with Megan, they commented on our relationship. Alyssa did her best to redirect the conversation to the movie.

Once away from the crowds and the media, our mini entourage found our seats and we settle in for the movie. Since we were no longer in the eyes of the media, we could stop the loving-couple routine. Now we were just two friends out to see a movie—a movie Alyssa happened to star in.

Sadly, because I'd been so involved in my own personal dramas, I'd had no idea what the movie was about. Her previous movies had been romantic comedies. And yes, the title, *Forgiven Chances*, didn't exactly scream chick flick, but I hadn't paid much attention to that either.

Alyssa's character entered a convenience store with a homeless teen she was going to buy food for. But the store was being robbed and one of the assholes overreacted. He wasn't armed with a gun like his friend.

He was armed with a knife.

My hand unconsciously shifted to where my father had stabbed me.

40

NOLAN

Six Years Ago

My father stood in front of Hailey and me, blocking our escape route. I tightened my hold on her hand, warning her to remain silent.

"We're leaving." I nudged Hailey to the side, keeping her as far from him as possible.

"Why was there a fuckin' cop car in front of the house earlier?"

I was surprised the house didn't shudder because of how loud he bellowed. Hailey stiffened next to me. She knew he got angry. This was the first time she had witnessed this small taste of it.

My father narrowed his gaze on me. "What kind of fuckin' trouble you get into now?" Before I could respond, he grabbed hold of my T-shirt with both hands. The stench of booze rolled off him in waves.

With more force than I expected given his drunken state, he shoved me into the wall. My head bounced back hard against it, and the world tilted as if it had shifted off its axis. I was vaguely aware of Hailey and Mom screaming, their panicked voices somewhere in the distance.

I shook my head, struggling to regain my senses. *Run*, I silently pleaded with my mom and Hailey.

With my gaze locked on my father, I told Hailey to go home. She didn't move at first, but after what felt like several minutes, she disappeared out the front door. My father didn't make any attempt to touch her. If he had, I would have killed him.

The front door clicked shut.

"Why was the fuckin' cop here?" he repeated, voice no quieter than last time.

"Why don't we eat dinner first, Gordon, then we can discuss it." Mom's tone was soothing through years of practice, but even so, it still wavered slightly. If my father noticed, he was doing a great job hiding it. His alcohol-bleary eyes studied me for a moment before he nodded and staggered after her into the kitchen.

A deadly silence suffocated the hallway.

I needed to get out of here. Mom would be fine. I was the one who had fucked up in his eyes.

Since he was preoccupied for a few minutes and wouldn't know I was gone, I snuck out of the house and shut the door quietly behind me. I needed to see Hailey. Just for a few minutes. Just so she knew I was okay.

Hailey's bedroom light was on. Her parents had gone out and wouldn't be back for a few more hours. I rang the doorbell and a minute later the door opened to reveal my best friend, no longer in the wet shorts and my hoodie. Now she was in her sleep shorts and flimsy tank top. My dick jerked to life, its typical response whenever she was dressed this way.

Her gaze searched my body for signs of injuries. "Are you okay?"

"Yeah, I'll be fine." But I didn't feel fine. I felt trapped.

Trapped and fucked, and I didn't know what to do about it. "Can I stay with you for a bit?"

"Of course." She reached for my hand and led me into the living room. "You want to watch a movie?"

I nodded even though what I really wanted to do was hold her.

I lay down on the couch.

An adorable frown crept onto her face. "Hey, where am I supposed to sit?" She eyed the armchair, which wasn't her favorite. She thought it was lumpy.

I patted the cushion in front of my hip. "There's plenty of room here."

The frown became an equally adorable pout. No other girl could pull it off the way Hailey could. No other girl looked as sexy as Hailey did. "But you get to lie down. Why do I have to sit?"

"Nothing's stopping you from lying here too." I scooted back. My back was pressed against the couch, giving her a little more space, but not a whole lot. We'd have to get cozy if she didn't want to end up on the floor.

And that was my goal. I wanted to move our relationship up a level. I'd known her forever and had been in love with her almost as long. I had no idea if she felt the same way about me. This would be the ultimate test.

She lay next to me, her body touching mine. I wrapped my arm around her waist. Her breath hitched, the small movement pressing her back against me. Her sweet vanilla scent had me visualizing all kinds of scenarios, most of them involving her on her back and me kissing her senseless.

Even though we had never watched TV this way before, it felt natural. Her body fit mine perfectly, like we were designed to be together this way.

My mind was only half on the movie we were watching— the other half was figuring out the best way to make my next move—when my cell phone pinged in my back pocket. Any other time I would have ignored it, not wanting to end this possibility between Hailey and me. But a warning in my gut told me I needed to check who was texting me, now.

I pulled the phone out and read the message from Sarah:

Where are you?

Hailey's.

Please come home. I need you.

Something was very wrong. Sarah never texted after she went to bed. She'd get in trouble if she did.

On my way.

"I've gotta go. It's Sarah."

Hailey scrambled up. "What's wrong?"

"I don't know. My father's probably yelling at Mom, and that scared Sarah."

She followed me to the front door. "Are you coming back?"

I wanted to return to Hailey and the couch and the movie. I wanted to continue where we'd left off, but I couldn't. I wouldn't leave my sister again. Not tonight.

I gave Hailey a sad smile. "I'll see you tomorrow."

"Text me once you get back to let me know everything's all right."

"Okay."

She must not have been convinced, because she said in a tone that warranted no argument, "Promise me, or else I'll call the cops."

"Okay," I said, this time with more conviction.

I ran across the street to my house and opened the front door. The place was quiet. No yelling. No slurred conversation. No TV blaring in the background. I entered my house and flipped the light on. Instead of the usual warm glow, the light was cold and harsh. But that wasn't what filled my body with icy dread.

Blood drops on the beige carpet formed a trail to the kitchen.

I strained to hear a sound, but my ears were met with nothing but silence. Darkness seeped from the room, and I walked toward it, my gaze glued to the bloody trail. A strong, unpleasant smell sat heavy in the air, and my stomach turned.

Ignoring the five alarms in my head telling me to get out of the house, I stepped into the kitchen and turned on the light. My hand recoiled at the sticky wetness on the light switch and I glanced down to see what it was.

And wished I hadn't.

Smeared bloody handprints stained the walls.

My heart slammed hard against my ribs, threatening to shatter them. My gaze traveled around the room. The island obscured my view of most of the floor, other than the pool of blood seeping across the tiles. Based on the amount of blood, I could only guess the person was no longer alive.

Somewhere deep in the recesses of my brain, a voice told me to get out of the house and call 911, but the rest of me didn't want to pay attention to the voice. My body, working on its own accord, moved forward.

The first thing I saw as I walked around the corner of the island was an outstretched female hand in the pool of blood, her fingernails painted a muted red. Next came the familiar long brown hair. I choked back a sob and rushed to Mom's side.

"Mom?" I said even though it was too late. Her eyes were wide, peering up at me but no longer seeing.

Call the police. Now, the voice insisted, but I couldn't move. All I could do was stare at what had once been my mother. Blood soaked through her cream-colored blouse, the fabric ripped in numerous places. It looked like whoever did this had stabbed her multiple times. She'd never stood a chance. Her hands wore defensive wounds from trying to protect herself.

I couldn't hold back the sob. "Mom." I sounded like a small child, lost, without hope.

A muffled bang from upstairs jerked my attention from Mom's body. That was all it took to break the spell. Sarah.

I raced out the kitchen and up the stairs.

As I approached the top step, a frightened scream ripped through the air. This transformed into a pained cry and grunts. Concern for my own safety shoved aside, I rushed to her room and threw open the door. I didn't give myself the chance to process the scene. I couldn't. I just reacted.

I hurled my body at my father.

My father was a large guy, only I was bigger from working out at the gym. But in this moment of unspeakable insanity, he possessed the strength of two men. He didn't even budge from Sarah's body. It was like moving a house with your bare hands —impossible.

I did, though, manage to break his attention from what he was doing to my sister. With inhuman strength, he shoved me away. I half flew, half stumbled backward.

Before I could avoid the impact, my body slammed into Sarah's desk. Pain shot through my hip. A level of anger I'd never seen before twisted my father's once handsome features. Finished with his assault on my sister, he shifted his attention to me.

"What did you do?" I choked out even though I knew exactly what he had done. The why was a mystery. People got drunk all the time. They didn't stab people to death and continue stabbing them long after the victim had died.

"They had to die," he said, voice deadly calm, his body covered in blood. Mom's blood. Sarah's blood. "They had to die so she couldn't have sex with anyone else."

"She?" My voice was the opposite to his. I was amazed I could even utter any words around the rapidly beating heart jammed in my throat.

He moved toward me, his body blocking my escape. My only hope was to talk my way out of this until help arrived.

If help arrived.

"Your mother," my father said.

"She wouldn't have had sex with anyone else. She was faithful to you." Otherwise she would have escaped this hell years ago.

"That's a fuckin' lie," he screamed.

I could barely breathe, and it had nothing to do with the stench of death choking the air from my lungs.

My gaze dropped for a brief second to the gruesome sight on the bed, and my strength gave way. If I hadn't gone to Hailey's, I could have prevented this. I could have protected my mom and my sister.

And instead of standing in front of me, getting ready to end my life too, Dad would've been in jail.

In that moment, instead of seeing my life flash before my eyes, only one thought crossed my mind. I'd never told Hailey that I loved her. I mean, I had told her I loved her . . . as a friend. But I'd never told her that I was in love with her, and now I'd never have the chance to tell her.

And I would never find out if she felt the same way about me.

A loud noise came from downstairs, like the sound of someone banging on the front door, followed by shouting. None of this bothered my father. His focus was entirely on me.

I kept my gaze locked on him and took a cautious step back.

Everything happened fast after that. My father lunged at me as movement in the doorway caught my attention. His knife sliced into my body, bringing with it a sharp pain. I cried out and stumbled back.

Yelling filled the air. My father moved toward me again, his knife ready to butcher me. A loud bang. And another. My father's body jerked forward, then slumped to the ground.

Unable to support me anymore, my legs gave out and I collapsed.

Pain engulfed me. Pain from my wound. Pain from what my father had done to my mom and sister. Pain from all I had witnessed.

A cop crouched beside me and spoke. In my numb state, I couldn't make out what he said.

Instead, I welcomed the darkness.

41

___

NOLAN

Present

My breathing came fast and hard at the memory. The movie continued playing on the huge screen, but all I could see was the blood covering the kitchen floor, my mom's open but sightless eyes, the blood-splattered bedding surrounding my sister's mutilated body.

I gripped the armrests, digging my fingers into the velvet fabric.

Alyssa leaned closer to me and whispered, "Are you all right?" She placed her hand on mine and lightly squeezed it when I didn't respond. "Nolan?"

Deep down I had always known the murders were my fault. If I hadn't been at Hailey's, none of the events of that night would have happened. I had bailed on Northbridge not only because I wanted to avoid the memories but also because I wanted to escape Hailey. I'd failed my mother and sister. I was afraid of failing Hailey too.

"I need to get out of here," I told Alyssa.

She must have realized something major was going on with

me. She whispered to her assistant, then told me, "Monica will escort you out and stay with you to make sure you're okay." She kissed my cheek, either for my benefit or for the benefit of the people witnessing me leave in the middle of the movie. Or maybe a little of both.

I squeezed past Alyssa and the rest of her entourage. My body no longer felt like it belonged to me. I was a walking zombie. The only thing I was aware of was sound of the movie and the scattered whispers following me up the aisle.

I almost sagged in relief when Monica pushed the theater door open and we stepped into the lobby. My father's final words, *That's a fuckin' lie,* pounded in my head. Had he been right? Had Mom been cheating on him?

Monica waved a staff member over. "I'm Alyssa Graham's personal assistant. Mr. Kincaid has a migraine and needs a private place to sit for a moment."

"Absolutely. This way, please."

We followed him down the dimly lit hallway and stopped at a door. He unlocked it and ushered us into the small room.

"Is there anything else you need?" he asked.

"No, this is fine, thanks," I said, dismissing him.

Once the door clicked shut behind him, I sat on the red velvet couch in the middle of the room. The space had been designed for comfort and for a quiet place to converse. But it was also like stepping into the past. Framed classic movie posters lined the light brown walls.

Monica locked the door. "Do you want some water?"

I could have used something much stronger, but I nodded. She handed me a bottle of water from the table against the wall. With shaky hands I opened it and drank the lukewarm liquid.

"I heard about what happened to your family. I'm sorry you went through that."

I gave a slight jerk of my head in thanks. While pretending

to be Tyler Erickson, I'd avoided those pitying looks and words of apology over what happened. At the time, it had been a relief because I had only wanted to focus on my future instead of my past. But something about the way she said the words made the meaning behind them sound different. She didn't say them because she believed they were the right words to say.

"A friend of mine lost her family in a robbery," she explained. "She was a kid at the time and witnessed their murder. She struggled for years with post-traumatic stress disorder." Monica bit her lip before powering on. "You have that too, don't you? That's why you looked like you were having a panic attack in there."

I wanted to deny it, but then changed my mind. Alyssa wouldn't trust someone she felt could end up betraying her and those who were close to her.

"I'm not sure," I said. "Until recently I couldn't remember anything from that night. But ... but I remembered it all during the movie."

"Are you seeing anyone?" At my confused frown, she added, "I mean like a therapist?"

I shook my head. "I saw someone after the murders. He told me I had dissociative amnesia and that I might or might not remember what happened. I decided to go with the might-not-remember option and avoided seeing anyone after that."

"Maybe things will get better now that you remembered what happened. But there's also a good chance it will only get worse unless you talk to someone. My friend struggled with guilt because she thought she should have done more to save her family. The guilt almost killed her. If you want, I can find out who she talked to."

"Thanks. I'd like that." She was right. I couldn't keep living like this. Not if I wanted a life with Hailey in it. I couldn't keep hiding from what it was doing to me.

We talked for a bit longer. Like Alyssa and Hailey, Monica

was easy to talk to. But that was probably because she just saw me as a regular guy. I wasn't some rock star she was fangirling over. She was used to being around celebrities.

She checked her phone. "The movie's almost finished. You ready to join Alyssa and the media circus?"

42

———

HAILEY

I flopped down on the couch and turned on the TV, needing a distraction from everything that had happened lately: the coma, Nolan returning to Northbridge, the amnesia, falling in love with him even more than before, the attack, Nolan leaving, his relationship with Alyssa, Chris's death . . .

To sum it up, I needed a distraction from life.

On the screen, a mob of people stood behind a roped-off area. The picture then flashed to a limo and Michael Seger, one of the sexiest actors around, appeared from it.

His fans spotted him and the intensity of their frenzied shrieks jumped up a notch. He waved at the crowd, further exciting them. The guy should come with a warning: *Caution: risk of ringing ears when you stand too close to my fans.*

"What's all the screaming for?" Kayla handed me a soda and made herself at home on the other end of the couch.

"Michael Seger. Who else would it be?"

She threw me a look. "Oh, I don't know. Your boyfriend's pretty hot too."

"Nolan isn't my boyfriend. News flash: in case you haven't noticed, he's back in L.A. now." With Alyssa.

"That's only 'cause you didn't have the guts to go with him. And if he isn't your boyfriend, then why did you turn down that guy who called to take you out for coffee?" She meant Craig, the man I'd met the day Nolan stopped to fix the flat tire for the man's grandmother.

"Because I didn't feel like going out with him." My heart wouldn't have been into it, and it wouldn't have been fair to let him believe he had a chance with me. "And because Nolan didn't ask me," I said, responding to her first comment about me not going to L.A. with him.

"Ask you what? To marry you?" The exasperation in her tone surprised me.

"No, but I didn't want to move there if I had no idea if he wanted to be my boyfriend for real. I didn't want to give up my job for nothing."

"So why didn't you ask him?"

Right. Like I was going to do that. I wasn't one of those people who got off on rejection. Although in retrospect, it couldn't have hurt any worse than it did now.

"I'm serious, Hailey. Instead of moping around feeling sorry for yourself, you should ask him if he wants you to move to L.A. to be with him."

"In case you haven't noticed, he's dating Alyssa Graham."

She shrugged in a way that said, *You know they're not dating for real.* Or maybe they officially were now. Everyone, according to the media and fan sites, agreed they made a gorgeous couple.

"Oh my God," Kayla breathed, her eyes wide as she gaped at the TV.

I turned to see what was wrong. The entertainment news was still on the same event, but now the reporter was interviewing Nolan and Alyssa.

My heart practically stopped beating at the sight of him. It was the first time I'd seen him in a tux, and *wow* wasn't enough of a word to describe how hot he looked in it. And when combined with his sexy smile, there wasn't a single fan at the event who wasn't swooning. Nolan normally looked mouthwatering in his usual faded jeans and body-hugging T-shirts, but Nolan in a tux was beyond rocker-boy sexy.

And that only made my heart hurt more.

"Not to be crass or anything," Kayla said, still staring at the TV, "but I think I just came in my panties from looking at him."

Despite Nolan being with Alyssa, who looked more gorgeous than I'd thought was possible (a fact that wasn't lost on my poor heart), I chuckled. "I'm sure your boyfriend would appreciate hearing that."

Kayla made a scoffing sound. "Are you telling me you didn't just cream your panties?"

I wrinkled my nose at her words, even though she was right. "Shhh. I want to hear what they're saying." Because I needed to torture myself a little more.

"Hi, Alyssa," the tall, skinny redhead said in that annoying way some entertainment reporters had about them. Like they considered themselves equals to the big name celebrity, when most of the time the celebrities had no idea who they were. "Megan Keyes with *We Talk*. You look absolutely gorgeous. As always."

Alyssa smiled. The warmth to it made her even more breathtaking. It really wasn't fair. "Thank you, Megan."

"And you . . ." The redhead looked uncertain what to call Nolan. Some fans and reporters now referred to him by his real name. Others stuck with Tyler. Which meant Nolan hadn't decided yet, or else the record label would've already issued a statement as to which name he was now going by.

"You can call me Nolan."

He glanced at Alyssa. She beamed at him, and he smiled back, further confirming they were officially a couple.

My insides tightened even though this wasn't news. It just hated the constant reminders.

"Nolan," Megan said, "you look particularly yummy." To Alyssa she added, a knowing grin on her face, "You have very good taste." She then asked a few questions about the film before the golden couple had to move on.

Alyssa waved to a group of screaming teenage girls holding banners that proclaimed NOLYSSA, WE LOVE YOU and NOLYSSA FOREVER!

I groaned at the name. It was just as bad as the last one. And seriously, what was it with giving celebrity couples idiotic monikers? We didn't give them to normal couples. No one went around referring to Kayla and Dylan as Dylayla. She'd probably slug me if I tried.

"Kiss her!" someone yelled. Alyssa leaned in and kissed Nolan's cheek. The fans screamed their appreciation. As much as I wanted to think of them as stupid, they weren't. They'd been sucked into the lie as much as the rest of us had been.

Neither Kayla nor I said anything, the truth sinking in about the status of the golden couple's relationship. As I stared numbly at the screen, Kayla theorized what was really going on between them. She even threw in a few alien-related theories that made me laugh. God, I loved her.

"You know what I think you should do?" she said.

"Make popcorn?" Then we could watch a movie. Preferably one not starring Alyssa, and one without any hint of romance. A terrifying psychological thriller would be good right about now.

"Go to L.A."

I liked my popcorn idea better. "And why would I do that?"

"Have you told Nolan that you love him? And I don't mean as a friend."

"He told me I was his heart and soul and, well..." What exactly had I said when he told me that?

Nothing. I'd kissed him, but that was it. Yes, I'd thought about how he was my heart and soul too, but I hadn't actually said the words. I wasn't sure if they meant the same for him as it meant for me. Maybe that was why I'd been hesitant to believe he was declaring his love for me. More than likely, in guy talk, he'd been hoping to have sex with me again.

"I kissed him," I said.

Kayla's mouth flopped open. She blinked. "Shit, girl. The guy says he loves you and you're sitting on this couch, hanging out with me, when you should be in L.A. with him."

"One, he didn't say he loves me." Except he did, in the note he'd left the morning he returned to L.A.

Kayla threw me a look to tell me I was an idiot. I couldn't disagree with her there. There was a small chance she was right. A very small chance.

Kayla continued giving me the look.

Okay, a big chance.

"It was implied in his words," she said. "In case it's skipped your notice, Hailey, he's a musician. And musicians are more poetic than your typical male." She threw her hands up. "I swear, sometimes you're as dense about these things as Dylan."

Ignoring her outburst, I went on. "Two, the record label is pushing for this relationship between Nolan and Alyssa, to save his reputation and to help the band become even bigger. A bad-boy reputation can only get you so far in the industry." A similar reputation had killed several promising careers in the past few years. Those musicians had never been heard of again. I didn't want that to happen to Nolan.

Kayla gave me the you're-an-idiot look again. If she wasn't careful, it might become permanently etched on her face. And her boyfriend might not appreciate that. "Right. Because everyone knows that celebrity relationships last."

I folded my arms. "Theirs could." Hell, why was I defending their relationship?

Kayla snorted. "You're right. His touring schedule and her movie schedule will be super-conducive to a solid relationship. The record label's stupid if it thinks their relationship—fake or real—will last and help Nolan's reputation in the long run. The paparazzi will be constantly hounding them, ready to do anything to poke holes in their relationship. That will be enough to destroy it. Happens all the time."

I laughed. "Tell me what you really think."

She shrugged. "I just think you and the label are wrong. Nolan doesn't need a celebrity girlfriend to save his reputation. He needs a sweet, loving, down-to-earth girlfriend. A girlfriend who isn't constantly in the spotlight."

"But I've already been in the spotlight," I pointed out.

"That's only because you, in the eyes of the paparazzi and fans, tried to destroy what Nolan and Alyssa supposedly had between them. But think about it. How many non-celebrity boyfriends, girlfriends, or spouses end up in the tabloids? None of them. Not unless they do something illegal or immoral that drags their celebrity lover into their mess. I don't care what you believe. You're perfect for Nolan's reputation."

She was right. But . . . "I'm not sure the label will see it that way."

"The label isn't what's important. Nolan should have a say in who he's dating, not the label. Look, all I'm saying is you need to go to L.A. and tell him how you feel. Tell him you love him and tell him that you're willing to move there to be with him." I opened my mouth to speak, but she didn't give me a chance to say anything. "I know you're scared of being hurt again, but you need to do this or else you'll spend the rest of your life wondering what if."

I released a long, slow breath. "You're right. But it'll have to wait until he's finished recording his album. The last thing he needs is for me to go to L.A. now and disturb him." Kayla opened her mouth, no doubt to argue against what I was saying. I raised my hand to stop her. "No, it has to be my way. This album's important to him and the band. If I'm gonna do this, it's not at the risk of that."

While my romantic-at-heart best friend would have preferred that I rush to L.A. in some grand gesture, she nodded, seeing I wouldn't budge on this point. No matter what happened between Nolan and me, his music career came first. He'd worked so hard and defied all kinds of odds to get where he was. I wouldn't take it away from him. He deserved everything and more.

My phone played a generic tune. I glanced at the number but didn't recognize it. I accepted the call. "Hello?"

"Is this the slut who's trying to steal Tyler Erickson away from the sweetest person alive?" The menace in her voice caused the air in my lungs to stop moving. I quickly hung up on her and stared at the phone as if it had turned into a viper.

"What's wrong?" Kayla asked. I barely heard her over the pulse pounding in my ears.

"Hailey?" She waved her hand in front of my face, breaking my trance.

I swallowed. Hard. "That was a member of the Nolyssa fan club."

Kayla's eyebrows drew together, forming deep crevasses. "What did she say?"

"She asked if I was the slut who was trying to steal Tyler away from Alyssa." I figured there was no point telling Kayla exactly what the fan had said about Alyssa. She was already angry enough as it was.

"You're fucking kidding me!"

I shared her sentiment. "I don't even know how she found my number. It's not like I give it to everyone I meet." Although who knew what I'd done during those five days I still didn't remember.

Kayla narrowed her eyes at me. "Don't even think it."

"Think what?" I gulped down some soda, stalling.

"You're going to use this call from some crazed fan to avoid telling Nolan the truth."

Kayla knew me too well. But really, who could blame me? This wasn't the life I'd signed up for. I didn't do well having people hate me. I'd always done things to avoid that. And for good reason.

"This wasn't a fan who wrote a comment on a fan site," I reminded her. "She tracked down my number. She might not have found out where I live or work, but that doesn't mean someone else can't. Someone who is even more pissed off at me."

The lines on Kayla's forehead deepened. "You need to tell Nolan."

I shook my head. "No, he doesn't need to know about this. And you can't tell Brandon either." Because he *would* tell Nolan.

"Then tell the police."

"And what are they going to do? It was one phone call. It's not like she threatened my life." Nor was it linked to what had happened to Chris and me in Northbridge. That was their bigger priority. They wouldn't care about some crazed Nolyssa fan.

Not unless she was connected to the attack and murder.

43

NOLAN

The final note of the song faded away and I glanced at Daniel Maynard, sitting behind the impressive mixing console in the control booth. He nodded, which was good, but I also recognized his expression and what it meant.

"That was good, Nolan," he said through the microphone. The rest of the band was standing behind him, listening. "But I'd like you to sing it again, this time with more emotion during the chorus. The song is about finding the girl you love after losing her. Show the listener how broken you were and how seeing her again gave you hope."

I nodded and waited until the engineer started the instrumental track of the song again before pouring my heart out. I thought about how this time tomorrow I would have told Hailey that I loved her and asked her to move to L.A. to be with me. True, she could say no and break my heart, but it was worth the risk.

By the time I finished singing the song, Daniel was grinning. "Perfect. She's one lucky girl." He winked at me, clearly knowing the song was about a real girl. But I had no idea if he assumed the girl was Alyssa.

The door to the control room opened and my supposed girlfriend walked in. At the unexpected intrusion, all six guys in the crowded space turned to her. I couldn't see their expressions, but I could imagine Mason's at the sight of Alyssa's short skirt, stilettos, and long legs.

She waved to me and spoke to the guys in the room. They nodded. In contrast to what the fans and media believed, the band knew I wasn't in love with her. They were aware I'd been doing exactly what the record label had requested. And even though none of them had protested at what I'd been forced to do, I could tell Jared wasn't thrilled with any of it.

I joined everyone in the control booth. They peered expectantly at me as I walked through the door, all curious about what Alyssa could possibly want with me.

She placed her hand on my arm. "Can I talk to you for a moment? It's important."

I looked over at Daniel, since he was the one calling the shots. As it was, he'd been very accommodating by allowing me an hour off twice during our recording sessions, so I could meet with my therapist. Talking to my supposed girlfriend was pushing things.

"Go ahead," he said. "We'll start laying down the final track. Just don't be too long."

I led Alyssa down the hallway to the office where my therapy sessions had been conducted. I knocked on the door. When no one answered, I opened it and waved her in.

Calling the room an office was generous. It was more like a cross between an office, a storage room, and a place where staff and musicians could crash for a few minutes during late-night recording sessions. A naked bulb hung overhead and cast eerie shadows around the room.

Alyssa gracefully navigated her way around stacks of sheet

music, books, and paperwork and sat on one side of the couch. I removed a pile of sheet music from a plastic chair and turned it around. The corners of her mouth momentarily twitched down as I sat opposite her.

"What's up?" I asked.

"Have you seen the social media and fan sites since the premiere?"

"No, we've been too busy." Not to mention that I never bothered with any of those things. Kirk and Jared were the ones who had taken over the responsibility of dealing with social media. Mason was banned from it because we were worried what he would say, especially if he'd been drinking.

"You don't know, then?"

"Know what?"

"About the rumors of our breakup?"

Shit, that had been fast, but I couldn't say I was disappointed. "No, but that's good. I'm flying out to see Hailey tomorrow and asking her if she wants to move in with me."

And if she did, we'd have to find a new place to live. One without Jared, my current roommate.

Alyssa cringed. "You might want to wait on that."

I frowned. "Why?"

"The rumors are claiming Hailey's the reason there's trouble in paradise. It was leaked to the media that you bailed on me during the premiere."

I felt the frown deepen. "I didn't fucking bail on you."

"I know that, but unless you go public with what happened, you won't be able to contain the rumors."

I grunted. "They'll pass. As soon as the next celebrity scandal comes along, everyone will forget that you and I were 'dating'"—I finger-quoted the last word—"and everything will be fine."

"I hope you're right." Her shoulders raised, then lowered

with a long exhalation. "There are some pretty die-hard fans when it comes to Nolyssa."

She tapped the screen on her iPhone, handed it to me, and left the room.

Confused why she'd given me her phone, I looked at the screen. At first I couldn't figure out what I was looking at. But then I pieced it all together. It was a fan site dedicated to Alyssa's and my relationship. Some of the fans were disappointed at the rumors the relationship was possibly ending. Others weren't too surprised, because most celebrity relationships didn't last.

But a few comments had me wanting to smash my fist into the wall. The individuals wanted to physically harm Hailey for being responsible for the demise of Nolyssa.

Deciding to spare the wall, I sent a knee-high pile of paper flying across the room. The pages scattered, creating a huge mess. Much like my life.

I stared at the comments for several minutes until a knock on the door intruded on my not-so-pleasant thoughts. When I didn't answer, the door opened.

I expected to see Alyssa there, but instead Jared stood in the doorway. "You ready to do this?" he asked.

"Yeah, sure," I mumbled.

I reached the door, but Jared didn't step out of the way. "Why do you look like someone keyed your car?" he asked.

I briefly explained what was going on.

"Shit. What are you going to do?"

"Nothing for now, I guess." Other than contacting the Northbridge police. But who knew if they would take it seriously. "It's just empty words. I can't see anyone actually tracking Hailey down." After all, they weren't the paparazzi—they were just fans. I hoped that Hailey realized that too, especially if she'd seen the comments. Otherwise, no way would she agree to be my girlfriend, let alone move to L.A. to be with me.

"Okay, that's a wrap," Daniel said five hours later, after we'd listened to the song's final mix. Smiling, he nodded at us. "I thought your debut album was good. But this one is much stronger."

Mason hooted and high-fived Kirk. "We'll kick the hell out of the charts this time."

We laughed at his enthusiasm, but I had to agree with Mason and Daniel. The album was our best one yet.

And it was the album that would show the world Hailey and I belonged together. The songs existed because of Hailey, like "This One Moment" from our debut album. I'd written it when I first realized I'd fallen in love with her.

As we packed up to leave, a nervous energy twisted inside me. My flight wasn't until tomorrow morning, but in ten hours I'd see Hailey again—and this time it wouldn't be in the hospital because she was in a coma. This time when I kissed her, unlike the last time when I first arrived in Northbridge, she'd be able to kiss me back.

She would be able to hear how much I missed her, how much I loved her.

44

HAILEY

"Are you home?" Kayla asked me on the phone as I packed my suitcase for the week.

"I am for a few more minutes, then I'm heading over to my parents'." They'd left for their Mexican cruise this morning and had asked me to house-sit.

"Have you received any more letters or phone calls?" she asked.

"Only the one letter from yesterday, and I haven't received any more calls since the last one." After calling me three times, the Nolyssa fan had given up phoning me when I'd quit answering her calls. The cops hadn't been able to identify where the calls came from, but they did have the letter. It hadn't threatened my life, unlike some online comments I'd seen. It contained a rather lengthy explanation as to why I was lacking compared to Alyssa when it came to being Nolan's girlfriend.

But the fact the girl knew where I lived disturbed me the most. If she could figure it out, then maybe so could some of the more ardent Nolyssa fans. Eventually things would die down when Nolan and Alyssa officially broke up and moved on with their lives, or once the rumors ended that they were headed for splitsville. But until then, my life was still poten-tially at risk.

"Have you told Nolan?" Kayla asked.

"No, I think he's still in the recording studio."

"But are you going to tell him?" Her tone wasn't so much a question of whether I'd do it or not. It was a demand.

I removed a couple of pairs of jeans from my closet and folded them into my suitcase. "If you're asking if I'm gonna talk to him, the answer is yes. As a friend." I missed him more than the last time he'd left, and that had been unbearable. This time it felt like all the air in the room had been sucked away, and I was no longer able to breathe.

"But you're not gonna talk to him about being his girlfriend and moving to L.A.?" The demand in her tone had been replaced by the desire to whack me on the back of my head for being such an idiot. But this was Kayla. I was used to it.

"No, I'll continue being his friend and see what happens between him and Alyssa." I'd decided on this in case he was falling for her, as the media suggested. I couldn't compete with her and I wasn't going to try. That was more than my poor heart could handle.

Kayla sighed. "Okay. I'll support you in whatever you do. But I really hope it works out for you two. You're perfect together."

If only Nolan's fans agreed with her. "I know. But it is what it is. I'm just happy for him no matter what he ends up doing."

We continued talking as I wheeled the suitcase to my car.

"Let me know if you need anything," Kayla said as I approached the trunk. I scanned the area for crazed Nolyssa fans. Other than an elderly couple I recognized from the floor below mine and a sleek blue car pulling into the parking lot, no one else was around. The late afternoon sun peeked from behind a random cloud.

At my parents' house, I parked my car in the driveway. My

parents had taken a cab to the airport, and their BMW took up most of the space in the two-car garage. I glanced at the neighbors' houses but did my best not to look at the one that would cause me the most pain.

A memory slipped in from the last time I'd been in the house. It was a memory that I had forgotten until now. Dad had called me, asking if I could find some legal documents in Nolan's house. He didn't have time to come back to find them, and wanted me to take a look.

That's when I had accidentally found the letters I wasn't sure Nolan had known about. Letters from his mother to her lover.

Unease spread through me at the memory, but I couldn't figure out why.

Still avoiding looking at Nolan's old house, I removed my suitcase from the trunk and wheeled it to the front door. I unlocked the door and entered the house I hadn't visited for a few weeks now.

I couldn't tell if anyone was at home in the houses on either side of my parents'. Not that it mattered. The neighbors I'd grown up with had long since moved away. I hadn't yet met the ones who now lived there.

After putting away the groceries I'd brought with me, I went upstairs. My room had changed since I'd left home. Once decorated with posters of my favorite bands and actors, it had long since been converted into a guest room. But Mom had gotten slightly carried away after watching a home decorating show, and the room now resembled one from a fancy bed-and-breakfast. The alarm clock was off by over four hours. I walked to the nightstand and adjusted the time.

After unpacking my suitcase, I went down to make dinner. Like the alarm clock in my room, the microwave clock was also behind by over four hours. There must have been a power outage after my parents left. I reset the clock.

My phone pinged. It was a text from Mom to tell me they had arrived safely in Florida, the first leg of their trip.

> Me: Have fun!
>
> Me: And make sure Dad doesn't forget the sunscreen this time. :)

Once dinner was ready, I carried the soup and grilled cheese sandwich into the living room. Purposely avoiding the entertainment news, I found one of my favorite shows. But somehow watching the FBI track down a serial killer didn't appeal to me when I was alone in a big house. And especially not when Nolyssa fans wanted to see me "removed from the planet" because I didn't "deserve to exist."

I eventually settled on a sitcom. By the time the closing credits came on, the world outside the window was a dusky black. I stood up to close the curtains. The Christmas lights on the house to the right of my parents' home were on, as were the living room lights. Nolan's house was dark. No big surprise there.

As the next show ended, the doorbell rang. I didn't feel like answering it, but since it was obvious someone was home and it might be important, I walked to the front door and peeked through the peephole. The guy looked familiar and it took me a second to remember why. It was Lindsey's stepfather.

Confused what he was doing here, I cautiously opened the door. He looked as surprised to see me as I was to see him.

"I didn't know you live here," he said.

Smiling, I opened the door a little wider. "I don't. I'm house-sitting for my parents. Is there something I can help you with?"

"I realized our flashlight batteries are dead, and my wife's worried we'll have another power outage like the neighborhood had last night. I was going to ask if you had any we could borrow, but since this isn't your house, you probably have no idea."

I laughed. "You obviously don't know my parents very well. I swear they can't survive unless they're fully stocked with batteries." I stepped back so he could enter, and I shut the door behind him. "What size do you need?"

"Double A's. Four of them." A familiar spicy aftershave brushed past me.

Why the hell did you bring her here?

Even though I was safe in my parents' home, my pulse accelerated, my heart slamming against my ribs in its haste to get away. *Whoa. What the hell just happened?*

"You okay?" Lindsey's stepdad asked, frowning in concern.

I nodded. "I just remembered something."

"What?"

"It's nothing, really. The batteries are in the kitchen. I'll be right back."

Pushing away the old memory, I entered the kitchen and went straight for the battery drawer. Yes, some families had a junk drawer. My parents had a battery drawer. I peered in at the organized array of different sizes.

Without warning, a thin wire dug into my neck from behind, cutting into my skin. Choking me. I grabbed it with both hands, struggling to keep it from ending my life. The familiar odor assaulted me again, and I briefly flashed back to that night once more. Of being hit on the back of my head. In Nolan's house.

Chris's words from just before his death echoed in my head, and a distant memory returned of a move I'd learned in the self-defense class I'd taken in college. I tapped my palm against the man's package. One tap, two taps, and then *wham!* I hit him hard, surprising him. His grip on the wire loosened.

While he was groaning and doubled over in pain, I jerked to the side and nailed his face with my fist. I didn't have time to wonder why I hadn't done this the night I was attacked; I just ran.

With my lungs and throat burning from the near choking, I hurled myself toward the front door. I snatched hold of the doorknob and twisted it. But Lindsey's stepfather must have locked the door before following me into the kitchen. It refused to open. *Shit.*

I scrambled to unlock the door, breath coming fast. But in my haste to escape, I'd forgotten it got stuck unless you push on the door while twisting the lock. Leaning my weight against the door, I reached for the doorknob.

Lindsey's stepfather grabbed hold of my arm and yanked me away from the door. Screaming, I wildly punched and struggled and squirmed. Anything to keep him from getting a firm hold on me. Anything to break free.

It worked. The hand holding me lost its grip, and I jerked my arm away.

Not expecting the sudden release, I stumbled sideways, the momentum pulling me toward the stairs and away from the door. With the man between me and the front door, I didn't have a choice. I scrambled up the stairs, pushing hard to escape before he caught up with me.

Just before I reached the top step, I tripped.

A hand grabbed my ankle.

I screamed.

45

NOLAN

I grabbed my overnight bag from the overhead compartment and waited for everyone in the aisle to start moving. I was ready to shove them out of the way if it took any longer—which wouldn't help my bad-boy image. Unfortunately, the flight had been delayed more than three hours due to bad weather.

As soon as I stepped off the plane, I rushed to where the cabs were waiting for new arrivals. The cold winter wind howled through me. Snow blanketed the ground; the roads and sidewalks hadn't been cleared yet.

I climbed in a cab and gave the driver Hailey's address. My leg bounced the entire ride there. I had no idea what I was going to say to her.

By the time the cab pulled up in front of her building, I still had no clue what I would say. I scanned the parking lot for her car, but it wasn't here. *Shit*.

"Can you hold on?" I asked the driver. "I just need to verify something first." I dialed her number on the new phone I'd bought after destroying mine against Mason's wall. She didn't answer. I called Kayla on the chance she knew where I could find Hailey.

She answered on the third ring. "Hello?"

"Kayla? This is Nolan. Do you know where Hailey is?"

"She's at her parents'. Why?"

"Her parents? I thought they were away on a cruise."

"She's house-sitting."

I was about to thank her and end the call when she added, "She's been having problems with some of your fans. One started phoning and warning her to keep away from you because you and Alyssa were meant to be together. And then the other day someone slipped a note under her apartment door, explaining why Hailey didn't deserve you."

Fuck. "Did she threaten Hailey?"

"No. She wasn't one of those psychopaths who've been making those threats online."

I gave the cab driver Hailey's parents' address. I'd planned to visit my old home while I was back in Northbridge—my therapist thought it would be a good idea, as long as I didn't go there alone—but this change of plan meant I'd have to deal with the ghosts of my past sooner than I'd intended.

"Where are you?" Kayla asked.

"On my way to see her."

"And why are you visiting her?" There was a definite smile in Kayla's voice.

"That's between Hailey and me," I said, unable to keep the laugher out of *my* voice.

I heard a muffled scream. "Yes!"

After I ended the call, my leg resumed its bouncing as the cab drove through my old neighborhood. I tried to focus on happier times and not on what had happened six years ago. I didn't want to revisit those memories tonight.

Tonight I would tell Hailey how I felt about her, and if

things went well, we'd be making love for the rest of the night. I could deal with my ghosts tomorrow.

As the cab drove down the street to my house, I avoided glancing at it and I pointed out which house I was going to. Hailey's car sat in her parents' driveway.

The cab driver dropped me off in front the house, and I paid him.

As the cab zoomed off, I checked over my shoulder at the home that held so many dark memories. Maybe it was better if I visited it alone after all, instead of with Hailey. I wasn't sure yet if I wanted her to know the full details of what had gone down that night.

I turned toward my house.

46

HAILEY

Fear. It's something we all face at one point or another. Some fears are small and insignificant but real all the same. Like the fear of spiders. We develop an irrational fear that they'll kill us if we allow them to come too close. Those fears can cause us to freeze up, make us unable to walk away.

Yet those fears are nothing compared to when you come face-to-face with death. Not the irrational fear of spiders and death, but of something very real. When the odds are against you. The only chance you have is hope, as weak as it might be. Hope gives you the extra surge of energy to fight for your life. Hope propels you forward and keeps you from giving up.

I yanked my leg away from his hand and half stumbled, half threw myself up the final step. The hallway at the top of the stairs was dark, but a soft glow of streetlight spilled from my room.

I sprinted to my bedroom and slammed the door shut.

Not that it made any difference.

Using his body weight, Lindsey's stepfather hurled himself

against the door, pushing me back slightly. I could've sworn he snarled when he did it, like a giant rabid dog ready to tear me to pieces.

I tensed my leg muscles, hoping it would be enough to keep him out. Purely delusional on my part. The force of his weight against the door caused my sock-clad feet to slide across the carpet.

The pressure against the door slackened for a second, then he threw his body against it again and I flew backward, screaming.

"You're not escaping this time, bitch."

The backs of my thighs hit the bed hard, and I tumbled backward onto it. The bedroom light clicked on. I barely managed to twist around before he grabbed my hair and arm. He then pulled me up by my hair to stand.

The sharp tip of a knife instantly dug into my lower back. Not enough to cut me, but enough to prove a point.

I let out a startled cry. "Why are you doing this?"

"Because I can't risk you remembering everything."

"I don't even know what you're talking about." Not that it mattered if I knew what he was talking about or not. He couldn't just walk away after attacking me in my parents' home. The odds of me telling the cops, even after I promised I wouldn't, were too high. I just didn't get why he was doing this. He wasn't the man who'd put me in a coma. That man was dead.

But then that night came back to me. He was the one who had attacked me in Nolan's house soon after I found the letters. But I hadn't just found the love letters to Nolan's mother. I had found a bunch of legal documents. I didn't understand most of them, but one thing was clear—Sarah and Nolan hadn't shared the same biological father.

"You were Sarah's father, weren't you?" I said, more to

myself than to him. I didn't wait for him to reply. "She and Tanya have been dead for six years now. Why now? Why did you wait so long to look for the documents?" I suspected that was what this was all about.

The knife dug in a little deeper, piercing my skin. I cried out in pain. Warm blood trickled from the wound. This time I couldn't get away like I had in the kitchen. He was making sure of it. If I tried anything, he would stab me. And if the wound wasn't enough to kill me, it'd be enough to take me down so he could finish the job.

"I couldn't risk the truth getting out. I was married to my first wife when Tanya got pregnant. We had used condoms, so the risk of the baby being mine was small. After she found out she was pregnant, we ended things. But I loved her and that never changed.

"My first wife and I divorced several years later, and I moved away. A few months before that asshole murdered Tanya"—the pain in his voice was unmistakable—"I moved back to Northbridge with my second wife and her kids. I didn't expect to see Tanya again, but I bumped into her, and just like that, we resumed our old relationship. But as much as I loved Tanya, I couldn't leave my second wife. If I divorced her, I would have lost everything. Tanya knew that. That's why she stayed with *him*." He practically spat the last word.

"Did . . . did her husband ever suspect?" But even as I asked the question, I already knew the truth.

"Before the day he confronted me, we had never met. I knew Tanya from high school. The asshole moved here after college. I don't know how he found out about us, but he did. He confronted me the night he killed Tanya and the girl."

The impersonal way he referred to his daughter chilled me, like shards of ice slicing me from within. "Her name was Sarah," I bit out. "Your daughter's name was Sarah."

"Yes . . . Sarah."

"Why didn't you stop him? Why did you let him kill them?" Tears clouded my vision. I didn't bother to blink them away. There was no point.

"I had no idea he was going to kill them." His voice came out as a croaked whisper. "He was drunk and angry. I had no idea what he was capable of. Had I known, I would have done anything to save them."

I couldn't tell if he was telling the truth or if they were just pretty words he felt he needed to say. And it didn't matter either way. The end result would be the same.

"Are you really my parents' neighbor?" I asked, stalling the inevitable.

"No, I saw you leave your apartment with the suitcase. I already knew where your parents lived, and since you weren't driving toward the airport, I took a chance you came here. I'd heard last night on the radio that this neighborhood was one of those hit by the power outage."

I was about to ask how he knew where my parents lived when Nolan spoke, his voice oddly calm. "Why don't you put the knife down and we can talk?"

Surprise, relief, and hope surged through me, and I silently prayed I wasn't imagining things. That Nolan really was here and wasn't a delusion brought on by intense fear.

The knife plunged a little deeper into my back and I gasped. The trickle of blood became heavier, streaming down my back, soaking into my jeans, taking with it what little hope I had left. Lindsey's stepfather tightened his hold on my hair and twisted us around to face Nolan.

Nolan's face was pale, and I could only imagine how this was for him. His mother and sister had been stabbed to death, and he hadn't been able to save them. And now the likelihood of him saving me was nonexistent. Instead, he'd be forced to watch me being killed. Or worse yet, Nolan could be stolen from me. Murdered like he was almost murdered the night his family died.

I couldn't let that happen.

"Don't come any closer," Lindsey's stepfather barked, the hand holding the knife in my back trembling—and I started piecing things together. This guy wasn't used to hurting people. As a firefighter, he was used to saving them.

This revelation was of little comfort with the knife cutting into me. Tears leaked from my eyes at the burning pain.

"Okay," Nolan said, hands up to show he was unarmed. "I'll stay right here if that makes you feel better." His gaze darted to mine. For a second, pain flashed in his eyes at the sight of me.

"No," Lindsey's stepfather grunted. "I want you to back away. Slowly." He backed away too, pulling me with him, cornering himself further in the room. No longer was I just someone he wanted to kill. Now I was his human shield.

The shakiness in my legs increased, helped along by the blood loss and pain. If he hadn't been holding me with his arm tight against my chest, I would've collapsed. But his arm was also making it hard for me to breathe. Each gasp was a struggle for oxygen.

Afraid that this was the last time I'd see Nolan, I kept my eyes on him. And maybe that's why I noticed his body jerk. The movement was so slight, it was only noticeable if you were paying attention to him and nothing else.

"All right," Nolan said. "Just don't hurt her, okay?" He stepped backward into the hallway, then moved to the side. I could still see him, but it was as if he was giving the man room to escape.

As soon as Nolan was away from the doorway, Lindsey's stepfather shoved me forward. But my strength was rapidly fading and I stumbled. The knife shifted in my back and I screamed from the intense pain.

"Hailey!"

I didn't know if it was my scream or the unexpected movement, but Lindsey's stepfather loosened his hold on me and I tumbled to the floor, the knife jerking out of me.

The world faded slightly. Black dots shifted in my vision.

Drawing on everything inside me—the fear, the determination, the love—I fought the desire to close my eyes. I didn't want to go to sleep. I wanted to be in Nolan's arms. I wanted to tell him I loved him.

There was a sudden movement in the doorway, and for a moment I thought it was Nolan.

"Police," a deep male voice yelled, the sound of it reverberating in my head. "Put the knife down . . . I said, put the knife down!"

A muffled thud near me on the floor almost made me cry out in relief. Needing to get as far from Lindsey's stepfather as possible, I dragged myself forward, biting my lip against the pain.

The cop entered the room, his gun pointed at the man.

Another cop came in after him and crouched down beside me. "We need a medic up here." He'd barely had a chance to finish the last word before Nolan was by my side.

As the cop coaxed me to lie back down, Nolan whipped off his T-shirt. Normally I would've appreciated the sight of a shirtless Nolan. What girl wouldn't? But right now he could have been completely naked and I wouldn't have cared. Much.

"Hey, Forget-Me-Not." The smile in his voice that was usually there whenever he used my nickname was missing. He pressed the T-shirt against my side. "I've got you."

Gasping, I jolted at the sharp pain.

I vaguely heard someone informing Lindsey's stepfather of his rights as Nolan brushed the hair from my face.

"I've got you, Forget-Me-Not, and I'm never letting go of you again."

I focused on Nolan's voice and only on his voice. If I could help it, I'd never let go of him again either.

I replayed his words in my head as the paramedics arrived, as they examined me, and as they drove me away in the ambulance. And true to his word, Nolan stayed with me.

47

NOLAN

Hailey squeezed my hand as we stood in front of my house. "Are you sure about this?" she asked. She glanced back at her parents' home and shuddered. We were going there after this, to help her deal with what had happened almost two weeks ago.

"Yes. I need to do it." I pulled her toward the front door and unlocked it. What had happened the night my family died wasn't my fault. I'd finally accepted that. For the longest time, I had been trying to convince my mother to leave my father. I couldn't have predicted the sequence of events or the outcome. None of us could have.

The cops eventually put everything together as to what had happened the night Hailey was found barely alive in Westgate. Philip Brady, the man Mom had been having an affair with, had attacked her in this house, and he panicked. He and his brother took Hailey to Westgate to kill her. They wanted it to look like a random attack. They never expected her to survive. The man I accidentally killed when he attacked Hailey while she was running? He was Philip's brother.

Initially it didn't make sense that Philip had waited so long to make sure there was nothing that could link him to my mother and Sarah. But then we learned that Philip had recently decided he wanted to go into politics, and so he needed to ensure all his skeletons stayed buried deep.

Chris's death was quickly determined to be unrelated, the result of a steroid drug deal gone wrong. His alleged killer had been arrested early last week.

I opened the front door and stepped inside my house. The night Philip had attacked Hailey at her parents', I'd been about to cross the street to my home when I heard her scream. Thinking that the person who'd put her in a coma and the person who had killed Chris was the same and was still running free, I'd called the cops. Fortunately, Hailey's parents had left the spare key in the same place as when she and I were kids.

Now, as we entered the house I'd grown up in, I saw that a layer of dust covered the furniture. The air held a slight musty smell. But otherwise, the place looked no different than I remembered.

I inhaled deeply and started coughing. "Hmm. It's a little dustier than I remembered." Hailey's parents had arranged for someone to clean every few months for the past six years. Her mother knew my mom would've appreciated it, even if she was dead. I had agreed to it, and the funds had come from my parents' estate. I wasn't sure why I hadn't sold it right away—why I had waited until only recently to finally decide to put it on the market. Maybe deep down I had assumed no one would want to buy a house three people had died violently in. Or maybe deep down I just hadn't been ready to let it go—to let go of the only home my sister had ever known.

Hailey chuckled, taking in the dusty state of the furniture and the house. "Just a little."

"I guess I should hire someone to deal with it before I sell the place." I pulled her into my arms and grinned. "Unless you want to delay our flight for another month. Then we can clean it ourselves."

She made a face. "No heavy lifting for me for a while. Doctor's orders." Doctor's orders also said she couldn't have sex for a few more weeks while Hailey recovered from surgery. Not that I was counting the days or anything. "Are you sure you want to sell the place?" she asked.

I glanced around. The house had long since ceased being part of my existence. The happy memories associated with it were tainted. "Positive." I squeezed her hand to let her know that she was my life.

Always had been.

Always would be.

Still holding on to Hailey, I walked into the kitchen. The blood from my mother's murder had long since been scrubbed from the wall and the floor by the cleaning service. I closed my eyes against the image of the last time I'd seen her, lying on the floor in a pool of blood.

Hailey wrapped her arms around my waist and rested her head on my shoulder. I opened my eyes and kissed her temple. "Thank you," I whispered.

She peered up at me. "You're welcome."

We climbed the stairs leading to the second floor. Hailey's movements were slow and slightly unsteady. I kept my arm around her hips and let her set the pace.

In my room, I removed from my back jeans pocket the laminated photo that I had held on to for all these years and handed it to Hailey. "Do you remember this?"

She laughed at the picture Mom had taken while I attempted to help Hailey master the guitar. We had been sitting on my bed at the time. "I can't believe you still have this."

"It was the only thing I held on to from my previous life. I loved you, Hailey. Even though I walked away from North-bridge all those years ago, I couldn't walk away from you completely. Every time I missed you, every time I was about to go onstage, I'd look at the picture. It was like you were with me." I gently kissed her. "It was what kept me going."

"I wish I had known that. I thought you had moved on and forgotten me."

"Never. I couldn't have forgotten you even if I tried."

Entering Sarah's room was harder than entering the kitchen. If she had still been alive, my sister would've been sixteen years old, with her entire life ahead of her. My gut twisted at seeing her bed and remembering the last time I'd been in the room. I pulled Hailey closer to me.

Sarah had loved Hailey. She would've been thrilled to see us together. The way we were meant to be.

It didn't matter that Sarah had been my half sister. I loved her no matter what.

I picked up the familiar framed photo from my sister's desk. Like everything else, dust blanketed it. With a T-shirt I'd found in her closet, I cleared away the dust, revealing a picture of Sarah, me, and Hailey.

When I had left home for L.A. six years ago, all I took with me was my guitar, clothes, and the one photo of Hailey. I'd fled the town without anything to remember my sister by—other than the tiger tattoo I got soon after arriving in L.A., the one that represented Sarah's favorite stuffed animal. I thought that if I had something of hers with me, I would never move on.

I had been wrong.

I hugged the picture, and after one last quick glance around the room, Hailey and I left to begin our new life together.

"YOU TWO READY?" ALYSSA ASKED HAILEY AND ME FOUR DAYS later. In the other room, the media were set up to listen to our press conference. It had been Alyssa's idea, and the record label grudgingly agreed to it after they learned about the threats to Hailey's life.

Not that they had much choice. Alyssa had planned to go public with the news one way or another, and there were plenty of other labels interested in signing her.

Hailey and I nodded, and Monica, Alyssa's assistant, opened the door to the room. The media knew only that Alyssa and I wanted to make a statement. They had no idea that Hailey was also part of the news conference.

The latest rumor was Alyssa and I were announcing our engagement. Or baby news.

I entered the room first, followed by Hailey, then Alyssa. Alyssa and I had planned it that way, to show her support for Hailey and our relationship.

I reached for Hailey's hand and squeezed it to let her know it'd be all right. We had already prepared her for this moment, as had the publicist from the record label. But despite that, her hand trembled in mine as camera flashes momentarily blinded us.

The small conference room was filled with reporters and camerapeople from numerous TV stations. The only individuals excluded were the paparazzi. Whether they were invited or not didn't matter; they would have twisted the story for their own benefit either way.

We walked to the podium, where three microphones were set up. Even though Hailey wasn't excited about the idea of talking to reporters, she understood how important it was that she did.

"Thank you for coming," Alyssa said, smiling. "I understand you all came here today expecting us to announce our engagement. But trust me, once I find a guy I want to settle down with, I won't be calling a press conference. My publicist will issue a statement. What we wanted to talk about is something more important." She turned to me.

"For months now, there have been speculations that Alyssa and I are involved. But none of it is true. There's only been one woman I've ever been in love with." I smiled at Hailey, and she smiled back, the nervousness from a few minutes ago gone.

Unable to help myself, I leaned down and kissed her. Nothing R-rated. It was a simple kiss. One that clearly stated my heart belonged to her as much as hers belonged to me.

The cacophony of clicking cameras grew in intensity, intruding on the moment. And for a second I wished we were alone so I could explore her sweet mouth again, this time more thoroughly.

"Why is it that only a few weeks ago," a male reporter asked, "Alyssa made a statement that you two were involved and Hailey was nothing more than a friend?"

That was my question to answer. "The record label believed that by announcing Alyssa and I were involved, it would remove the attention from Hailey. At the time, I hadn't realized Hailey would want to uproot herself from her life back home to be with me in L.A., and Hailey hadn't realized I wanted her with me. Obviously we need to work on our communication skills a little more."

Knowing chuckles greeted us.

"So what made you decide to come forward now?" a female entertainment reporter asked. I recognized her from the movie premiere, when she had helped feed the speculation about the whole Nolyssa crap.

"While the idea of standing in front of all you and discussing my private life scares the hell out of me," Hailey said to the middle microphone, "I was tired of the unfounded hate Nolyssa fans had toward me. Some individuals threatened me online. I received hate phone calls from one person, who also sent me a letter. The cops in my town have questioned the individual and charges are possible." It had turned out to be someone in Hailey's apartment building. "People who didn't know me were threatening me or saying hurtful comments about me just because they were supporting something that wasn't real."

Alyssa placed her hand on Hailey's shoulder. "I've had a chance to get to know Hailey over the past few days, and the negative press she received is undeserved. And unlike the media and Nolan's fans, who didn't get to know him because of secrets he felt he had to keep, I've gotten to know the real Nolan over the past year. He's a great guy, and he and Hailey are the ones who are perfect together. It never should have been about him and me."

We answered several more questions. Some were about my past, which I told them was behind me and was in no way an indication of who I was. Some were about Hailey's and my plans for the future.

"I'm still recovering from an attack prior to coming here," Hailey stated. "Then I hope to continue what I was doing back home." She didn't say what that was, though. She wasn't the one whose career was based on being in the spotlight. She wanted to keep that part of her life private. We could only hope the media would respect her decision.

"Was this an attack from a Nolyssa fan?"

"No," Hailey said. "It was a home invasion that had nothing to do with Nolan or Alyssa. That's all I can say about it."

Eventually the questions ended and we thanked everyone for coming. Monica opened the back door for us and the four of us left. She and Alyssa said goodbye to us and walked out to the car waiting for them.

Grinning happily because I was finally going to have Hailey all to myself for a while, I grabbed hold of her hips and brought her flush against me. "So, what do you say, Forget-Me-Not?" I murmured against her ear, and I could've sworn she whimpered. "Why don't we go home and I can help you relax?"

"What do you have in mind?"

"You'll see." I languidly ran my tongue along the shell of her ear. She moaned softly. "And maybe tomorrow we can start looking for a place to live. Together. Without Jared."

She laughed. "Sounds good."

I pulled back. "Which part?"

The smile on her face made my heart do a quick step. "All of it. As long as it's with you."

EPILOGUE
HAILEY

Two Months Later . . .

From the throw line in the middle of the sports bar, I tossed my beanbag toward the red bucket. If this had been soccer, I could've dazzled everyone with my fancy footwork. Not that anyone cared. The sole reason the ten people behind me were here was to drool over my boyfriend. Okay, maybe not so much the guy at the end of our line, but definitely the guy on Jared's team. He'd been checking Nolan's ass out, like the rest of the girls at the radio-station sponsored event. But I couldn't say I blamed him. As long as he and the girls realized that only I had Nolan's heart.

The beanbag effortlessly landed in the bucket with a hard plop. Nolan didn't have a chance to congratulate me. He was up next. His team cheered and oohed as he hurled his beanbag at the same target. And he, too, easily made the shot.

We walked together to the end of the line, his hand on my butt. A few girls shot me a jealous glance, but that didn't bother me. It was an improvement compared to a few months ago. Fortunately, once Alyssa had accepted me as a friend, the entire

Nolyssa mess had blown over. Not that I had seen her much lately. She was busy in the studio recording her debut album.

"So, Hailey," Jared said as we waited for the next game to be set up, "you're coming with us on our promo blitz, right?"

"I hope so. Depends on if I can get the time off. Plus we're expecting . . . a new family member." How I managed not to laugh at Jared's shocked expression was beyond me.

"Well, um, congratulations." He hugged me and gave Nolan a one-armed man hug. The rest of the band was too preoccupied giving Mason a hard time to overhear us.

Nolan burst out laughing. "She's not pregnant. We're adopting a puppy."

I laughed. "Sorry. Couldn't resist it."

"Not funny," Jared grumbled, which seemed like an odd reaction from him. Then the fleeting emotion on his face, which I couldn't get a firm grip on, vanished, and he smiled. "So, when are you getting the new addition?"

"Today."

I couldn't even remember when the idea of adopting a puppy had first come up. It wasn't one of those "Hey, let's get a dog" conversations that happened one morning over coffee. It started with Nolan's subtle yet wishful glances at golden retrievers as we strolled past them when they and their owners were out for a walk. Then a few weeks ago Nolan stopped to pat one dog we'd seen a number of times, and his longing for one almost knocked me over. We spoke to the owner for a few minutes, and the next thing I knew, we were contacting the breeder from whom the man had adopted his dog. The woman and her dogs came highly recommended, and one of her dogs had recently given birth to a new litter.

Somehow I survived the agonizingly long wait before the radio event finally finished. All I could think about the entire time was our adorable puppy and how he was soon coming home with us. To be a family.

After we said our goodbyes, we drove to the address we had been to one other time. Adopting a puppy from a breeder wasn't like picking out a puppy at a pet store. We had already visited the breeder so she could determined whether we were the right couple for one of her babies.

"Are you sure about this?" Nolan asked. But any uncertainty he might have felt wasn't about getting a dog. Rather, it was because he was leaving soon on a long tour to support the new album Pushing Limits had just released.

"Positive. It'll be nice to have someone to keep me company while you're off flirting with all those groupies." My tone was light and breezy, and I smirked as he pulled up to the breeder's home. I was kidding, of course. I knew he would be friendly with his fans, because that was part of his job. But there was a thick line between being friendly and flirting, and I trusted that Nolan wouldn't cross it.

Without a word, he parked the car in front of the simple two-story house and we climbed out. Unlike back in Minnesota, spring had paid L.A. a visit more than a month ago. The trees and plants and sweet fragrant flowers in the well-tended garden were lush and green.

Nolan was still oddly silent as we walked toward the path leading to the front door. I was about to tell him I was kidding, in case he hadn't figured it out for himself, when he grabbed my waist and pulled me close.

"The only flirting I'll be doing is with you." He leaned down, his mouth close to my ear, and murmured, "When you're talking to me on the phone. Naked."

"Oh, you think so?" I murmured back, my legs weak at the thought of hot phone sex with my equally hot boyfriend while he was on the road. At least I had something to look forward to, other than his safe return.

"I definitely think so." He ran his tongue along my neck,

and heat ignited between my legs. God, the man was such a tease.

But the part I'd said about having someone to keep me company was true. Other than Alyssa, I'd only made a few new friends since the move to L.A., and they were more like casual work acquaintances—not people I could see getting close to. A puppy was exactly what I needed to keep me from missing Nolan too much while he toured with the band.

Nolan stepped away, and my body instantly missed his closeness. "As much as I want to taste you," he said with a groan, "that's gonna have to wait a little longer." He threaded his fingers with mine, and we walked along the path to the front door. The freshly awoken ache between my legs cursed him the entire way.

I rang the doorbell, and less than a minute later Gail opened the door and we were ushered into the house. It might have been a simple two-story house on the outside, but inside, the home was warm and welcoming. Gail was originally from Scotland, and while her accent might have softened over the years, her love for her Celtic roots hadn't. She also loved plaid. I mean *really* loved plaid.

"They're looking forward to seeing ye." No sooner had she said the words than six chubby seven-week-old puppies bounded toward us from the kitchen. Their cuteness factor was way over the top, and I wished we could've adopted them all. Choosing just one had been next to impossible.

They tumbled into each other in their haste to get to us. The slightly curled up edge of the rug sidetracked one puppy, who chewed on it instead.

"How 'bout we go into the backyard with them?" Gail walked toward the kitchen, where the back door was located. They must have sensed where she was going, because they all charged after her, including our little boy, Rocky. The name was both a tribute to Nolan's first dog, Lucky, and a symbol that

Nolan would always be my rock star—both in the musical sense and otherwise.

We followed the bundles of cuteness outside and played with them for a while. Like last time, when we'd first fallen in love with Rocky, it was clear that the puppy was as taken with Nolan as I was. Even when the other puppies chased after the ball Gail had thrown, Rocky stayed close to us, waiting for Nolan to toss the ball he was holding.

I sat next to Rocky on the grass and stroked his soft fur. At my touch, he rolled onto his side and gave me those adorable puppy eyes that melted my heart. "So what do you think?" I asked him. "You wanna come home with us?"

Rocky gave a little puppy yap that I interpreted as meaning "yes," and then attacked the laces of Nolan's sneaker. I laughed as Nolan gently dissuaded the little fur ball from his goal.

While Nolan played with Rocky, I watched the man I loved with all my heart prove that nothing about him was a reflection of his father. For years Nolan had been deprived of the love he deserved from someone who was supposed to love him unconditionally. Watching him with the puppy, it was easy to see how none of his father had rubbed off on him—and what an amazing dad he would be one day. I had no doubts about that.

I also had no doubts that nothing was hotter than a sexy tattooed rock star cuddling with a puppy—even more so when that sexy rock star was all yours.

READ ON FOR AN EXCERPT FROM MY SONG FOR YOU

JARED

Loneliness was a bitch. True, that wasn't the most convincing statement to say when surrounded by a group of screaming girls in a sports bar, eager to touch any part of your body they could get their hands on. And try telling that to a horny twentysomething guy. This place was a smorgasbord of groupies interested in a quick lay.

Not that I was complaining.

So far I loved what I did for a living. I loved the fans, and I loved hanging out with the guys in the band, even during our last grueling tour. But that didn't stop the nagging feeling that despite the music, the fans, and the band, despite how hard we had worked and how much we had sacrificed to get this far, something was missing.

But hell if I knew what it was.

"Oh my God," the girl in a super-tight white tank top shrieked, jumping up and down on the polished floor. Her huge tits bounced like overinflated beach balls. "I can't believe it's you. You're like my favorite guitarist of all time."

I flashed her the smile that always left girls sighing. Mason, the drummer for Pushing Limits, claimed the smile guaranteed

I'd get laid. I wasn't so sure about that. "Well, thanks. You just made my day." I had already used the same tired line five times in the past fifteen minutes. But as long as the girls at the radio-station-sponsored event didn't compare notes, they'd be fine.

Flipping my lucky guitar pick between my fingers and across the back of my hand, I glanced at Nolan with his mob of fans. His girlfriend, Hailey, was standing to the side, talking to Kirk's sister. Neither of them paid attention to the eager fans pawing at the individual members of the band. It wasn't like the two women hadn't seen it before. Although I had to admit I was impressed at how Hailey took it all in stride. Not all girlfriends were like that.

A kiss on my cheek dragged me back to my own group of screaming fans. The girl with beach-ball tits grinned at the smartphone in her hand. Had she just taken a fucking selfie of her kissing me?

"Okay, everyone," Rebecca, one of the radio personalities, said through the speakers. It was early afternoon and the brightly lit sports bar had been rented for the event, which meant the TVs weren't on, much to Kirk's annoyance. I chuckled. His occasional glares aimed at the TVs meant one thing: he was missing out on a hockey game featuring his favorite team, the L.A. Kings.

"May the games begin," Rebecca continued once she had everyone's attention. "And ladies, no mauling our special guests. You wouldn't want to scare them off, right?"

"Boo!" Mason's loud voice exploded through the stale, beer-scented air. His lazy grin, bright against his brown skin, was visible above his groupies' heads. He wasn't the only one disappointed at her suggestion. The girls crowded around him would've been more than happy to continue groping the bulky drummer—and the feeling was mutual when it came to Mas. I wouldn't have been surprised if he already had some of their phone numbers.

"Is everyone still in their assigned group?" Michael, the other radio personality, asked. His question was met with a chorus of yeses, shrieks, and hollers. "The first event is the beanbag toss. The winning team is the one with the most bags in their bucket at the end of three minutes." He and Rebecca had us line up behind the throw line in the middle of the room. In total, fifty participants, with the girls easily outnumbering the guys, had won the chance to join us today.

The two radio interns herded Nolan, Mason, Kirk, Aaron, and me to the front of our respective lines and handed us each our first beanbag. I returned my guitar pick to my back jeans pocket. And the game commenced.

Cheers and groans filled the air as each person at the throw line quickly tossed their beanbag into their team's bucket. I might have not been brilliant when it came to basketball, but I could hold my own. The beanbag landed smartly in the white bucket. I moved to the back of the line.

The next person, a brunette in a tight black dress and stilettos, hurled her beanbag at the bucket as if the damn thing was burning her hand. She missed our bucket and almost scored a point for Aaron's team.

Before I knew it, all nine girls and the one guy in my group had finished their turns, and I was up again. Like last time, I nailed the bucket, but it wasn't enough. A quick glance at the guys' buckets warned me my team wasn't doing too hot.

A hand from behind me squeezed my ass. "My turn," the I-want-to-fuck-you-all-night-long brunette said.

I gave her both a brief nod and the grin that was reserved for groupies—the one that said any other time, I might've been interested—and walked to the end of the line again. The empty feeling trailed alongside, and I glanced at Nolan and Hailey. Both were lost in their own little world, despite the fans screaming and cheering around them. They smiled softly at each other in the way I was all too familiar with after being their roommate for a short time, ever since Hailey moved to L.A. to be with Nolan. Usually the look meant he was about to become one very happy guy—as my thin apartment walls could attest to.

The ass-grabber joined me, and her gaze tore the jeans and T-shirt off my body. She leaned in, her breath against my ear. "I'd be all for you playing me like a guitar afterward."

I barked a laugh. And here I thought guys were the real winners when it came to lame pickup lines. "Thanks, but . . . but I have somewhere to be after this."

She flashed me a pout. "Maybe afterward?"

"Maybe some other time."

She brightened, failing to see the lie for what it was, and slipped her fingers in my pocket. I had no idea if she was giving me her phone number, but she took the moment to cop a feel. And from the way she smiled at me, she liked what she felt.

I stepped back and grabbed a beanbag from the bucket at the front of our line. But as I tossed it at the intended target, the brunette brushed her hand against my ass, again, and the bag missed its mark by a foot.

The loud blast of a whistle ended the game. I didn't need to count the number of beanbags to know we'd lost. Not that I really cared.

"We won!" Mas hooted.

"Wait till they've counted them, dumbass," Kirk said next to him. He gave the drummer a brief glance before returning his attention to Rebecca, who was counting the beanbags. A former hockey player, our bassist was as competitive as they came.

"I don't need to wait, douchebag. My group is just that awesome." Mason unleashed his grin on them again, and I swore some of his fans came in their panties, if their glazed expressions were any indication.

"Maybe so, but up against my athletic prowess," Kirk said, "you're toast."

Mason smirked. "Bring it on, puck boy."

Rebecca jotted on her clipboard, then counted the bean-bags in Aaron's bucket.

"Do you have a girlfriend, Jared?" asked a girl who could best be described as jailbait. The rest of my team waited for the answer with bated breath.

I shook my head. "Not right now."

"So you aren't dating Tiffany Grainger anymore?" the girl with giant tits asked.

"No. We're just friends." I almost snorted at the "friends" part. I didn't think we had ever been friends. Just on-again, off-again whatevers.

"That's too bad. You guys were perfect together."

I shrugged. "With our work schedules as they are, it was too difficult to spend time together."

The only other guy in my group chuckled. "Must be a tough life, dating a supermodel."

He didn't realize how right he was, even if he had meant it another way.

"And the winner of the beanbag toss is . . ." Michael paused for dramatic effect. "Kirk Helmson's team."

Kirk's group cheered, the girls jumping up and down like hyped-up cheerleaders. One actually did do a cartwheel, but her technique was far from impressive.

"I demand a recount," Mason yelled. His fans giggled. The rest of us laughed.

"Man up, Mas," Kirk replied. "My team won and you know it."

Mason folded his arms, chin raised. "You just watch. My team will destroy yours in the next game." Mock defiance gleamed in his eyes.

"Bring it on, drummer boy."

Welcome to what it had been like touring with them for the past year. They were always trying to outdo each other in whatever competition they had going. The rest of us had long since learned to ignore them . . . and maybe place the occasional side bet.

"Good to know nothing has changed between those two," Nolan said to me as we waited for the next game to be set up. "I'd hate to lose our entertainment for the next tour."

"You mean you'd hate to lose out on winning more money from me." He and Aaron, our keyboardist, beat me hands down when it came to our little side bets. The little side bets that neither Mason nor Kirk knew about.

"Damn straight."

"So, Hailey," I said, "you're coming with us on our promo blitz, right?" Maybe then I'd have a chance of doing better in our betting game. She would unintentionally distract her boyfriend and he would screw up his bet. Or that was my plan, at least.

"I hope so. Depends on if I can get the time off. Plus we're expecting . . . a new family member."

Holy fuck! That was the last thing I'd expected. They had only been together for a few months, but who was I to judge? If anyone should know how easy it was to get a girl pregnant, it was me.

"Well, um, congratulations." I hugged Hailey and gave Nolan a one-armed hug. Fortunately, the fans were too busy listening to the sideshow entertainment between Mason and the radio personalities to notice our conversation.

Nolan burst out laughing. "She's not pregnant. We're adopting a puppy."

Hailey grinned. "Sorry. Couldn't resist."

"Not funny," I grumbled, doing my best not to let them know how I really felt. Joking about pregnancy was never a funny matter.

Shoving away the pain and betrayal from my past, I smiled, the move genuine. "So, when are you getting the new addition?"

"Today," Hailey said.

From the look on my best friend's face, you'd have thought Nolan was four years old and it was Christmas.

Rebecca announced the next game—darts—and we returned to our respective teams. I spent the next hour flirting with the fans, signing autographs, and finding out what they loved about our songs and about the band. This was one of the things I enjoyed most about what I did: interacting with the fans. The real fans. Not the groupies who were hoping to add us to their I-slept-with-a-celebrity tally. They usually couldn't tell us what they loved about our music. We were just hot bodies as far as they were concerned.

"And the grand prize," Rebecca announced, "goes to Kirk Helmson's team."

Cheers broke out among the teams, including Mason's.

"Hey, bro," Mas said with a laugh, "you finally won the Steward Cup."

Kirk snorted. "You mean Stanley Cup."

"Sure, whatev."

Kirk collected the tiny metal trophy on behalf of his team and congratulated everyone as if they really had won the most coveted prize in the NHL.

"You guys want to meet up for drinks later?" Aaron asked after we had packed up our instruments to leave. As part of the event, we had agreed to play a couple of our songs off the debut album. The president of the record label had been quite clear: under no condition were we to play anything from the upcoming album. And basically whatever he said, we did. No questions asked.

"Count me in," I said. Kirk and Mason also agreed to meet up at our favorite bar.

On my way to my apartment, I stopped at a grocery store and wandered up and down the aisles, grabbing whatever appealed to me and didn't require much thought. Cooking wasn't one of my favorite pastimes.

As I pushed my shopping cart down the cereal aisle, I spotted a woman I'd never thought I'd see again—a woman I had known back when we were kids. Only I didn't remember her looking quite so hot back then, with her long copper hair in a messy ponytail. The woman who was my ex-girlfriend-from-high-school's little sister.

The woman signing with her hands . . . to a four-year-old boy.

MY SONG FOR YOU is now available.

ABOUT THE AUTHOR

Born in Brighton England, Stina Lindenblatt has lived in a number of countries, including England, the US, Finland, and Canada. This would explain her mixed up accent. She has a kinesiology degree and a MSc in sports biological sciences.

In addition to writing fiction, she loves photography, and currently lives in Calgary, Canada, with her husband and three kids.

For news about her books, social media sites, and to sign up for her newsletter, check out her website at stinalindenblattau thor.com. Newsletter subscribers will receive a bonus short story.